# BLUE
# CRYSTAL

# BLUE CRYSTAL

## Philip Lee Williams

## GROVE PRESS
New York

Copyright © 1993 by Philip Lee Williams

Published by Grove Press
A division of Grove Press, Inc.
841 Broadway
New York, NY 10003-4793

Published in Canada by General Publishing Company, Ltd.

Library of Congress Cataloging-in-Publication Data
Williams, Philip Lee.
    Blue crystal / Philip Lee Williams. — 1st ed.
        p.        cm.
    ISBN 0-8021-1499-7 (acid-free paper)
    I. Title.
    PS3573.I45535B57 1993
    813'.54—dc20                                    92-44232
                                                              CIP

Manufactured in the United States of America

Printed on acid-free paper

Designed by Jack Meserole

First Edition 1993

10 9 8 7 6 5 4 3 2 1

*This book is for Brandon and Megan*

# BLUE
# CRYSTAL

1

*Sunlight* begins to fill the town square. Sam Preston stands in front of his hardware store with a steaming mug of coffee and lets his eyes drift slowly over the gentle outlines of Sheppard, Kentucky. A few cars politely pass through town, almost apologetic for disturbing the early morning's peace. Swifts pour from the courthouse spire and bank into the light. Across the square at the Texaco station, Mose Johnson drops a tire tool, and the clang on concrete sounds like a bell.

Preston Hardware, much deeper than wide, spills its clutter into the aisles behind Sam. He's not much for keeping it ordered, though it's always clean. Since the divorce, Sam might come in at dawn or not show up until nine. He and his friend Jimmy Jones run it, and businessmen in Sheppard don't understand completely why Sam closes it on Fridays and Saturdays, the best days of the week. They just say it's that cave and let it go at that.

Mary McClain's opening the *Sheppard Tribune* across the square. She's a fine journalist and has been asking Sam about writing a feature on Blue Crystal Cave, but Sam won't give in. He's friendly about it, laughs, but he won't talk about it. He remembers one thing from his father: *Never talk out loud about private matters.* Two doors down from the *Tribune,* stern, corpulent Lem Wilkes is looking through his key ring, as he does every morning, then opening the Sheppard Finance Corporation. Lem never smiles and eats enormous lunches at the Sheppard Cafe, from whose kitchen the fragrant aroma of bacon and eggs settles over the town.

Sam turns further and notices Mary Beth Price, juggling a bundle of mail as she opens her bookstore, Mountain Pages. They're having dinner Friday night. They've had a few friendly dates, but he feels closer to her now. It's something he has not felt in a long time. She wrestles with the lock, turns the key. Then she steps back and looks straight at Sam and waves and smiles. He smiles and waves back and yells, "Good morning," but she can't hear. She goes into the store. He'll wander over there later to spend a few pleasant minutes. In Sheppard, you can leave your store for a while and not miss much.

Sam turns again and looks down past the *Tribune* and sees, like a gilded ribbon beyond the square, sunlight laying a golden sheen on the Coollawassee River. Above him in the pale summer sky, cirrus clouds twist, feathers of ice that hint the weather is changing. Sam's looking at the clouds and barely notices the sheriff, Tom Meade, walking slowly toward him.

In the years Sam's lived in Sheppard he hasn't had a better friend, though Tom is sixty, old enough to be his father. Sam's thirty-five, a tall, lean man with light green eyes, but Tom's even taller, with a head of iron gray hair closely cropped and penetrating brown eyes that seem to miss nothing.

"Looking for God up there?" asks Tom. Sam laughs, shifts his cup to his left hand, and they shake. Tom's grip is heavy and firm. He looks you in the eye when he shakes hands. Tom's been sheriff of Sheppard for thirty years, watching it change from a dusty rural Kentucky town to the self-proclaimed "Gateway to Cave Country."

"You think I'd see him if I looked long enough?" asks Sam. Tom looks up at the cirrus clouds.

"I think you can see anything if you look long enough," he says. "Angels dancing, Mary's hair floating in the wind. Probably everything that's ever been." Sam looks at Tom's eyes as they pass over the clouds. Tom can do that, say something entirely unexpected, words that let you know he's a reader. At lunch he goes home, and his wife, whom everyone calls Miss Patricia, cooks for him, and then he reads.

Several years ago, not long before the divorce, Sam lost an eye. He was trying to blast a new entrance into Blue Crystal Cave, and the charge went off too early. Sam was going to get a glass eye, but Tom said if it were him he'd wear an eye patch, so Sam does.

"Rain for the weekend," Sam says. Tom stretches and looks around the square.

"Well, it's good for flowers and such," he says. "I was going to water the annuals we planted at the cemetery, anyway." Sam nods, hardly knows how Tom can talk so easily about it. Thirty years earlier, Tom's only son, Andrew, died when Blue Crystal Cave collapsed. Sam's father ran it, the first successful commercial cave in Sheppard County, though Sam paid hardly any attention to it.

A church group of children from Little Rock was taking the tour when something belowground shifted and the limestone gave way. Andrew Meade had gone with the group since his first cousin was in it. It took four days to dig the bodies out, all seventeen of them. Sam's father, Allen Preston, who was wealthy and had built a fine house in the hills above Sheppard, fell apart and took the family to Richmond, where Sam was raised. They told Sam almost nothing about the disaster, and he didn't read the papers. His mother cried for weeks, and a year later Allen Preston locked himself in the attic of their Richmond home and put the barrel of an old Colt to his temple.

Sam didn't really know much about the children until he looked up the microfilm the year he was a junior at the University of Virginia. He cried as he read about how they had survived the rockfall, only to huddle against the wall in total darkness and slowly suffocate. He couldn't say he was ever the same after that. He quit school that winter and married Ginger, his girlfriend of two years, and brought her back to Sheppard, where he bought the hardware store from a man named Ownie Smith. In the quiet times Sam began to explore, through sinkholes and other entrances, the part of Blue Crystal Cave that his family still owned along with several hundred acres of land.

"What did you plant?" Sam says finally.

"Asters," says Tom. "Patricia planted asters. Course, I don't know, one flower's like another, and so forth." Tom doesn't speak of his son often, but when he does, his voice often trails off, and he'll simply nod several times, each a gesture of some unspoken word.

"I got gerbera daisies around the house this year," says Sam. "They add something. You can water them, and you feel like you're doing something."

"Speaking of doing something, I got to get to the office," says Tom. "Reports to file. Lord only knows what Leon's doing." His chief deputy, Leon James, is something of a dullard but well liked. People help Leon because they worry about him.

"Well," says Sam. He wants to say more, to sit through a long night over beer with Tom and tell him a few things. He admires Tom more than any man he's ever met, his quiet strength, his even temper. He wants to look him in the eyes and do something he's never done before, to say he's sorry about Andrew, that since the day he first read the old papers in the microfilm room he's never gotten over the thought of those children in that cave.

"You take care of yourself, boy," says Tom. They shake hands again, and Tom moves off down the sidewalk, gently slapping his leg and nodding as if someone had asked him a question and he answered yes.

It's late morning, and Sam leaves the store with Jimmy Jones, who's fifty and loves to talk to customers. Jimmy's slow-motion life calms everything around him. Sometimes Jimmy can just be wandering endlessly through a sentence about Kentucky politics, and Sam will lean back and smile, not caring if Jimmy ever gets to the end.

As he crosses the square, people stop Sam and talk to him, ask him about baseball or the weather. The older ones, some who live in years that unwound long ago, can't forget the cave-in and say to themselves that Sam Preston looks just like his daddy. But most people find him companionable.

The center of the town square is a park, and Sam walks across the cobbled pathway, crosses Main Street, and goes into Mountain Pages. He can't see a customer anywhere except Miss Elma Leonard, who's looking through the Hallmark cards. Mary Beth's by the counter in the back, and she smiles when she sees Sam.

She feels something now for him. Two years earlier, her husband, who was a salesman, had driven off a cliff near Gatlinburg, Tennessee. They had found no skid marks and decided he'd fallen asleep. The car fell eighty feet, tumbling down a green gorge into a glen filled with wildflowers. The papers said no one knew the car was there because the country was so inaccessible. He was missing for four days before they found the wreck. He was supposed to be on his way to Cincinnati. Nobody knew why he was in Tennessee, and Mary Beth's anguish was tinged with suspicion. Now she's thirty, and the bookstore is doing well. She'd opened it just before the wreck, and for a while the women in town brought her lunches, came and held her hand. She was a city girl, but their care touched her so deeply that now she says to herself she'll never leave Sheppard.

Mary Beth waits for Sam to come to her. He's kissed her twice now, the first time on the cheek and the second time on the lips after they'd gone to a movie in Bowling Green. She'd awakened hours later, the bed sheets balled in her fist, crying and saying his name. She lives a few miles from Sam on the ridge above town where the caves start.

"Good morning," she says. Her smile spills light into the room, Sam thinks. She's compact, not more than five two, with short brown hair that shines and steady blue eyes. She loves to laugh and has a vegetable garden behind her house.

"Morning," says Sam. He gets to the counter and leans against it. He could just stand here looking at her.

"Is this a social call or could I show you the latest Stephen King?" she asks. She sells both new and used books, and the aroma of pages, thousands of pages, mingles with the faint flowery echo of her perfume.

"How about the large-print edition of *Our Wonderful Caves*?"

Her laughter spills through the small room. They'll joke about that book, written by Sheppard's mayor, Douglas Dickens, and self-published. Sheppard County has five commercial caves now, from Sweet Sally to Confederate Caverns, but most of the people in town get tired of cave talk.

"You already spend too much time in caves," she says. She leans on the counter, her face in her hands. She whispers, "Miss Leonard's been looking for the right card for twenty minutes. Her next-door neighbor's got a new grandbaby."

"An everyday occasion," says Sam. "And you're right about caves. In fact, that's sort of what I wanted to tell you about Friday." Her face starts to fall, but she composes herself before Sam can see the edge of her disappointment. "I'm working through a new section, and I'm close to finding some things. I was wondering if you'd like to eat dinner at my place instead of going to Bowling Green again."

The air seems to drift from her chest. This is better, an intimacy she wants but does not know how to approach. She could fall into his arms and beg for that touch.

"I dunno," she says coyly. "Depends on what you're cooking for me."

"You pick," says Sam. "Either bologna sandwiches or spaghetti."

"Elegant choices," she says.

"Well, both *are* Italian," says Sam. Mary Beth can't stop laughing as Miss Leonard comes up and pays for her card and makes eyes at Sam. When she gets out, Mary Beth's eyes are still sparkling with delight.

"I'll take the spaghetti," she says. "Remember, red wine goes with that."

"Well, you sure are picky," says Sam. "I could ask Miss Stone. I bet she'd like whatever I cooked her."

"I bet she would," says Mary Beth. "All these little old ladies in town seem to love you to death."

"You know why?" says Sam. "It's because I'm a good boy."

"That remains to be seen," she says.

They talk a while longer, about the weather, about business, other things. They set the time, and she can't quite believe it when he starts to leave then looks at her hand on the counter and slowly draws his finger over it from the wrist to the tip of her finger. Even after he's out the door she can feel a heat in her hand, halfway up her arm.


Tom Meade comes through the back door, letting it slam lightly as he always does so Patricia can hear. He can smell cornbread and black-eyed peas cooking. They've lived in the same house for thirty-three years, a small brick structure on Thomas Street not far from downtown Sheppard. When they built the house it was in the country, but a neighborhood surrounds them now. Vast white oaks shade the house.

He walks through the den and into the kitchen, where Patricia stands before the stove stirring the peas. Her hair, as always, is cinched into a tight gray bun, and she looks up and tries to smile at Tom, but it's more of a brief nod.

"How was your morning?" she asks.

"Fine," says Tom. "Yours?"

"Jane Green called, and her mother died," says Patricia.

"I'm sorry, but she'd been sick a long time, I hear," says Tom. He gets plates, forks, and napkins from the cupboard and takes them to the small dining room that adjoins the kitchen. Patricia keeps it too clean, almost formal, as if they were expecting important guests.

"A year in September," says Patricia.

She serves the food, and they sit in the dining room and eat silently for a while. The fan blows on them. Tom looks up at Patricia's pictures. She has pictures on the walls of Jesus praying in the garden, of the dark day of the crucifixion, of Lazarus being raised from the dead.

"I went by the cemetery this morning," says Tom. He knows she can't stand to talk about it, isn't quite sure why he said it.

"They said on the radio that we could get heavy rain this weekend," she says. She won't look at him. She hasn't looked him in the eyes for a long time.

"You can see the cirrus clouds," Tom says. She gets up and goes to the kitchen and gets the salt and comes back and sits.

"Patricia, why won't you talk about the cemetery?" he says. He didn't come home to say this, can't figure why he even brought it up. They never argue, don't often discuss more than the day's events.

"Tom, don't," she says.

"Honey, it's been so long," he says. "At some point we have to, I mean . . ."

"Tom, don't," she warns him.

———

*10*

"I just don't think we have ever dealt with it properly," he says.

"I've heard this speech before, and I don't care to hear it now," she says coldly. "Are you finished?"

He looks at her and then through the window to his shady lawn. It's no good. She won't even say Andrew's name. He nods and helps her clean up the table and take the dishes to the sink. He goes into the den and gets the book he's reading, then walks back into the kitchen, where she's started to wash.

"I talked to Sam Preston this morning," he says.

"How's he doing?" she asks. Tom can see that she's relieved he has changed the subject.

"He's a good boy," says Tom.

"He's no boy," says Patricia, scrubbing the plate after it's completely clean. "He's certainly not a boy."

"No, I didn't mean it that way," says Tom. "I just meant that he's somebody I like a lot, that's all. He's trying to make a good life here."

"That's nice," says Patricia.

"I mean, after what happened, his daddy, you know, and all . . ."

Patricia turns angrily toward Tom, wiping her hands on her apron. She is trembling, and Tom feels foolish, as if he's driven to say something he knows he shouldn't.

"Tom Meade, stop it!" she says. "I won't listen to you living in the past. I've told you this over and over. I won't listen to you living in the past. I can't do this. I can't!"

She walks quickly through the house. He hears her close the bedroom door. Tom walks back into the den and sits in his recliner and tries to understand what he's feeling. All he can do is hold his finger at his place in the book and whisper two words. The first one is *Andy* and the second one is *Sam*.


Mary Beth's house nestles on a hillside amid a luxuriance of perennials and annuals, each with its proper place and color. A row of foxgloves shakes its bells in the wind. Fleshy portulacas spread out their spidery arms. From the porch, on rainy days, she can smell the marigolds.

She kneels in the soil now and pulls weeds from the raised bed of ferns and papyrus, exulting in the fecund smell of the earth and its textures. Once she bought a pair of gardening gloves, but she hated touching the soil with them. She can sit and crumble it in her palms for hours. After Charles died she would flee from the silence of the house and come into the yard and dig. Friends might come to check on her and find her sitting up a slope out back, pulverizing clods amid a military row of flowerpots she'd bought at a nursery in town. Gardening, keeping her hands in the soil, brought her back to life.

She thinks a little of Charles now. He was thoughtful but quiet, as if some valve that regulated ebullience had become stuck in childhood. When they'd first met, she valued that silence as the antidote to her own volatile nature. She thought that he would become more like her, but she was wrong. They were married four years, and she never even knew his favorite color. She'd asked him that once, and he'd said, *Whatever*, and she'd laughed and poked him in the ribs, but now she knows he meant it. When she thinks of Charles now, a veil descends over his features so that he seems like someone she saw in a movie or remembers from a book. She never looked at him after the accident. The funeral director said, *Mary Beth, maybe it would be better if you remembered him as he was.* His parents took it badly, though his brothers and sisters ate well and laughed sometimes during the mourning. His mother's name is Brinsley. Mary Beth has not talked to her now in eight months, knows she probably never will again. Mary Beth buried Charles in the Sheppard Cemetery, which is on a plateau above the Coollawassee River. She went once a week for two months, then once a month, then hardly at all.

Charles liked to play cards, and he could pick a twelve-string guitar, though not very well.

Mary Beth stands and brushes the dirt from her jeans and looks at the ferns and papyrus and nods: they are clean and healthy. She's thought of making paper from the pulpy stalks of papyrus, but she won't this summer. She'll save that for another year. After Charles died she thought that she had to do everything quickly because death could end it all without warning. She wore herself out, and her doctor put her to bed.

She goes inside and eats a light supper and puts on a CD of Natalie Cole and thinks of Sam. She sits on the sofa in the comfortable den and thinks of Sam Preston. If it isn't love, it can't be far off. He flirts with her. He's going to cook spaghetti for her.

She tries to understand his obsession with Blue Crystal Cave, but she can't see it. She knows all about the children who died, and how it ruined Sam's father. She knows Sam's father killed himself in Richmond, and she tries to think of how Sam felt when it happened. They share this unspoken bond of loss.

When they were eating in Bowling Green he'd laughed and told her a secret: *There wasn't any blue crystal*. At least it had never been found. Stories about it had started in pioneer days when the Indians used caves as gathering sites. During the War of 1812 soldiers mined saltpeter all through these hills and used it to make gunpowder because of the British blockade. A rumor started that in one cave north of Sheppard, a magnificent blue crystal was locked in limestone at the end of a lost chamber far underground. His grandfather, sensing the value of the cave as a tourist attraction, had sent off to South Africa for a hundred-pound amethyst crystal and put it in the cave along with lights and signs. The family kept improving the cave as the years passed, and it was making a fortune when it collapsed in 1958. The original entrance is now gone, but Sam first got into the cave through a sinkhole up the hill behind his house.

Mary Beth doesn't care about these channels beneath the earth, has only been into a few caves around here. She thinks of them and she is afraid. But when she thinks of Sam she feels safe and loved. She crosses her arms over her chest now and sings along with Natalie Cole and smiles. She feels safe. He's going to cook spaghetti for her.

Sam's house is a mess, but he doesn't care. The back porch nearly sags with rope, pitons, hammers, boots, carbide head-lamps, flashlights, and bags of rock samples. Friends will visit and say his house looks more like a hardware store than the real thing. He knows it does, shrugs it off.

When he and Ginger first came here, he sold the old family home, which had been rented out, and moved into what was for years a modest tenant house. After she left he'd stayed, and now it fits him well, several cluttered rooms off a central hall-way that cuts the house in half and ends on the kitchen, which extends along the back wall.

Now he's on the back porch sitting in cutoff jeans, checking his carabiners, metal snap rings he sometimes uses in climbing underground. He's listening to an old Little Feat album, which is on the stereo inside. He takes a sip of his beer and thinks of the section he's reached in Blue Crystal Cave now. One section goes north toward Sweet Sally, and for several years he looked for a connecting passage but never found it. These days he's working in a different sinkhole and exploring toward the south. When he thinks of it long enough, thinks of the children, he'll quit for a few days, but he always goes back down into the darkness.

The carabiners seem fine. An auto-belay's Prusik knots are secure. He adjusts the eye patch and swings his head back and forth to take in the piles of caving equipment. He thinks maybe this is an obsession. A waste. As a boy, he'd seen *Journey to the Center of the Earth*, and now he half believes that he can find a passage that goes down and down, to an ocean in the hot middle of the globe. But he knows that his rules of caving are confused. He wants to save those children from Little Rock. In his dreams, he can be moving along, following the beam of his carbide headlamp, and suddenly he sees them, huddled against the wall, faces black as coal-mine children's from Wales. They'll squint in the light, arms out toward him; they are saved. Their deaths will not be his family's fault or his own.

No one blames Sam for the disaster, but no one has forgotten. Each cave operator, in a fury over some worker's corner cutting, will say, *Remember what happened at Blue Crystal.* Sam's dreams upset Ginger. She'd tell him to quit going down there, just run the hardware store and leave the past alone. She said it all the time, *Nobody can change the past,* and it made the bitterness spill from him. After the explosion, when he lost his eye, his anger would not go away, and she left him.

Now he knows how stupid he was, that Ginger was right all along. He wrote her a long letter apologizing, but it was too late for them. He knows now that he should quit it, give it up finally. Only fools cave alone, much less a fool with only one eye.

But he has this idea. Going south, he might find the blue crystal. It's spilled into so many dreams. In one, the children stood as he arrived, huddled around the blue crystal, which glowed with its own light. Somehow it had guided him to their safe port. He'd awakened believing they had never died, and it took an hour before he knew nothing had changed, and he wept.

No reason to remember that now, he thinks. He sips the beer and goes back in the house and changes the record, putting on James Taylor. The music makes him think of Mary Beth, wonder what will become of their friendship. With his eye patch, he should be a seer, reading the future in the stalactites below the earth.

He's thinking of flowstone formations when he hears a car out front. He walks down the hallway to the front porch and sees that it's Tom Meade, getting out of his own car, a faded green Chevrolet.

"If you're looking for my moonshine still, it's in the north-west chamber of Sweet Sally," says Sam, and Tom laughs.

"I could take a beer as a bribe to keep my mouth shut," says Tom.

"Bribing lawmen is a specialty of the house," says Sam, who's glad to have some company. It gets lonely up here sometimes. "Come on up and let's get a cold brewski."

They walk through the house, and Sam gets them a Stroh Light each, and they sit on the edge of the back porch, feet not quite touching the ground. An owl cries urgently up the hill. Crickets and cicadas snicker in the weeds. The gibbous moon swings up just above the elms and oaks.

They agree ticks are bad this summer, and fleas. Tom tells him about a wreck out on the highway that afternoon. A woman from Florida died. She drove into a parked transfer truck on the side of the road. Sam says it's going to rain for the weekend. He wonders what Tom really wants to say, decides he can wait.

"I was just thinking it's hard," says Tom. He looks at Sam, shows him a thin smile.

"What?"

"Keeping it all straight," says Tom. "You know, everything. Things. Keeping it all straight." He sips his beer.

"Right. Keeping things straight is impossible," says Sam. "Half the time. I mean half the time it's like, huh?"

"You can't do it," says Tom. "You think a thing's done and gone, and then it's there in front of you. It's not done and gone, is it? It's not gone at all."

"It's never gone," says Sam. "You find that out quick enough."

"You try and talk to somebody about those things, and they can't face it," Tom says. "You keep thinking that if you don't believe in it, it never happened. But if you don't believe in one thing that's real, you can't believe in anything real. You start believing in things that never were true. You can't keep things straight."

16

"It's just like that," says Sam. "It's crazy."

"Well," says Tom.

He finishes his beer and notices that the moon is rising red and nearly full. They talk about owls and then hawks and then about how dangerous the roads are. Bridges fall apart all the time. Sam walks him back through the house, out to his car. Tom shakes his hand, holds it a second longer than usual, looks into Sam's eyes, and just nods.

"You tell Miss Patricia I said hello," says Sam. Tom nods and says he will. He pats Sam twice on the back, gets in his car, and drives off.

That night Sam dreams once more that he bursts into a section of the cave he's never seen, that he saves the children.

## 2

*They stole the car* in Chattanooga. Hermie is driving now, far into Kentucky, and Bobby is huddled against the door in the backseat, staring at the summer countryside. The colors are all gone. Leaves seem like a memory of green. Bobby holds the Camel between his lips and ignores Misty, who is nearly in his lap.

"Oh, come on," pleads Misty. Her feet are tucked under her slim hips. Her fingernails are thick with ruby polish, and Bobby glances at them and thinks of bugs. Small bright bugs creeping up his arm.

"He gets like this," says Clay. He's in the front with Christiann and Hermie. "You don't know him like I do. Sometimes, he goes like this for days."

Misty Ward leans back a little. Since she ran off with Bobby, leaving her husband of six months behind, she probably ought to try and understand. She watches Bobby Drake. He's small but muscular, and that turns her on. His fingernails are so clean. He can laugh and have a fine time, but he broods, too. And that tattoo of a blind snake on his arm chills her.

"Hon, let's talk about Kentucky," says Misty. She leans away from Bobby as if that will snap him out of it. "I never been out of North Carolina."

"It's a place to be passing through," says Bobby. She can't believe how he looks. His hair is so black it's almost blue. His eyes are green. When he'd come to work at her husband's garage in Cullowhee, she barely looked at him for two weeks. Then one day, when she was hanging out the wash, she saw him standing not ten paces away. J.D. had sent him back to the house to get a set of wrenches. J.D. was such a bastard, had beaten her the first week they were married. She spent part of every day thinking of leaving him. She couldn't quite say why she'd married him. When Misty looked up, she saw this level gaze coming back at her. She later told Bobby it felt like a whirlpool had formed behind her navel. She *knew*. She'd never known with J.D.

"Then how come we don't go to California?" says Christiann Mizelle from the front seat. She is Misty's best friend and still isn't sure why she ran off with them, except that she felt so badly for Misty living with J.D. They've been gone from Cullowhee for two days now. It's not because of Hermie. His gut spills from beneath his shirt, and he's balding and wears a silky mustache. Maybe it's Clay. He's tall and blond. She sits between them. She doesn't know much, only that Clay and Bobby did time in prison and that Hermie was Clay's friend years before.

"Hush up," scolds Misty. "Bobby says we're going to this town to find that cave, idn't that right, hon?"

Bobby looks up at Misty. The cigarette is nearly burnt down, and he takes it from his lips with the thumb and forefinger of his right hand. Hermie's driving on secondary roads. Misty's small features are taut with anticipation. Her hair is very dark brown, eyes a shade lighter. Her teeth are so white they look like petals of milk to Bobby. Misty doesn't smoke. The teeth are all slightly askew, though, moving around her mouth like an out-of-step marching band.

"Blue Crystal Cave," says Bobby. He wants to say more, tell her what he heard at Reidsville, but her acceptance, her eager approval, chills his tongue. *You can rule this world with silence*. His own father, chest sunk with bitterness and coal dust, had showed Bobby that, taking seven months to die. Bobby was twelve. For the last three months the man had not spoken a word. The morning he died he lay in bed, shaking with fear, refusing to let his anger go. Bobby had shaken his thin shoulders when the gaze got stuck and the lips parted. *Daddy, wake up, wake up*. But that silence was permanent then. It followed Bobby. After he killed Elijah Morton with a tire tool, Bobby felt the silence enter his bones. The killing had been almost an accident. He never wanted to hurt anybody, but that silence had entered his bones. Something about Elijah drove him into a brief madness.

"I think there's money buried there," says Clay. "Been closed up for years."

"Y'all want to stop and get some beer?" asks Christiann hopefully. Clay's thigh is tight up against hers. He doesn't seem too interested.

"I could go for a cold beer," says Misty. She takes a lipstick from her purse and rises high enough to see her face in the rearview mirror. Bobby watches her smear a dark red streak across her upper lip and then smack.

Hermie suddenly laughs, a dry flutter attached to nothing in particular. Christiann looks at him. She feels creepy. He's chewed his fingernails down to the moons, and sometimes spit forms at the corners of his mouth and he doesn't lick it off. Christiann licks her lips. Then she takes a lipstick from her purse, shades lighter than Misty's, and wipes it across her heavy lips. Her elbow nearly hits Clay in the mouth, but he just moves slightly toward the window. Christiann is just shy of fat.

"Anyway, I need to stop," says Misty.

"How far you reckon it is to this Sheppard, anyway?" Clay asks Bobby. Bobby stares at his friend. They'd met at Reidsville. Bobby starts to say something, then feels the maternal tug of silence. It was that way in the coal mines. When he was nine, Bobby's daddy took him down to show him why he should get out of West Virginia. The vein was pure black, the machinery grinding, eating it away. Men stripped to the waist in poor light hacked and coughed as they filled buckets and cars. The heat and stench were unbearable. Only after an hour, a thousand feet underground, did Bobby realize that the weight of this world was over him. He could imagine this tomb-shaped vein beginning to crumble and fall. He screamed. His daddy tried to hush him, but Bobby screamed so much they had to bring him up. The foreman docked his daddy a full day's pay. Once back into the pure air, Bobby gasped oxygen until he became giddy and fell, faint, into a wash of blackened sand.

After that he always feared death.

"Bobby?" asks Clay after a long time. Misty watches him, waiting for him to say something.

"Still a long piece off," says Bobby. "Hermie, stop at the next station for Misty."

"And we can get some beer," says Christiann. She's turned the rearview mirror toward her face and is fussing with her hair. She makes a face. She can't get it right in here. It's too cramped. "And a motel. I'm so tired of riding I could puke."

Hermie laughs again and turns on the radio. A shouting country preacher is talking about hell and redemption. Hermie finds it hilarious.

In the backseat, Misty is trying to blow her breath on Bobby's neck. That makes men crazy. Her friend Kathilou said so, and for once Kathilou was right. But Bobby says nothing, doesn't move.

"Ow!" cries Bobby. They turn from the front seat, all but

Hermie. Bobby's accidentally let the cigarette burn down and singe his fingers. He flicks the butt out the window. Misty takes his hand and thrusts the burned fingers in her mouth. She gently licks them, glancing up at Bobby. Christiann feels as if her deodorant is starting to go bad. She can't explain it.

"Go, baby," says Clay. He laughs.

"Better, hon?" asks Misty, finally removing the fingers. Bobby smiles at her, kisses her cheek. The radio preacher is talking about eternal darkness. Christiann notices that the rich aroma of honeysuckle briefly fills the car, overpowering the smell of cigarettes. Already in the hill country, she watches the earth begin to mound and hump, trees and vines rising and falling. She wonders what they're thinking back in Cullowhee. Her mother's probably about to lay an egg.

"Fire," says Bobby softly.

"Fire," nods Clay. It was a game in prison: finding a focus that would help them past the pain. There was *fire*. There was *steel*. There was *blade*, and there was *ice*.

"What's this, like some secret language?" asks Christiann.

"You hush," says Misty, warning her friend. "My Bobby says fire, it's fire, right, hon?"

Bobby grins but can't find anything to say.

"There," says Clay. He points to a sign that says Sheppard, Kentucky, is sixty-four miles away. "I hope that jerk was right about that cave."

"Who told you about the cave, anyway?" asks Christiann. Her hand rests loosely on Clay's knee, but he doesn't even seem to notice.

"Con used to live in Sheppard," says Bobby. A thunder-shower to the east hangs a curtain of violet and flame. Bobby watches the forked tree of a bolt and waits for thunder, but it's too far away or the car's making too much noise. "Said the family owned this Blue Crystal Cave got rich, but then it fell in. Always talked about how rich old man Preston was."

"Rich is my middle name," says Christiann. Her face is very

close to Clay's, and he thinks her nose is too fat on the tip. The preacher on the radio says that at the Last Judgment, the trumpet shall sound and the dead shall be raised incorruptible.

"There's a service station," says Misty. She's bent over and looking straight ahead. Hermie pulls the Taurus into the gravel lot, up to the pump. A dusty cloud following them catches up, lingers for a moment, and then swirls on ahead. "Come on, Christiann. Let's go tinkle together. You never know what's hidin' out in a place like this."

Hermie laughs. He gets out and starts to pump the gas. Bobby and Clay get out and walk to the back of the car. They've taken the license plate off and stuck on a crudely cut piece of cardboard that says LOST TAG. They light up and stretch.

"Bro, you tell me what you think's up there," says Clay. His father was Mexican, and his last name's García. But his hair is blond, almost ash like his mother's. He never met his father. Drunk one night, his mother admitted she'd barely met him, either.

"It's there, the money," says Bobby.

"Right," says Clay.

Bobby sucks up the smoke from the Camel. Once, a few years back in Reidsville, he cried in his bunk at night. He couldn't believe it. He was so frightened when he awoke that he hit a con named Jernigan in the stomach. Hurting in the head was his life. He had thought about it after that and could not remember a single time he'd ever been happy. He only wanted enough money to sit tight, think about things. One score. That was all. Clean. Almost like science. He missed Doc. Guy named Barber doing time for killing his wife. High school science teacher or something. They called him Doc. Nothing got under that man's skin.

"I just want to find if there's a score," says Bobby. A wind stirs the dust. Hermie finishes pumping and heads inside to pay. The girls gave him gas money. They were good for that. Bobby kicks at the gravel. "What about you and Christiann?"

"I guess," says Clay.

"Hermie doesn't like girls?"

"Hermie's on a different wavelength," says Clay. "He could do anything without thinking about it. Like there's a filter missing or something."

"Yeah," says Bobby. "Okay."

In the rest room, Misty and Christiann look at themselves in the shard of stained mirror. Christiann can't believe her hair. The mirror's corner is broken off cleanly.

"Tell me what you think of Bobby," says Misty excitedly. "Idn't he something?"

"He scares me," admits Christiann. She tries to sweep her hair down a little over the forehead, and that's better. "It's like he's always about to blow up."

"I know," squeals Misty. "Something, ain't he?"

"If you like that kind of thing," says Christiann. "I mean, I wouldn't suck his fingers or nothing."

They laugh, touch each other's shoulders. A clap of thunder pours down the Kentucky hills and rattles the doorframe. When they come outside, the air has changed. Something could happen soon. Neither one minds.

Thunder comes once more, and the earth seems to vibrate beneath them, as if it might rise up or suddenly give way, collapse into veins of darkness.

3

*S*am *Preston* lies on his stomach, sliding downward in an inch of fetid water. The tube has narrowed dangerously until Sam's shoulders will barely slip across the slick flowstone. A fissured ceiling channel only inches above holds a tuft of angel's hair, gypsum needles that fill in brief glory with the light from his headlamp as he passes.

He has never been this far past the breakdown in the south end of the cave. He knows that any moment he could feel the air change, the tube widen as he slides into something grand. Barely a month before, Sam had found a grotto hung with translucent calcite curtains and tufted stalactites. But that was in the east spread of Blue Crystal Cave, and this is far south, where the walls are often crumbling and rotten.

"Oh Lord," says Sam softly. He can see the word on cool mist. He has pushed forward so fast that his shoulders have lodged on the side of the flowstone. He turns his eye directly toward the receding hole in front, sees only small darkness where the light ends. He's taking a chance by caving alone. His friends all think it's foolish after the explosion. Not only going beneath the surface alone but with a single good eye.

Sam exhales. His shoulders come in half an inch, and he pushes against the walls. He does not move. He closes his eye. Through the lid he can see light from the carbide lamp. He can see nothing through the pirate's patch on his left eye. He'd made them leave the eyeball, but it is sightless. Sometimes he looks at it in the mirror. A dank odor of sulfur comes from somewhere in front of him.

He pushes backward once again, face red from the exertion, and this time his shoulders slide free. He groans with relief, moves faster and faster, crabbing, not bothering to glance upward at the angel's hair. In thirty seconds he falls backward out of the tube. Sam coughs, leans against the wall. This section of the cave is going nowhere.

He checks his watch. Mary Beth is coming over for dinner in less than an hour, and it's forty minutes back to the sinkhole where he gets into Blue Crystal Cave these days.

After half an hour of following his own light he sees a glow ahead in the corridor where he's strung electric lights. He'd planned to relight most of the cave, but he's only done the room just below the sinkhole. It is half a mile from the original entrance to the cave, but he never goes that direction. After they dug the church group out, the cave collapsed again, and they sealed the entrance. He could reach the old commercial area, the Grand Room, the once-famous bacon-rind drapery, but he never goes that direction either. He keeps seven or eight flashlights in here.

When he gets to the sinkhole he sees rain coming down. Funny, he thinks, how there are two levels to this earth and one holds its darkness like a dream.

* * *

Sam can be lying in bed, and he'll think he can see with his left eye. Some mad variant of phantom limb syndrome, he supposes. He might have been dreaming of a bad knot on his auto-belay, thinking of falling. Often, he leaps up windmilling, arms grasping air. Sweat-soaked, he'll sit up for a moment, planets, suns revolving around him in the small bedroom. He'll turn to his left and see things. He'll palm the eyeball gently. A man with heavy biceps is coming into the room. He will close the right eye and sweep his head right and left, but the scene doesn't change, like turning a television screen, and he knows that image is somewhere inside looking for a fissure to escape, not out there in the room trying to get in. He lies back then and tries to trace the man or the sunset or whatever image lingers inside that blank pupil. The man might speak, but Sam can't hear his words. Sometimes, water is running. On moonless nights it might take him several minutes to separate one world from another. Then, he's floating or flying, knowing that he's finally done it, become hopelessly lost in Blue Crystal Cave. But if he turns to the real light when morning comes, a curtain of sun in the pines and oaks, he will know an unimaginable urge to gather back the night.

Sam found a tribe of blind salamanders and brought the natural-resources boys up for a look. They said it was nothing special. But Sam had spent days watching them navigate the icy holes by instinct and touch. Sam thought love might be an acquired sense. He did not seem to have missed it when Ginger left, but that might have simply been anger, he reasoned. When Sam first found out about Blue Crystal Cave, his anger had changed him. A kind boy who played clarinet, he became sullen and introspective. He wrote Little Jackie Moss's aged parents one time, but they didn't answer. He was seventeen then. Sam would chop wood, stay away from people. He thought of Ginger, but she might have been the face from a favorite movie seen many times.

27

When he'd first noticed Mary Beth, she had not long before lost her husband. She ran the bookshop, but she also grew flowers and tended her house. Sometimes Sam drove past. She was always touching flowers. On her knees, rocked backward on her hips, she was planting, watering, turning petals. She looked upward to the sun, then back at the new buds.

Sam dreams of Mary Beth, but it's a different one. The girl at night touches his ear with her lips, and he can feel her words sliding down the channels of his body, lodging squarely in the heart. You awaken breathing hard from a thought like that. But he can't feel it awake, not sexually, anyway. Sometimes when they're sitting on his front porch or hers, watching the sunset tug west, he'll dream a parallel life for them, children, Sunday dinners, baptisms in the Coollawassee River.


She's sitting on his porch steps when he walks down the three hundred yards from the sinkhole. He's late. He comes up adjusting the patch. She's never seen his eye without it. Often, he'll catch her looking at it, as if she might pull it away in his sleep, as if he's the Phantom of the Opera.

"I'm just plain sorry when it comes to time," says Sam. Mary Beth is wearing a long dress and holding two yellow roses. "Here I am inviting you to supper, and I'm the one who's late to my own house."

"You're pretty sorry," she says. She smiles. When he gets to the steps, he pushes the black hair back from his eye. She hands him one of the roses, and she keeps the other. He sniffs it.

"A rose," says Sam. "I'd forgotten how nice they smell. Isn't this sexist or something, the woman bringing flowers?"

"You get a shower, and I'll have a glass of wine," she says. "You did get wine, didn't you?"

*"Mais oui,"* says Sam Preston.

She can't understand why he lives in this small, cluttered house. Sometimes one corner of a room will seem to be freeing itself of ropes, lamps, brake bars. The next time she comes, equipment has crawled there, heaving itself into the chairs, taking over everything. He has money, but he knows the shape of this disorder. Her house is frantically neat and dustless, and now, in the kitchen, even with the fragrant aroma of vinegar, the ghosts of recent meals, she can't resist an urge to tidy things.

The kitchen is a rectangle on the back of the house with room for a table and two chairs that Sam made himself. They have a rough charm. Off the kitchen is a small covered porch shaded by oaks. The grass needs cutting out there.

Mary Beth finds the wine in the fridge and pours herself a glass. Water is running in the bathroom. The house drums, rushing toward Sam's shower. She can be in town at the shops, and she'll look across the square and think of Sam.

Just beyond the edge of the yard, the hills spill upward. He keeps saying he'll take her up there, down into Blue Crystal Cave, but she doesn't want to go. She'll pass on geologic wonders, hold flowers and books instead.


Sam feels full and lazy. After wine and spaghetti they sit on the front steps. A cardinal and its mate hang in the dusty lower boughs of a red oak. They're chirping, nearly barking at each other. Mary Beth's cleaned the kitchen. Sam told her to leave it, but she just couldn't.

"I think I almost didn't get out today," says Sam. Fireflies wander around them like pleasantly lost angels.

"What are you talking about?" They're sitting next to each other but not touching. Something's different tonight. Storms might be breaking to the north, but here it is very still.

"I was in a tube, going down about seven, eight degrees, and I just kept pushing," says Sam. "My shoulders got stuck. I didn't think I was going to get out."

"My God," says Mary Beth. They're quiet for fifteen seconds.

"I was scared," says Sam.

"I wish you wouldn't do this," she says. "What was at the other end of the tube?"

Sam smiles. That's the problem. Seeing everything down there, the benign and the brutal, the beautiful.

"There's a cathedral down there," he says softly. He sounds almost apologetic. Mary Beth's been looking at the fireflies and the heat lightning, but now she looks at Sam. He stares at his hands. They're weaving air, fingers fumbling. "I'm going to break through all that rock down there, and I'm going to come into this glorious room full of spires and windows. It'll be as quiet as a benediction."

"Sam," she says, not sure why she simply calls his name. He looks up at her.

"Sometimes I'm down there, Mary Beth, and I hear my own name coming back to me," he says. "Heaven could be beneath the earth. I don't think angels live just on the clouds."

"You believe in angels?"

You can come around a corner down there into unfurled calcite wings. You could imagine they are fallen angels. Or not. *Everything trapped is not trying to escape.* Sam can't find the right words to say it.

"When I was a little boy, I believed an invisible elf lived in my closet," says Sam. Mary Beth's laughter spills up, unforced, pleasingly natural.

"You ever see invisible elves down there?"

"I think I saw Elvis once," says Sam. She laughs again, leaning against his shoulder, then back. "Don't you ever see Elvis when you work in your garden?"

"Never," she says. "Maybe Jimmy Hoffa, though."


It's late now. She has to go, and Sam walks her to the dusty Cherokee. A quiet wind mumbles in the leaves. The night seems starless. It's dark anywhere you look.

"We'll have to do this again," says Sam. He swings his head

———

30

back and forth to take in the scene. It's an irritating habit, but he feels afraid sometimes because his depth perception is so poor.

"Yeah," says Mary Beth. Sam leans down to kiss her cheek. She watches him move close. When his lips brush her cheek, her hands grasp his shoulders. The touch surprises him. For a second or two they stand like that, his face close to hers. He wants to kiss her lips, as he's done only once, but he can't bear the idea that she might disapprove.

"You take care," Sam says.

"You, too," she says.


It's much later, and Sam could kick himself. Her lips were that close, so near he could smell her lovely breath. Tonight he's restless, thinking of the tunnels underground, where they all might go. He dreamed once that all the channels and grottoes were wayward threads, going into one awe-inspiring room, ranks of speleothems like organ pipes spread around him, upward to a glory. But what then? He can't see himself owning another commercial cave in Sheppard County. Besides, even four decades later they remember those poor children.

Lying in bed, relieved to have the patch off and hanging on the bedpost, Sam thinks of his anger. Once it had seemed like his own child, growing in there, monstrous, ready to choke him. He could look at Ginger, and she'd smile, and something of pure clotted madness would rise up. It wasn't even the blood of his father. He didn't know how much of it was anyone's fault. Someone should have known part of the cave was unstable. No one did. Ginger was hurt so easily. When she finally left Sam tried to apologize, to think of anything that made sense, but little came.

"One day you're going to go down there, and you're going to decide not to come out," she said. "I'm not going to be sitting around here waiting on that."

He could think of nothing to say to her, that cute sandy-haired girl, so pleasant, open. Here in his room, he gently bounces his fingers off the blind eye. Colors and lights seem to appear. He wants to dream a new route to the heart of the earth, to see if it's all liquid, all fire.

Sam's up early, already half a mile back in the east wing again. He peers into the opening of the tube where he was stuck the day before, decides to go no farther. He wants to photograph the gypsum needles in there someday but not soon. The tube has the shape of tombs. Perhaps this is his own family pyramid. While they're packing them in at Mammoth Cave, while thousands are marveling at Luray, Sam's alone in the acetylene glow of his headlamp. This cave system goes everywhere, arrives nowhere.

Sam's father explored these passages as a young man, convinced they'd connect to Sweet Sally, Sheppard County's best cave. But all he found was a descent of impenetrable darkness.

This place is not unfamiliar: a collapsed chamber full of jagged sheets of stone on the floor. You crawl over them, hoping not to get cut. Far off, water is moving. It could be another Ruby Falls or merely echoes of something above ground. All the karstland of Kentucky sinks down limestone sinkholes toward places like Blue Crystal Cave. Forty feet higher, a brief ledge juts over Sam, and he senses a tube might twist off it.

He looks for footholds, crevices in which to wedge his strong hands. He hammers a few pitons in as he ascends, threads his guide rope through, but he's playing at it. He wants that ledge. The cold, damp stone moves its vibrations through his gloves into his hands. Sam scans the ledge, moving his head back and forth. The ceiling is closer now, and he breathes heavily.

His chest is heavy. He groans for breath. It feels as if someone is holding him around his heart, embracing him half to death. He reaches the ledge, and with a last effort pulls himself up to it.

He sees another wall. The ledge goes ten yards, crumbles away. There are no tubes, no grottoes. No carved names. No human has ever sat on this outcrop and looked down into the room before him.

"Crap," says Sam. His voice is deadened. The sound carries only a few inches. He'd imagined it: this shelf connected by a narrow passageway to a spreading gorge, something that might hold demons with bat wings. You could come around a slab of rock anywhere here and find heaven or hell. He remembers a picture of Satan from his boyhood, and even *he* had wings.

Sam should be moving back down the rope now. The day is barely started. He should let the gravity of the earth's core pull him toward the center of things. Instead, he thinks of Mary Beth and the closeness of her lips. What could he offer her? It would not be his vision, real or imagined. It would be his map to this place, his veins and capillaries. He could lean close to her and say that nothing you stand on in this life is ever as solid as you think.

## 4

*B*obby Drake needs a beer, and his face is pressed against the backseat window frame. He's staring at the poor countryside. Misty's feelings are hurt, and she's clear on the other side of the seat, looking at the massive crossing contrails of two long-gone jets. Misty had touched his shoulder and called him hon, and Bobby had snapped at her.

They'd slept until noon, up all night drinking at this flat-roofed motel called The Bear Hut. Bobby's head hurts. Hermie's listening to a call-in show about home canning with some extension agent. Clay and Christiann are kissing sometimes up there. She'd finally jumped him the night before.

Christiann wants to go to California with Clay. "You could be a movie actor," she'd told him. He was so drunk he can't remember that part, so she's told him again, and he just laughs. He can get money faster than that.

Storms exploded in southern Indiana that night. They got two rooms, as far as the money went. Bobby and Misty got one. Clay and Christiann and Hermie took the other one.

The rooms didn't even have televisions. Clay had drunk six beers, and Christiann was looking better. He was sitting in a rickety green chair at the foot of the bed. Christiann was cross-legged on the bed. She sipped a wine cooler. Hermie was on the other bed, reading a crumpled copy of *Dune*. He'd read it thirty-six times. He could tell you the entire history and life cycle of sand worms.

"You better not hurt me," said Christiann.

"It's okay," said Clay. He set his beer on the air conditioner that jutted from the sill. It clattered and rumbled, spilling slightly cool air into the room. He came on the bed and sat beside Christiann. Clay reached out and with his right index finger traced a slow line from the middle of her forehead, across her nose and lips, down her chin and neck.

Hermie barely turned his head when they began to noisily make love, but it lasted only a few minutes, and when he was through Clay put on his shorts, got another beer from the sink, and opened the door and listened to the rain.

When they got up that morning, nobody wanted to talk much except Hermie, who had come out near three A.M. and gotten a West Coast baseball game on the car radio. Some pitcher had walked in the winning run, and Hermie still couldn't believe it.


They don't get to Sheppard until nearly two, and the sky is clouding and steamy now. Your eyes can be slits, and it still hurts. Hermie drives past the city limits sign, and everyone stirs, even Bobby. Hermie pulls into a rough-looking bar and grill called Mama's Crossroads. Christiann kisses Clay on the neck once just before they get out.

"Cut that out," says Clay, wiping his neck off. "Feels like a damned fish. Your mouth's cold."

Hermie's dry laughter, high-pitched, almost sad, bounces around the car. Hermie's fat, so the car sits higher, groans in relief as he gets out. Bobby gets out one side of the car, Misty the other. Christiann comes around to Misty, whose face is dark and drawn. Bobby hasn't said a word about Misty's shorts outfit, curve-hugging lime green. The men move a little toward the front. Bobby lights a cigarette and then puts his hands in the pockets of his tight jeans.

"Did he hurt you?" whispers Christiann.

"No," says Misty. "I just don't know what to say to him."

"You know how men are," says Christiann. She's quiet for three steps. "I think me and Clay might be going to California." Misty giggles and grabs Christiann's arm.

"He got you last night, didn't he, girl?" says Misty.

"Or I got him," says Christiann, and they both giggle.

The men are at the door, and Hermie's told a joke, but he's the only one laughing. Bobby smells something outside the door, a salty or mildly foul odor that reminds him of Reidsville. A couple of years, they made him work with the garbage. The smell got in his hands, and he'd awaken on his bunk in the night, fingers to his face, and he'd nearly retch from the smell. A year after he was working on the prison farm he could still smell traces of garbage on his right index fingertip.

"What the dope, bro?" asks Clay, noticing his friend has stopped.

"Reidsville," says Bobby, and Clay just nods. Hermie's still giggling about his joke. His copy of *Dune* rides in the hip pocket of his jeans. Hermie's gut is enormous, and his shirttail flaps as he walks, but he has no hips.


The money's starting to run out, and Clay counts it twice while they're waiting for the hamburgers to come.

"I bet your husband's about to scream," says Hermie to Misty. Hermie's got some peg game. You're supposed to jump one peg over another, removing them like checkers, until they're all gone. He's slow, but most of the pegs are gone.

"Hush up," says Misty. Hermie makes her blood turn to ice water. Christiann's a little embarrassed because he saw her naked, but he doesn't seem to care about anything.

"You're just trying to make her mad," says Christiann. The men are on one side of the booth, crammed in, and Misty and Christiann are on the other. Bobby and Clay are smoking, looking around the room. Bumper stickers, metal signs, free brochures, all say *This Is Cave Country*.

"He's just probably trying to figure out what happened to his baby doll," says Hermie. His grinning upper lip pushes the mustache up. Clay is between Hermie and Bobby.

"Don't," says Bobby, turning in the seat and looking behind Clay. Misty notices his hand is shaking a little, and the cigarette ash falls on the table, missing the tray. Clay has an odd expression, as if he's enjoying all of this. He's a lifter, and his upper shoulders are huge, pressing against his T-shirt.

"Hey, I was just reporting the news," says Hermie.

"You leave her alone," says Christiann. "You love somebody, don't nothing stand in your way, idn't that right, Misty?"

Christiann is smiling at Clay, but Misty doesn't say a thing. She looks at Bobby for some sign, but nothing's there.

The waitress comes out with a tray of food. They're all suddenly ravenous. Bobby and Clay put out their cigarettes. The waitress has the name Deenie stitched on her blouse.

"Who's got the cheeseburgers?" asks Deenie, and they sort things out. Bobby watches the food.

"We're looking for a cave," says Bobby Drake.

"Don't take a genius to find a cave in Sheppard County," says Deenie. She gets two of the orders in the wrong place, then gets them right. She's popping gum. She looks over the food, and it seems okay. She tucks the tray under her arm. "We got caves that have caves. That's an old saying around here."

"It's one specific cave," says Bobby, seeming suddenly softer as he eats. Misty puts her foot in his lap under the table, but he doesn't even look at her. "Called Blue Crystal Cave."

"Blue Crystal Cave fell in when my mommer was a little girl," says Deenie. She blows a bubble. It pops, and she harvests the pink film with her tongue. Clay notices that Deenie has very small teeth. "Nothing up there now but Sam Preston. He's a nice guy, though. Runs a hardware store in town. Ain't there on Fridays or Saturdays, though. Everybody knows that. You wanna see a cave, you orta see Sweet Sally. It's the one we're famous for."

"How about Deenie's cave?" asks Hermie. A piece of lettuce is hanging from his lip.

"You wish," says Deenie, looking at a fingernail suspiciously, then yawning.

"Oh, ha ha," says Misty. Christiann starts to laugh.

Bobby has stopped eating. He's looking at Deenie, and Misty feels some dark jealous knot behind her breastbone.

"Preston?" says Bobby.

"His daddy owned Blue Crystal Cave," says Deenie. She looks around the place for customers, but nobody else is there this time of day. "Got rich is the story you hear. Moved away after the thing fell in on them children."

"The cave fell in on children?" asks Christiann.

"Oh, musta been like a hundred of 'em," says Deenie. She bends her knees slightly, sees her reflection in the window-pane, fusses with her hair. "From Louisiana or somewhere. Got killed when the thing fell in. It was big news. My uncle, he owned a cave, said it like to have put them all out of business. Y'all need anything else?"

"This Preston man's rich, then," says Bobby.

"Who knows?" says Deenie.

"Madame," says Hermie, waving a hand in papal circles, "I'd like for you to bear my children."

"If they looked like you, I'd drown 'em," says Deenie. Christiann almost chokes, she's laughing so hard, and even Misty,

---

who's trying to stay angry, can't help it. She's laughing, too.

Deenie wanders off blowing bubbles. Bobby seems to forget about his food, and Misty wants to act that way exactly, but she's starving, so she eats, and it's not bad. Hermie's manners are almost sickening.

"How can you eat like that?" asks Christiann finally. "It's enough to turn my stomach."

"What's cooking, bro?" asks Clay. Bobby's taken out a cigarette and lit it.

"You gone eat that?" asks Hermie. Bobby shakes his head, and Hermie grabs the other half of Bobby's burger.

"Rich folks," says Bobby.


You ask directions, people will tell you anything. They might remember a landmark, a turning to the left at some fence post, or they might enjoy directions, give too many. The grease monkey at the gas station gave them to Hermie, but they're lost now in some hills north of Sheppard.

Clay's trying to remember something about circling that he read in a paperback book when he was in Reidsville. He read all the time, spy novels mostly, and he'd give them to Bobby. It took Bobby eight months to read one of them. Clay can't remember about circling now.

"None of these roads is marked," says Bobby. " 'Take Flat Rock Road'—hell, it ain't marked. These hicks think everybody in the world knows their damned roads."

"Welcome to Cave Country," says Hermie. His dry laughter puts Misty's nerves on edge.

"Are we lost?" asks Christiann nervously.

"Keep your panties on," says Clay.

"Didn't say that last ni-ight," singsongs Hermie.

Bobby's dad took them to his grandmother's house once when Bobby was eight, all the way to Raleigh, but he'd taken a bad route somewhere. When his father got upset or excited he'd begin to cough from the coal dust, and they spent an hour on a country roadside with him coughing and hacking, wheezing, trying to get his breath back. Bobby sat in the backseat, terrified his father would die. His mother couldn't drive. He'd have to walk for miles and miles to find a house; anything could happen then. After twenty minutes his dad started coughing blood, then he fell asleep. When he awoke he was weak but not coughing. They'd only been half a mile from the intersection on the map, but it might have been ten years into hell. Bobby didn't sleep for two days. His grandmother could hardly recognize him; he'd grown so much and he looked old and tired, like his father. Just getting another breath terrified him.

Misty watches him. Bobby can't help himself. She can calm him down.

"What are y'all gonna do if we find this Preston man?" asks Christiann. She and Misty are still in the backseat, the men up front. They've bought beer with their dwindling money. Everyone has one open.

Bobby turns in the seat.

"He's rich," says Bobby. "Nobody rich has a right to keep it all to themselves. We'll ask him to share it."

"Share," snorts Hermie.

"Are we gonna rob this man?" asks Christiann.

"You hush up," scolds Misty. "My Bobby don't do a thing he don't have to, idn't that right, hon? He just asks the man to give us some money, and that's all."

"Well, doing a robbery's what got my Clay in prison," says Christiann.

"Stop running your mouth," says Clay. He turns to Bobby. "Blade."

"Blade," says Bobby, shaking his head.

"Blade?" says Christiann. "Sweet honey, what are y'all talking about with this stuff?"

"Leave it lie," says Misty.

"There's Sweet Sally," says Hermie. He's been humming

some old hymn and interrupts it to speak, then resumes it. A huge sign with an arrow says it's two miles to Sweet Sally, Sheppard County's grandest cave. Over one hundred thousand visitors annually. "You want to go there first or something?"

"Keep driving," says Bobby.

"Hey, look at that," says Christiann.

"What?" asks Misty. She leans over her friend's lap and looks out the window.

"I thought I saw a rainbow," says Christiann. Misty looks right and left.

"I don't see nothing," says Misty.

"You ain't Judy Garland," says Hermie.

"How come a hundred thousand people a year pay to go down in some cave?" asks Clay.

"Like going to hell and escaping," says Bobby. Misty moves back to her side of the seat.

"Like being in prison," says Hermie.

"Shut up, Hermie," says Clay with a sigh. Hermie's changed. He used to be weird and fun, good to drink with. He's read too many things in the past five years. He talks like a damned book, has odd ideas.

"Or a bad marriage," says Hermie.

"Oh, ha ha," says Misty angrily.

"There's the sign for Fall Creek Cave," says Clay. "Here's where we turn."

"Being lost is a relative thing," says Hermie.


Bobby had attacks in prison. He'd be working on a detail or lying in bed, and he'd feel as if his brain were melting. He could feel it begin to liquefy. He'd press his hand to his ears so fluid wouldn't leak out on the sheets. His breath would get fast, and he could see his brain crumbling apart. He'd seen pictures of the brain once in a book at Reidsville. A con named Lucky said your brain could melt and run right out your ears. When he'd killed the man with a tire tool, Bobby had hit him so hard his brains broke through the cracked bone.

When Bobby had his attacks he would try to concentrate on something until it went away. He'd look at the blind snake tattooed on his arm. It would rise up a little and look around, crawl up and down his muscles. Once, the snake had crawled into Bobby's head, and he'd gone blind for two days, thrashing around.

They took him to the hospital and gave him a shot, and when he came around he didn't know who he was for a long time.

# 5

*Sheriff Tom Meade* wipes the sweat from his eyes and looks down at the shoals in the Coollawassee River. The weatherman said the cold front has stalled and is gaining strength. Tom smells the gasoline on his hands and wipes them off on a rag. He has finished cutting his son's plot, kept going and cut two or three others that needed it. The old folks can't get out to keep them groomed. He sees heat rising from the old push mower.

The inscription on Andrew's stone just says *Darling boy*, and he's never liked that. Tom thinks that Andrew's grown up now and will find it silly, but that's what Patricia wanted. She hasn't been out here in more than ten years now. When some spinster dies, when she has to come to a funeral, she'll act as if the stone

,were not here at all. Tom comes all the time, and he can't decide what hurts more, seeing it or pretending it isn't here.

When he bought the plot he got enough space for himself, the boy, Patricia, and other children they might have. He wanted to have more children, but she did not. He wanted a family plot, but she didn't even want a family.

He squats before Andrew's stone and wipes off the grass that's blown there from the mower. He whispers a few words. He stands back up in time to see Sheppard Mayor Douglas Dickens walking toward him, smoking a cigarette and looking worried. Douglas is wearing a white seersucker suit with pale blue pinstripes. His shirt is white, and the tie neat and snugged into the collar. He is short and chubby, always looking mildly ill or worried.

"Well, the public works people have just gotten nowhere stringing the bunting for Sheppard Dollar Days," says Douglas. "I was thinking you could give Jack a nudge."

"He's your employee, Douglas," says Tom, "not mine. I don't work in City Hall, remember?"

"Oh hell, Tom, I know that," says Douglas with a dry laugh. He stays with Tom step for step, and as they reach the pickup he touches Tom on the sleeve. "It's just that Jack's got it in for me because I'm recommending a cut in his budget. If I tell him to get on with it, he'll sit down like a mule and do nothing. You know how people like that are."

"I do," says Tom. He squats and lifts the mower with his powerful arms and sets it in the back of the truck.

"For God's sake don't give yourself a coronary," says Douglas. "Anyway, everything's off schedule, and the Merchants' Council is getting edgy because there's no bunting and no flags. You can't have a sale without flags. Hell, everybody knows that."

"Everybody knows that," says Tom.

"Besides, these weathermen are saying it's going to rain for the weekend," says Douglas. He lights another cigarette. "Of course, what do they know, right? The cave operators are counting on this bringing lots of people into the county. You know what this means for business."

Tom gets the gas can and puts it in the truck.

"I know what it means," says Tom.

"I knew I could count on you," says Douglas. "It's a matter of planning. Everything's a matter of proper planning, Tom. That's right, isn't it?"

"That's right."

"These weathermen don't know squat," says Douglas. "They never have. I bet we won't get a drop. See, it's all a matter of proper planning. It's like the cemetery. It's too close to the river. Been here a hundred years, and it's too close to the river. This wasn't proper planning."

Tom gets in the truck and closes the door. Douglas stands next to him and looks down to the river, then back.

"The river changed course over the last century," says Tom. "When they built the cemetery, it wasn't this close. You know that."

"Anticipation," says Douglas, pointing at Tom with his cigarette, then smiling. "You anticipate problems, that's part of proper planning. I knew Jack would stall like hell getting the bunting up. And the flags. Don't forget the flags. Without those flags we might as well not have Dollar Days at all. You can't do business without those flags."

Tom stares past Douglas at the river and then back.

"Not everybody on the Merchants' Council wanted to use flags," says Tom. "Sam Preston didn't."

"Dang, Tom, you of all people," says Douglas. "Defending somebody from that family." Douglas shrugs as if he can't quite believe what Tom's said. "I mean, you of all people."

"I was just saying not everybody agreed on the flag thing," says Tom wearily. He starts the truck. The engine needs servicing and splutters and shakes.

"Sam's a great guy, and he means well," says Douglas.

"Everybody likes Sam. *I* like Sam. But it's been decided now, and Jack's just sitting down like a mule because of budgets. Jesus, I'm responsible here. It's my call. Nobody can say I haven't done the proper planning. You can avoid problems if you do the proper planning."

"We'll see," says Tom.

"We'll see?" says Douglas with a nervous laugh. "That's what you say to a kid to put him off."

Tom glances at the sky and nods.

"Douglas, you know what?" he says.

"What?"

"To me, it looks like rain," says Tom. He puts the truck in gear and rolls down the dusty cemetery road before the mayor's mouth can close.


Tom's office in the courthouse is full of mementos. He was Kentucky Sheriff of the Year in 1977. The governor gave him an award. The attorney general named him to a panel on law enforcement reorganization in the state, and he was praised by everyone for his evenhanded work. They started calling it the Meade Committee. The commonwealth gave him a special certificate. He left it rolled up for a month before Patricia had it framed.

The office needs cleaning, but Tom can't bring himself to throw things away. He has a view of the town square from this office on the second floor. A framed picture of James Madison has been on the wall since the early part of the century. Tom has a picture of Patricia on his desk, but it's an old one, and it's obscured by stacks of papers anyway.

He has a window air conditioner unit, but it doesn't work well. He gets up from behind the desk and walks to the window and looks out at the town. Things just keep on as they always have, he thinks. A community doesn't stop for one man, one event, any motion, or change in time. It's a tightly wound clock that will never stop.

Tom's up for election the next year, and now he's thinking that he should retire, buy some land on a lake, and sit on the porch for the rest of his days watching the play of the sun. Maybe they should move far away, to a different state.

Clouds have come now. The cirrus have given way to heavy cumulus. At the corner of Main and Jefferson, a couple of city workers are starting to hang flags on the utility poles.

He should just retire. They'd never miss him anyway. He could leave all these pictures and plaques. They'd take them down and store them for a while, then someone would find them in a few years and toss them out.

"Tom, is everything all right?" asks Marie Morris. She's been his secretary for twenty years, gray-haired now like Tom. She has grandchildren who come to visit from Owensboro.

"Sure," he says, turning. "Why did you ask that?"

"You seem to be thinking a lot lately's all," she says. She's been in the doorway, but now she comes on into the office and tries to straighten a stack of papers on his desk. Tom laughs and moves from the window.

"Gad, a thinking sheriff," he says. "Kentucky may never be the same." She blushes. She hates it, but she's blushed all her life.

"I didn't mean that," she says.

"I know," says Tom gently. He turns and walks back to the window and looks out. "Do you know that Douglas Dickens asked me to call Jack and nudge him to get the flags put up for Dollar Days?"

"You didn't hear me say this, but our mayor is such a ninny," she whispers. "I mean, I play bridge with Runelle."

"I don't know, Marie," he says. "I have this feeling I'm too old for this job, that I'm not supposed to be doing this anymore. I haven't done anything that would really help a living soul in this county in so long I can't remember it."

"Tom Meade, you should be ashamed," says Marie. "You help people every day of your life. All kinds of people depend on you."

47

"They don't, you know," he says. He comes back and sits down behind the desk and smiles at her kindly. "They don't. A sheriff's supposed to do extraordinary things. Now Douglas Dickens wants me to help get the bunting put up."

"Oh, screw Douglas Dickens!" she says. She puts her hand over her mouth, and her eyes register shock at her own words. Tom throws his head back and roars with laughter.

"Marie, you're on your way to becoming an even better public servant," he says.

"That wasn't like me," she says.

"It's okay," says Tom. "Sometimes we just have to take a good hard look at things and speak the truth."

"You're wrong about not helping people," she says.

"Maybe it's that we always think we help the wrong ones," he says. "You can't always save the right ones. Maybe you can't ever save the right ones."

Tom helps with the flags anyway, not by calling Jack but by helping the crew hang them down Jefferson Street. The merchants all seem relieved, but the thickening clouds draw a few disgusted comments. You can't ever depend on the weather.

Tom drives around for an hour, then stops by the Sheppard First United Methodist Church on Library Street, goes in. The sanctuary is always open. He sits in the back. The vaulted room isn't so hot, and Tom looks at the stained-glass scenes, mostly of Jesus and the little children. He would come here after Andrew died and imagine him being in that picture with Jesus, who must speak very softly and intensely, he thought. At the funeral, Preacher Elliott said that it was the will of God, and that nobody could understand the will of God. Tom had almost come out of the pew and screamed, *No!* God would not ask the sacrifice of seventeen children. If God had done that, he was not a benevolent God, or worse, there was no God.

After that day, Patricia kept on coming to church as usual,

praying more urgently, working with churchmen twice her age. She seemed old after that day.

Patricia let her hair go gray. She would not speak of their pain and so acted as if it had never happened. She was always afraid or angry, and Tom thought she always blamed it on him. Maybe it *was* his fault. Maybe spending the rest of his life paying for something he could not understand was a simple command by whoever ran this world. The world needed its unloved as well as its loved. He knew that he still loved Patricia and that he had not always treated her well.

Preacher Elliott has been dead for years and years. His stone says *Man of God*. He'd baptized Andrew.

Tom sits in the silent sanctuary and tries to pray. He asks that he be given some kind of answer, a direction for his days. He feels as if nothing makes sense anymore. He wants to go to the window of Jesus Ascending into Heaven and put his hands on the nail-scarred feet and ask if Andrew is all right, if heaven exists, if Patricia will ever love him again.

He just sits there. He picks up a hymnal and flips the pages, but the words run together without his bifocals. He leaves them in his shirt pocket.

Tom drives to a special spot on the Coollawassee River a mile outside of town. You can park on the side of a tar and gravel road and walk down a slope through a grove of beech trees and sit on house-sized boulders and watch the water flow past. He trips going down, then gets up and makes it without stumbling again. A few drops of rain fall, then stop.

Tom's thinking of how a man could float all the way to town, when he looks down the slope and sees a fissure in the stone he's never noticed before.

He picks his way down the rocks. He must be careful because the slightest bump gives him a deep bruise now. He can take a walk and be so sore the next morning that he can scarcely get out of bed. He gets there without falling. The river is much louder now. He never knew it was so loud down here.

Tom peers into the fissure and sees that it's black, extends back into a cave. Everything in Sheppard County leads downward into the earth. The land is all limestone, riddled with sinkholes and broken places.

Tom carries a lighter and a large pocketknife. He hasn't smoked for fifteen years, but he still likes the feel of a lighter in his pocket. He thinks of making a torch with a pine knot, but there are no pines here. Instead, he climbs the rocks back to the car and gets his flashlight. Once back down, he turns it on and steps into the fissure.

It's a small cave, but the floor is littered with beer cans, torn magazines, broken glass. They've spray-painted their names on the limestone walls. He follows the cave, and it curves once, then ends as the ceiling comes to the floor. He can hear water running, but he can't tell if it's the river or some other source of water behind the wall. That's how they found Sweet Sally, a small cave like this that broke after a heavy rain. Tour guides will tell you "The Legend of Sweet Sally." Jerry Carter, who bought the cave from the farmer who found it, made up the legend.

Tom shines his flashlight around the cave. Names, names everywhere. You could paint your name, he thinks, even carve it, and that's all that might be left of you. Not a single kind deed or heroic action can survive a man or woman. You can't save anyone, not really. You save them for a while, but sooner or later they are always taken away.

He starts to grin now. High on the ceiling in still-black paint is Sam Preston's name and the date, 9-9-88. He'll have to give Sam some grief about that. He could come up with some phony legal charge just to make Sam laugh.

Tom turns off the light. He turns it back on, then off again. He sits in the enveloping blackness. It is final. No one would roll the stone away from this tomb. He could stay here and disappear. He wants Patricia to love him again. He'd give up the job, get on his knees and beg her to forget that he couldn't save

Andrew. That was what did it: she believed Tom could save him. But the earth was stronger than a single man. Tom came home and told her that they'd gotten to the children but they were all gone. Patricia didn't understand; she thought he meant they'd moved somewhere else in the cave. *No*, he said, *they've all passed away.*

Tom climbs up the boulders, gets in the car, and drives back into Sheppard. They haven't made much progress with the flags. Rain starts to fall harder. Well, the farmers will like it. Tom thinks of the farmers, of his own father, who's been dead since '54. The farmers will like the rain.

The rain stops and the sun comes back out. It's steamy. The day's been wasted.

He goes back into the courthouse, back up to the second floor, past Marie, and into his office. He closes the door, sits at his desk, and takes a fresh sheet of paper from the drawer.

At the top he writes his name, then this:

*For health reasons, I have decided to retire effective immediately as sheriff of Sheppard County.*

He looks at the sentence as if he can't believe it's there or that he wrote it.

*It has been the greatest pleasure of my life to serve the fine people of this county. I believe in my twenty-three years I have tried to do my best. I have tried to give an honest day's work for my pay.*

*I believe it is time for a younger man to do this job.*

He taps the pencil eraser on the desk. His handwriting isn't very good. Sometimes, Marie will have to ask him twice what something says so she can type it. She fusses at him about his handwriting.

*I don't feel like a man anymore.*

He can't quite believe he's written that sentence. He stares at it and feels silly. The door opens, and Marie comes in, holding a form and talking at the same time. He reaches for the sheet before him, balls it up quickly, and holds it. She stops and stares at him.

"What are you doing?" she asks. "Is that something you need today?"

"What do you mean?" he says. It sounds angry, all wrong. He tries again. "Oh, it's nothing, Marie. I was just making a grocery list. I forgot. Patricia went shopping yesterday. I'm getting senile."

"I spent twenty minutes looking for my glasses Sunday morning before church," she says with a laugh. "They were in my hair. I'd pushed them up there when I was doing the crossword. We old folks would forget our heads if they weren't tied on."

Tom looks into her eyes. She has faith. She could make him believe that there's a God of love who forgives every evil action or thought of men.

She gives him the form to sign, and his name looks strange to him as he signs it, the mark of a man he never knew.

The rain's holding off now, and they're still doggedly and very slowly putting flags up around the town square. If only there were an accident, a robbery, a man to transfer to the state prison. A warrant to serve.

The sky is slate. Large raindrops begin to fall again. At lunch, Patricia said the weatherman was calling for extremely heavy rain. Tom barely heard her voice. Tom looks across the square at the hardware store. He could go talk to Sam. No. Sam doesn't work on Fridays or Saturdays.

Tom gets in his car and drives around town, watching the flap of the windshield wipers. He goes down Jefferson, and there's no sinkhole there. Men and women shop, move through the motions of the day. Tom laughs, feeling relieved he's not responsible for saving the town. Everybody thinks he can protect them. He can't protect anyone or save anyone. It's all a lie. There's no one to tell.

The rain seems to be stopping. Maybe everything will blow over. Maybe there's a reason for everything on this earth.

$S$*am sits* beneath a willow tree eating lunch in midaf-
ternoon. He's brought sandwiches on thick wheat bread,
wedges of cheese, and a six-pack of Molson Golden Ale. He
smells the mustard and the ham as he takes a bite. Light filters
through the fronds of the willow, spangling him with green and
gold.

He'll do this sometimes, bring a lunch, eat it outside of the
cave. That morning he had rappelled down a chimney toward
the northern end of the cave. He'd been there before, but it had
been a while. Maybe he'd missed something. The talus, fallen
rocks, seemed more brittle, and a small stream came through,
disappearing into a fissure. He could feel air from a four-inch
squeezeway, but that was useless.

He hears the sound of footsteps now. The path to the sinkhole is well worn, up the hill behind Sam's house. He takes a sip of the ale and stands. At first, the sound comes from everywhere. Then he sees Mary Beth. Sam waves.

He'd been thinking of her all morning. He's stunned now. She's never come up here. Sam sets the rest of the sandwich on wax paper and walks toward her carrying the bottle by the neck.

"What in the world are you doing here?" he asks, immediately thinking it sounds stupid. He could have said something about her hair, the way the sun throws light through it. Mary Beth is wearing a T-shirt with a dinosaur on it, blue jeans, and boots.

"I closed early," she says. "I thought you'd be miles underground. I took the afternoon so I could just come see where you go down."

"Want a sandwich?" he asks, but she's eaten already, and they sit in the shade. She does take an ale. A bird sings.

"What kind?" she asks.

"Semiedible," he says.

She laughs, and it's nearly too deep for a woman, and Sam feels a sweet edge. He could kiss those lips right now. They talk, and he tells her that sometimes he dreams about baseball games, going through all the innings, strikes and balls, pop fouls. Nothing might happen all night long. Just the usual. Slow summer swings.

"I dream I can see with both eyes again," says Sam.

"You do?" she asks. "Can you remember that? How could you remember that?"

Sam finishes his sandwiches and puts the wax paper in a brown kraft bag. He's brought a Winesap apple, and he takes out his heavy Buck knife, slices it, and gives her half. Her lips fold back as she bites the white pulp. Sam can see her teeth.

"It's like memory," he says. She nods and eats her apple. She's in no hurry for explanations, and Sam likes that. "What made you come up here? Really."

She makes a face as if she's thinking, but she knows. She

knew all night. She could make up this fantastic tale about geology.

"I wanted to see you," she says. "I don't know. It's just that . . . I don't know."

Sam wants to say something, but he feels a pressure in his throat. The light suddenly seems harsh, a blade through the trees, unbearable.

"I want to take you down there," he says. She's been looking at his face, but now she looks toward the worn path to the sinkhole twenty yards away. "I want to show you what it's like. You've never seen a place like this."

"I've heard about Sweet Sally," she says. "They say it's cold and wet."

"That's a tourist cave," says Sam. "This is where God's marrow begins. It's just a rope ladder down twenty feet. It's easy. Nothing will happen to you."

"I'm scared of rope ladders," she says. "It's a family thing. My great-grandfather was scared of rope ladders, too."

"Come on," he pleads. He stands and takes her hands and pulls her up. For a moment, their hands stay clasped, then he lets them go. "It's not scary down there. I promise."

"Tell me about it first," sighs Mary Beth.

Sam does. He walks around, hands in the hip pockets of his jeans, telling her Indians first used the old entrance more than a thousand years ago. He tells her about his grandfather and his own father, about how Blue Crystal Cave was named for a legendary but never-found blue-tinted crystal. He explains what he's mapped now.

"But it doesn't connect to Sweet Sally or anything?" she asks.

"Far as I can tell, it doesn't connect to a damned thing," says Sam. He tells her about spongework and dogteeth and solutional tubes. Sam strays toward the hole, finishing his ale and dropping the bottle in the grass. Mary Beth follows him, taking small, wary steps. A brief wind makes the trees tremble, then a crow coughs once. He brings her to the sinkhole, and she warily looks down toward the lights. The generator hums softly.

"Oh, it's full of lights," says Mary Beth. Just this room, Sam says. He takes his headlamp and refills it with carbide. He has another headlamp there just in case. He hands it to her. "You have anything in a teal? This isn't my color."

"Basic yellow's it," says Sam. He strikes the flames in both lamps, and the acetylene glows sharply. Sam goes to the edge of the ladder. "Come on. You won't fall. I'll go down first and hold the ladder steady for you. I want you to see this."

Mary Beth knows. She'd be wing-walking, hanging over building ledges to please Sam at this moment. Hasn't she dreamed of being in this cave with Sam? She believes he could protect her from anything, even the shadows of descent.


They're just past the last lights. It's open here, the ceiling high, studded with dripping draperies and growing stalactites.

"Here's the Colossus," says Sam. The cavern opens below the sinkhole into a large domed room, and a column eight feet thick squats with the ceiling hunched down on its shoulders. "I named everything in here, so you'll have to forgive the hyperbole."

"Seems pretty colossal," says Mary Beth.

"Here's where we need to be careful," says Sam after they've gone several hundred yards. He tells her about block-creep caverns. The way is long and narrow, past cracked and broken stone. Sam's tied them together with a heavy nylon rope. Cavers don't do that much anymore, he says, but Mary Beth's not a caver.

"Good grief, how deep is that?" she gasps.

"That's the pit, but it's only about forty feet," says Sam. "Don't worry, though. It doesn't go anywhere. You're not missing anything."

"Shoot," she says. He's ahead of her, stopping every few

feet as they edge along the wall. After twenty yards the pit passes behind them. Her heart is beating so fast she can't breathe.

They walk for a time into the cave's passageway, then come to the crossover trail, another cave that bisects this one, going northeast, slightly higher. They don't take that passageway, though, just stay straight as they have been walking.

The ceiling begins to cramp down. The place is tight, smells of wet stone and something almost musty. The immensity of it staggers her.

"I can't walk long like this," she says. "It hurts."

"We're almost there," says Sam. And forty steps later the cavern opens into a high-ceilinged room, and in its center a still pond that reflects the twin beams from their lights. Sam doesn't tell her he has a battery-powered lighting system in here, lights along the walls. He'll come in this room sometimes and read.

"This is incredible," she whispers. He tells her to stay where she is, and he walks around a trail curve. She's suddenly terrified but says nothing. He turns a switch, and the room is bathed in a soft white glow. "Oh!" Sam turns off his headlamp and comes walking back with a broad smile. Her face is transfused with surprise, almost ecstasy.

"Welcome to my church," says Sam. "All the wisdom of the ages rests here."

"I can't believe how beautiful it is!" she cries. She moves from one formation to another, touching them lightly. She looks back at Sam. The darkness is not so oppressive. She felt that weight when her husband had gone off the cliff face. She'd awaken and feel herself free-falling, what he felt, certain death and seconds to think of it. She'd felt that passing the pit. Now, this world is seamed with thick jewels.

"This is Lake Preston," he says, jumping over two half-submerged stones to the small, still pond. "I know it's presumptuous, but as the discoverer, it's my prerogative."

"How deep is it?" asks Mary Beth, joining him.

"It's a great mystery," intones Sam. "From all points it appears to be at least a thousand feet, but it's actually nine inches at its deepest."

"That's not much of lake!"

"I'm not much of a namesake," says Sam with a shrug, and her laughter travels from one formation to the next. She's standing beside him now, afraid again of being down this far, afraid of what she feels. Sam unties the rope between them.

"It's wonderful here," she says, not able to form the words she could say so easily.

"Yeah, it kind of grows on you," says Sam, but his voice falls toward the end of the sentence as he turns and sees her looking at him that way. "Why'd you come to see me today?"

She knew he would ask. *She* would have. Mary Beth fears saying the wrong words now.

"I thought about you last night," she says. She realizes she's whispering, but her voice won't get louder. "It was like I just wanted to see you today." She feels his eyes in her heart. "I thought I had to see you today."

"I know," he says. "Me too."

They move forward, imperceptibly at first. Water is dripping somewhere far away. A deep sudden tremble comes through the cave. The alarm rises in her eyes.

"Sam?"

"It's thunder," he says. "This high, you still feel the weather sometimes. I could take you places you'd never even dream about the surface of the earth. The air compresses from the top here. It's thunder. We're okay."

"I thought it was . . ." But she's whispering so softly the words fade into crumbled syllables then disappear. She realizes she's still wearing this ridiculous headlamp, and she takes it off and sets it on the cave floor next to Sam's. She can feel more than the thunder in this air. She starts to say something, and her mouth chews a word, won't release it.

Sam knows now. He can smell her hair, not long from the shower, smell the soap. The chamber shrinks, the chill vanishes. Their faces are six inches apart now.

"I'm going to kiss you now," Sam whispers.

"Okay." She nods.

She closes her eyes as he leans down. Their lips meet gently, the slightly yeasty taste of ale still there, ghostly. It's almost friendly at first, but her tongue becomes restless, and two seconds later they are embracing, kissing and hugging. Her right hand moves up and down his spine, sweeps over his muscled hips then back up. He kisses her neck. Their breathing is audible.

Sam kisses her again. She says *yes* when their kiss breaks. They kiss again.

"Do you want to make love?" he whispers.

"We could go to your house."

"Okay," he says. She kisses him again.

His lips are on hers when the lights blink once, come back up dimmed, then go out.

"Sam," she says. He tells her not to move, and he kneels and feels the damp stone until his hands find the headlamp. He thumbs the striker, and there's a flash in the room. He adjusts it, and the acetylene begins to come back warmly. He puts it on, finds Mary Beth's headlamp, starts it, and hands it back. "What happened?"

"Damned connection to the batteries," says Sam. "The moisture's been corroding it. It's getting worse. I'm going to go unhook the lights. You stay right here."

She watches his image wobble with the lamp, recede across the cave, move around a bend. She hears him talking, but she can't distinguish his words. She looks around fearfully and realizes that the earth's crust is over her, and even her desire doesn't weigh that much. She remembers the ledge. Mary Beth can't shake the image of falling: water from great heights, a plane nosing into the Pacific, a child leaning too far over the railing at a scenic overlook. She feels that falling in her stomach.

Sam fusses with the connection, and the lights come on once in an explosion of splendor, die as quickly. Not the cave, but the dream of a cave. He curses and sets the wire to one side. He'll have to mess with it later. No time now. He stands, realizing the puff of light has stunned his eye. He sees concentric rings, galaxial images from a show on public television. Sam steadies himself against the cave wall, waits until his eye adjusts to the beam from his headlamp.

"Are you all right?" calls Mary Beth.

"Be right there," says Sam, shaking his head. He gets back to her in ten seconds. "It's the damned connection."

"I'm so scared," she says. Sam's thinking of getting them out, then he takes her again and kisses her. The hard hats tip and bump.

"It's okay," he says. "I know every inch of this place. Nothing will happen to you. I won't let anything happen to you."

"Okay."

He takes her hands, and soon they're striding across the flowstone and at the edge of the pit. Her foot tips some loose clastics, and the stones fall. She stops, and it takes a second or two for them to hit bottom. Sam's tied them back together with the nylon rope, and he keeps it snug now, him in front, but close.

"Don't ever look down," he says.

"Because I might lose my balance?" she says.

"No, because the trail's always in front of you," he says. It takes her five seconds to know he's kidding her. She mutters a cheerful oath, and they move very slowly along the cliff face. She can't imagine how anyone navigates this bitter world, why they would. She wants light so bad her head aches.


She goes ahead of him up the rope ladder, thinking she can't make it. He's right behind her a few rungs. She finally rises to the surface of the earth, pulls herself out. Her legs are trembling so badly that she sits twenty feet from the broad mouth of the sinkhole.

She's breathing hard now, thinking again of what they did down there. He'll think she was a fool. He'll see her up here now, think she's nothing special. They'll laugh. She feels sick. The sky is dull and dark. More storms today, they said. Sam asks if she's all right. She nods, and he takes their headlamps and turns them off. He sits next to her in the grass.

"Things happen down there, you can't know what next," he says.

"I was afraid," she admits. "I'd be afraid all the time down there. I never felt so alone."

She's been staring at the trees wondering where their colors went. She turns now, and Sam's face is near hers. She wants to cry or choke out some pledge never to descend into that world again.

"I'm sorry," says Sam. "I thought you might like it."

She's going to say something, but she's looking at his mouth. It's close. She wants his lips on hers. She will do this. If she is a fool, she can't help it. She's going to say she really sort of did like it, anything, but then they're kissing again, lying in the grass, holding each other close. Thunder shakes from the east.

"Let's go to the house," he whispers to her, and she nods.

He sees half of this world, half of this growing love, half of the storms, half of the darkness below him.

He'd been unconscious for two days after the blast, and the first thing he saw on awakening were the thick features of a fat nurse as she leaned over him to adjust the pillow. She had lost some dimension: a flat plane, an absence of depth, the room behind her reeling from its poor focus. Sam had felt the heavy bandage over his eye, the cotton wadding stuffed there. He'd tried to sit up, and the fat nurse said, *Now then*, and held him down. Then he'd begun to tear at the wadding, and she'd held his arm back as if his strength were a child's. *Stop, sweet sugar,* she said. The fat nurse smiled and laughed. Her teeth were spaced widely apart. But then she stepped back, and Sam saw that she was kindly, nearing fifty perhaps, a sweep of pity in a turning gesture.

He will be tender with Mary Beth. He will not rush her or stop listening. He will hold her in the weak light of a daytime bedroom or the tarred blackness of night. There might be a passageway back to this life.

Sam wonders if Mary Beth has ever seen Richmond.


She glances at him as they walk. He isn't handsome, and the patch doesn't make him seem dashing. He isn't a pirate. In the past few weeks, they'd sit and sip their ale and watch sunsets and talk about politics or literature. They made rough jokes.

Now, her body slowly begins to remember a man's hands. She has not felt such things since her husband went off the cliff. After that she seemed old, a widow left with insurance money and no plans but planting flowers and tending them.

She feels a rising lust and a sweet tenderness for him. Yes, she will lie with him. She will show him her body, and he can praise it or not. He can leave the patch upon his eye or take it off.

There is nothing beneath it that she has not seen many times before.

A dark wall of rain is moving down from the north, along the ridgetops.

# 7

*At Reidsville,* they made Bobby talk to the prison psychiatrist. For the third year of his sentence Bobby hadn't said a word to another living soul. Clay came the next fall. The psychiatrist was a fat man with a pinkish blue face, the color of ripening blueberries. His rings were stuck on his fingers. Bobby would sit and look at those stuck rings and wonder if they hurt. His name was Gonsalves. His hair was black as the big ace on a playing card. His eyes were black. He never moved his head when he spoke. His eyes didn't move.

Gonsalves told Bobby that his anger was very deep and that his silence was a grave in which he had decided to bury himself. When Clay first came, Bobby started saying single words to him, *blade,* and *fire,* and *water.* Clay understood that tomb of silence. Clay had an uncle who smoked on the front porch, rocked, and never said a thing. So what?

"What was your mother like?" Gonsalves had asked. "Was she a happy person?"

Gonsalves's voice was almost a flat line, expressionless, soft, insistent. His cube at the prison had a forty-watt bulb and two worn cloth wing chairs that must have been ugly when they were new.

"I'll tell you about *your* mother," Bobby had said. It was the first thing he'd said to another person in eleven months. The words felt dry, as if spoken for the first time. Gonsalves sat up and his head moved. This was their fourth session, and the first time Bobby'd said a word.

"*My* mother?" asked Gonsalves.

"She's crying her eyes out in a whorehouse in Mexico because her son's a shrink," said Bobby. Then he smiled, something blind and icy. Gonsalves's professional steadiness rocked. Bobby felt the power flowing from his own eyes into the room.

The next Tuesday they didn't come for Bobby. Somebody stamped THERAPY TERMINATED on his file. Just at quitting time four months later, Dr. Gonsalves got in his car to go home, shut the door, and died. It was his heart. The cons all thought Bobby had something to do with it, and he rose in their estimation.

The new psychiatrist, making a clean start, threw away all the inactive files. Bobby would think about Dr. Gonsalves, lying fat six feet under the ground, rings still stuck on his fingers. He could be in that hole for years before the rings fell off.


Clay first got into trouble in the seventh grade. He stole money from a classmate's locker. Then it was a bicycle. His parents had never spanked him. They didn't believe in it. His sister, Ilene, was six feet tall, a member of the Beta Club, and an all-state clarinet player. Clay tried to play the trumpet, but he could only make it groan.

He got caught on the third robbery when he was twenty-five. He cried when they sentenced him, but then he met Bobby. Clay loved to read books. A few of the cons called him Perfesser, but it didn't catch on.

"I'm sorry," says Bobby. He's in the backseat, and Misty's back there with him again. He's just yelled at her.

"It's okay," she says. "I get so mad sometimes I can't sleep. It's okay."

Christiann whispers into Clay's ear. Hermie's gotten them going again, and he's turned up the radio. A preacher has told them that God will soon come back to this earth and defeat the devil, take the faithful.

"Hush now," whispers Clay to Christiann. She takes his hand, but it's cool and limp, barely responds.

"Just find the house," says Bobby. Misty slides close to him.

"Yassuh, boss man," says Hermie. Misty kisses Bobby's ear, but he asks her to stop. He says it softly, though, and she doesn't mind. Anything's better than sitting at home back in Carolina, waiting for J.D. to come home with grease under his nails. They'd be lying in bed at night, and his hands would start up her thighs, and all she could think of was the grease around the moons of his nails. They'd finish, then he'd hit her.

They come around a long, slow curve, and there's the turn-off, an old barn with a rusting roof. The words SEE ROCK CITY are flaking off. Hermie goes *whoops*, hangs a right on the poorly paved road. Bobby sits on the edge of the seat, looking. A mile down the road they see the large rock.

"That's it," says Bobby.

"We're home, dear," Hermie singsongs. Hermie pulls up the long driveway and stops in front of Sam's house. They all spill out. The rain hasn't quit or gotten much harder. A Jeep Cherokee and an old truck are out front.

"This sure ain't the house of no rich man," says Christiann.

"And God divided the darkness from the light," says Hermie. "And the darkness he called day, and the light he called night."

"You got it backwards," says Misty. "I had to memorize half that stuff when I was a little girl."

"I heard of a man living in a shack had four hundred thousand dollars sewed into his mattress," says Clay. Bobby's just staring at the house, shaking his head. Everything's going wrong.

Bobby and Clay both have guns, a pocketful of cartridges. Bobby stole them from Misty's husband before they left. Clay tells Hermie to open the trunk, and they get the guns.

Bobby looks at the earth. Somewhere beneath them is a blue crystal, hidden treasure sparkling when anyone comes close with light.


They've been standing in Sam's bedroom kissing.

Sam's kissing her neck when the sound of the car crackles on the gravel out front.

"Somebody's here," says Mary Beth, turning to the window. The bedroom's on the front, and while Sam goes to the window to look out, she rebuttons her shirt nervously. "Who is it?" Sam's looking through a break in the curtains.

"Beats me," he says softly. "Four or five people in one car. I'll go see what they want. Probably lost, looking for some cave or something."

Sam goes out of the bedroom and into the hallway, which runs centrally through the length of the old house. Mary Beth's right behind him. He comes out to the porch with her. The others walk toward the porch to get out of the rain.

"Can I help you?" asks Sam. Misty sees his patch and giggles, and Christiann looks at her like, *What?* Bobby's out front now coming right up to Sam.

"Are you Preston?" he asks.

"Who are you?" says Sam. "Can I help you?"

"Yeah," says Bobby. Hermie leans against a porch post and starts to laugh. *Reckon I could,* Hermie whispers, shaking his head. Sam braces, takes Mary Beth's arm. Something's wrong here. "Maybe we could go in out of the rain and talk about it."

"Out here's fine," says Sam. He looks back and forth trying to see what Clay's doing. He's moved to their right. Misty's looking at a nail that might be cracking. Christiann glances from Sam to Bobby and back.

"No, it's not," says Bobby.

"Should I call the sheriff?" asks Mary Beth softly. Her desire has swept out of her. She's suddenly terrified. Her knees feel as if they're changing to something half liquid.

"What do you want?" asks Sam.

"I've heard you're a rich man," says Bobby. He takes his gun from his hip pocket and shows it to them. Mary Beth steps slightly behind Sam, holding his arm.

"Go on in and take whatever you find," says Sam. "There's nothing in there worth much, but you're welcome to it. I don't want any trouble."

"You're Preston, aren't you?" says Clay, coming alongside Bobby and taking his gun out too. Sam can't think clearly. Mary Beth's hand trembles on his arm. He sees Bobby raise the pistol and point it at him.

Sam hesitates. Thunder crumbles along the ridges above them, and Sam tries to think of anything to do, some strategy, but nothing happens. He feels numb, his features thick with fear and stupidity.

Bobby cocks the hammer of the pistol and puts it in Sam's side. Mary Beth inhales sharply.

"In the house," says Bobby.

"Just ask him nice," says Misty. "That friend of yours in prison said he had plenty, didn't he?"

"Just shut up," says Bobby softly. Clay curses and shakes his head.

Once they get in there, Bobby makes them sit on the cluttered sofa in Sam's den, on the other side of the hall from the bedroom. Copies of outdoor magazines spill off the seat, and hanks of rope, cans of carbide, bundles of pitons fill every corner.

"Look at this mess," says Hermie. "He had two eyes, I guess he'd know what a pigsty this is." Christiann starts giggling. She looks at Sam, and that black patch is just the funniest thing.

"Go see if there's any beer," says Clay to Christiann. "Just get out of here right now."

"Well, excuse me for living," says Christiann.

"Come on," says Misty to her friend.

"He looks like the sign at Long John Silver's," says Christiann, and they bundle together in laughter as they disappear toward the back of the house.

Clay takes his knife out and shows it to Sam and Mary Beth, flicking it open. Mary Beth flinches. Clay then gets a bundle of rope, cuts lengths, and ties their hands behind their backs.

"Let her go," says Sam. "She's just a neighbor. I hardly even know her."

"Wish I could do that," says Bobby. He sets the gun down on the coffee table next to the latest *National Geographic*, walks slowly around the room. He sighs. This isn't going right. "You own Blue Crystal Cave?"

"Never heard of it," says Sam. Bobby nods, comes back to Sam, stops briefly in front of him, then slaps him hard across the face. Mary Beth screams. Sam looks up now, and blood trickles from the corner of his mouth.

"Blue Crystal Cave," says Clay. "We know all about you."

"I don't have any money," says Sam. The left side of his mouth has gone numb from the blow. From the back, Misty cries they've found beer. Then Christiann giggles and says something about a patch. Sam turns to look at Mary Beth, and Bobby hits him again, this time even harder. Mary Beth screams.

"Gag her," says Bobby, and Clay pulls the curtains down

68

suddenly, tears a strip from them, and roughly binds Mary Beth's mouth. Sam tries to stand to stop him, but Bobby grabs the front of Sam's shirt, pushes him stumbling across the room, where he falls hard on his jaw. Sam looks up to see Mary Beth crying, her eyes huge with terror.

"Hey, baloney," says Hermie, coming out the back carrying a sandwich and a cold beer. "It's a regular pirate's den of delicacies around here."

The rain's coming straight down now. A violet haze rises up from Sheppard toward the hills as the day begins to wash into night. You could dream. You could feel her hands on you, suddenly releasing some ancient desire, as if you'd forgotten how to walk or see.

Ginger had planted aromatic shrubs, and they're in bloom. The heavy scent drifts through the open windows. It's so thick you could taste it. When the rain began the day before, the earth's rich, fecund odor was bracing, but now it's gone slightly sour, marshy. Lightning spaces itself across the Kentucky mountainside, nearby crashes and distant peels. The close ones you can feel in your teeth. The windowpanes are slightly loose, and a close clap makes them rattle. Sam's been meaning to get around to that.

You can look out the kitchen window and see a rivulet bubbling down a usually dry ditch at the corner of Sam's yard. Hermie's standing there watching. He can't figure it. The stream seems to stop. It's sliding snakelike into a sinkhole, one Sam long ago knew twisted into an unexplorable crevasse. It's a river that stops halfway down the hill.

Mary Beth feels sick to her stomach. Her sister is a nurse and once told a story about a man who'd been gagged and was then sick, aspirating his own vomit, suffocating. Mary Beth thinks about that poor man. When she was twelve, her family had driven to a steak house, and an ambulance was pulling off. A fat man had just choked to death on a piece of steak. She didn't eat for two days. She lay in bed and remembered that pulsing red light, in no hurry, the silver ambulance crunching the gravel of the parking lot. The ambulance was a hearse, too. It was silver with black trim.

Her abdomen aches. Sam's in the back somewhere, and she doesn't know what they're doing to him. An hour before, she'd heard muffled blows, slaps on flesh, then thuds. She keeps thinking, Why is this happening? At her husband's funeral the preacher had said that *nobody knows God's plan*. She nearly leaped up and ran out. She'd almost shaken her fist and said, *Because there is no plan*. But she didn't.

"Come on and watch the TV," says Misty. They've made a pile of sandwiches from what's left in Sam's kitchen. Hermie's turned on the TV, but there are only three channels. He's watching *Mister Ed*. Bobby's smoking, staring at her. The house has five rooms. An equipment room and a small library are in the middle, a kitchen's on the back, and a den and Sam's bedroom on the front of the house. They're in the den. Sam's in the equipment room alone now, tied to a chair. Mary Beth's with them in the den, hands still tied painfully behind her back.

"Leave me alone," says Bobby.

"You get a sandwich, hon?" Misty asks. Hermie bursts into cool laughter that stops at the wrong place. Mister Ed's just made Wilbur look like such a fool.

"Leave me alone," says Bobby. He turns and walks down the central hall to the back of the house and hears, words trailing at his steps, *Excuse me for living*. He goes into the equipment room with Sam. It's dark. Wind makes the curtains undulate, waving, waving at them.

Sam is sitting perfectly straight. He's trying to plan for what comes next. The pain is intense from the left side of his jaw, down his neck, and into the collarbone. His hands are fat and stiff from the lack of circulation, but he won't slump now.

In the half hour he's been alone he's licked the blood from the corner of his mouth, and it tasted warm and sour. His fear and anger bind him in a majestic silence.

Sam's feet are tied so tightly that his toes are numb. Birds are huddled under the eaves and offer damp phrases that sound loud in the room. He turns when Bobby enters the room, then looks back, straight ahead. Bobby sits on a rough stool Sam sometimes takes into the cave. He'll sit on it and think, listening to the dense silence for clues.

Bobby smokes, sucking up the acrid burning tobacco, holding the air then letting it fire from his nostrils.

"You don't know about me," says Bobby quietly.

"Who *are* you?" asks Sam, surprised to hear his own voice so high, so insistently and fearfully curious.

"I'm nobody either," says Bobby.

"I don't have any money," Sam says, trying to fill the words with truth, urgency. Bobby smokes the cigarette down to a glowing nub, grinds it under his heel, lights another. "Just leave us alone."

"I can't," says Bobby softly. "Your girl might help, though."

"You leave her alone," says Sam. Bobby leans back and puts one finger over his lips and cocks his eye.

"I killed a man with a tire tool one time," says Bobby. "When I did it, you know what I felt?" Bobby gets up and walks to the window and looks at the darkening sky. Birds fly off. "I felt like God himself was inside of my fingers. I hit the man three times, and they couldn't tell the front of his face from the back of his head. I put my hands in it. I put my face in it, and I smelled it like steak." He comes back and sits on the stool. "I still smell it. I can't ever stop smelling it."

"Let her go," says Sam. He's thinking of how to do it. They don't know this country. He could get them away from the house. He's thinking of stories.

71

"Everything hurts," says Bobby. Sam wants to change the subject, to choke back his fear, but he can only struggle.

Bobby takes a drag from the cigarette, turns the lit end red. Without pausing, he takes it from his lips and pushes the fire into Sam's cheek. Sam screams from the pain, curses, struggles. Bobby holds it on his cheek for two, three seconds. Sam's gasping, breathing hard, shaking his head.

"Everything hurts," says Bobby.

"Please don't," says Sam.

In the front of the house, Mary Beth weeps at the sound of Sam's shout. Misty's brief glance at Christiann is anxious, uncertain. Clay can't believe Hermie's on his fourth sandwich.


A gust of wind blows the antenna off the roof, and as they hear it crash, the picture disappears from the TV.

"Aw, hell," says Hermie. "And *Get Smart* was coming on."

"This place gives me the creeps," says Christiann. She gets up and comes over to Clay. "Baby, why don't we leave here before something bad happens and go to California? Think about you and me out there in California."

"You could be on *The Dating Game*," says Hermie.

Bobby comes out and gets Mary Beth, takes her to the library next to the room where Sam's still groaning. Misty gets up and starts to follow him.

"Misty, get back in the other room," says Bobby.

"What are you gonna do to her?" asks Misty. She pouts a little.

"Nothing," says Bobby. "Clay?" Clay unfolds from the floor and comes down the hall. "I need you. If Misty's not back with them others in two seconds, I want you to slap the hell out of her."

"Okay, bro," says Clay mildly.

Misty starts to laugh.

"Well, if you think this is going to—"

Clay steps into the arm motion and hits her with stunning force across the face. She stumbles backward and falls against a telephone table and lands hard on her shoulder. Misty's gasping, eyes huge in shock just before she begins to cry, to bawl in choking sobs. Christiann comes into the hall and sees her friend roll up on her bottom, holding her face, crying.

"What'd you do to her?" she yells, looking at Bobby.

"It was me," says Clay. "She wouldn't do what she's supposed to."

Mary Beth starts to gasp against the gag. She feels the floor rising up to her. The hallway gets very dark and then very light. She feels she's outside in the dome of heaven, then packed into a hole. She falls against Bobby.

"You pig!" cries Christiann. She kneels beside Misty and puts her arms around her. Christiann starts to cry too. Misty's face swells slightly on one side. Bobby curses as he feels Mary Beth sag. He pushes her against the wall with his shoulder, then, with one hand, pulls the gag down. She groans and draws air into her lungs. The hallway is moving slowly, turning back and forth at old-film angles.

"Don't call me that," says Clay softly.

"They gone kill us!" cries Misty. "They gone kill all of us!"

Christiann helps her up. The thunder comes back now, the sound of armies outside, returned from some foreign adventure. Misty's starting to stop crying, but she looks with deep anger at Bobby, who's still propping Mary Beth up.

"Anybody see a radio around this place anywhere?" asks Hermie. He's come into the hall, and his shirttail is completely out.


Mary Beth's untied now, ungagged, sitting on the sofa in the small, cluttered library. Sam's bookcases hold musty rows of books on caving, Civil War battles, things like that. Bobby's sitting on the windowsill, smoking.

———

73

In the next room, Sam's head is down, and the pain from the cigarette burn on his cheek is searing, beyond belief. The pain had been like this when he broke his ankle down below two years earlier. Then it became numb. Now, the stinging won't go away.

Clay's back out front watching Hermie fiddle with the knob on a cheap radio, getting nothing but static. Misty and Christiann are sitting on the sofa, holding each other. Misty's face is swollen now.

"You'da done what the man said, I wouldn'ta had to hit you," says Clay. He's sitting on the floor. He's in no hurry to do anything.

"Hit a woman on the face," says Christiann. "I ain't going to no California with you if you don't cut this stuff out."

"I never asked you to go nowhere with me," says Clay.

The lights flicker once, go out. They come back on for less than a second, catching everyone frozen into some posture of surprise.

In the library, Bobby's silhouette against the window is all Mary Beth can see.

"Where is the money?" asks Bobby.

"There's no money here," cries Mary Beth. "Why won't you believe it? He's never had any. The cave's been closed for forty years."

Mary Beth realizes she's wandered over some line, so she sits in the darkness trying to think of what to say next. Bobby comes to her now, very close, his face three inches from hers. She's never felt so completely stopped with fear. Mary Beth turns slightly. Tears well up.

Bobby grabs her arms and ties her wrists again, then, with another piece of rope, her feet. Bound once more, she can't summon the will to struggle. The power comes back on, and Hermie's voice from the other room shouts approval. Bobby's face is so close now that she can see the pores in his nose. With one swift gesture he grabs the front of her shirt, tears at it, breaking buttons, tearing it half off.

"No!" screams Mary Beth. "Leave me alone!"

Sam's head bolts upright. The pain disappears from his cheek. He feels the adrenaline pouring into his blood. Mary Beth screams again, and Sam jumps, the chair falling over sideways.

"Leave her alone!" Sam screams. He listens for what comes next.

Bobby looks at Mary Beth's exposed breasts. He feels nothing.

"Leave her alone!" screams Sam from the next room. *Just leave her alone.* "Come here. Just come here."

Bobby licks his teeth and shrugs. Maybe, he tells Mary Beth, her luck is running good.

Bobby goes into the next room and sees Sam lying on the floor and starts to laugh at him. Clay comes slowly down the hall and into the room. Bobby tells Clay to pick him up, and Clay does, with little effort.

"It's getting dark," says Bobby. "Money."

"Okay," says Clay softly. Mary Beth suddenly screams, *No,* and Bobby and Clay look at each other. Bobby's lip curls up into a snarl. He storms back into the hall, then into the library, to find Hermie standing in front of Mary Beth, unzipping his pants. She looks at Bobby in terrified confusion.

"Hermie, I told you," says Clay. The women come into the hall from the den and stare. Clay shrugs.

"Hey, man, you ain't gonna keep this to yourself, are you?" asks Hermie. Bobby pulls the gun from his hip pocket. His eyes seem to wander, unfocused, seeing different planes. "Put the piece down, man." Hermie laughs. "You're no John Dillinger."

The gunshot is sudden. Misty screams and screams.

"*It's Leon,*" says Patricia. "From the office."

Tom looks up from his chair and wonders what Leon might want. Sometimes it's a shotgun killing or a two-car wreck. A really bad thing can happen, and Leon will call, his high voice wavering. Tom gets it in the hall. Leon has that sound again.

"Tom, we just got a call from the National Weather Service," says Leon. "They say this weather system's gonna sit on us hard. We gotta expect the river to go past flood stage."

"They've already said it's coming out?" asks Tom. "They said that?"

"They said it," says Leon excitedly. "Sure as hell, and I've talked to Bud, but I mean, should we be filling sandbags or calling people or what?"

"Let me eat right quick, and I'll be on down to the office," says Tom. Leon's relieved. Tom walks back into the kitchen, where Patricia's putting peas and pork chops on a plate. Tom looks at her, at the loose skin beneath her arms and her tight gray bun. She doesn't smile much.

"Troubles?" she asks. She hands him the plate, and he walks into the dining room.

"It's the river," he says. "The weather bureau says it's going to flood. This might be bad. We're going to have to get out there and see what we can do." She prepares her plate and comes into the dining room and sits at the small table across from Tom.

"You can't stop that river," she says. He looks up at her in surprise. He smiles wanly and tries not to say anything. "My daddy saw the big flood in '26. Took half the town away. They farmed more then. More runoff or something. Before caves got big in these parts."

"Patricia," he says.

"Well, it's true," she continues. "We keep building and building along that river. We keep building and building, and soon you have places that will be lost when a flood comes."

"It's human nature," says Tom. "We can't stop people from doing that kind of thing, and you know it."

"I know it," she says coldly. "They should never have expanded the cemetery down that hill. Never."

Tom is stunned. That's where Andrew is buried, in the new part of the cemetery on the downslope toward the river. Patricia has not mentioned it, even obliquely, in years. She looks into her plate and keeps eating.

"Well, it's done now," Tom says. "Lots of things can't be changed, and there's no sense worrying about them. You can't undo some things."

"No," she says, "you can't, can you."

Tom looks at her as he eats, but she won't look at him. He finishes, scrapes the leftovers into the disposal, rinses the dishes and puts them in the dishwasher. He gets his keys and is walking toward the door when he hears Patricia coming after him. When he turns, he sees her eyes are full of unspilled tears.

"I don't know how long I'll be," he says softly. "Will you be all right?"

"Yes," she says. "Tom, be careful. You be careful tonight, okay?" She stands close and touches a button halfway up his shirt, just touches it and runs her finger around it. His arms come around her, and she emits a small groan or a cry and leans heavily on him for a moment. As he goes into the gathering night, he can scarcely see for the dense, relentless rain.

Douglas Dickens is walking back and forth in front of the courthouse with a brown umbrella over his head. He holds the umbrella with one hand, a cigarette with the other. The streetlamps are on, and the flags are soaked and limp. Tom pulls into his reserved parking place and gets out, putting on a rust-colored raincoat and his waterproof sheriff's hat. He likes the smell of the rain. The drops are huge.

"Tom," says Douglas, rushing toward him, "this is bad. Did you hear what those jerks at the weather service are saying?" Douglas laughs bitterly and smoke puffs out his nose. Tom thinks he looks like a small, foolish dragon. "They're basically saying, I mean like, basically saying that we're going to be under the damn water by the morning. And I'm like, how can that be? We haven't had a flood that bad in years and years." Douglas shakes his head sadly. "It just had to be during Dollar Days. Just had to be."

"Maybe God doesn't want us to have Dollar Days," sighs Tom. Lights are on in the courthouse. Leon's up there, maybe a couple of the other deputies.

"God loves for a man to make an honest dollar," says Douglas firmly. "That's why God's on America's side, Tom. You know that. My God, man, you were in Korea. You think it was an accident how we kicked ass in Desert Storm?"

"No," says Tom. "I think it's because Iraq didn't have an air force or a navy."

"There's an evil feeling to this," says Douglas. "I mean, you know me, I'm not superstitious or anything, but maybe we're being repaid for something, you know? Do you believe in retribution?"

"I don't believe in much anymore," says Tom. He turns and walks into the courthouse, leaving Douglas Dickens standing there not quite believing what he heard.

Tom goes up the broad wooden stairs two at a time. The lights are too dim, but few people come in the courthouse at night, anyway. There's a hallway on the second story. Convicts built the floor of black and white tiles. When it's wet, your feet can slip or squeak. At one end is the courtroom, and down the hall are the sheriff's office and the probate judge's chambers. Bathrooms are at the other end.

"Tom, Zeke Watson wants you to call him," says Leon. "He's ready to go into the plan."

"The plan," sighs Tom. "Zeke's been wanting to go into the plan for years. He's probably about to wet his pants." Leon laughs lightly and crosses his arms over his chest. His features are thickening too early. His nose is rounded on the end and his chin's a little weak. He has brown hair and eyes.

"This time old Zeke might be right," says Leon. "There's a phone message from the weather service in Lexington, too. We might ought to be getting out the sandbags."

"Okay," says Tom. He thinks for a moment of Zeke, who's in his sixties and the volunteer head of the Sheppard County Office of Civil Defense. "You call Zeke and tell him to start rounding up his boys and be down here in an hour. And call Barney Timmons. The fire department boys can help on this."

"Ten-four, Chief," says Leon. Tom winces as he passes Leon. The boy just loves police lingo. When Tom has to use his car radio, he says *okay* and *thank you* and *goodbye*. He doesn't ask, *What's your ten-twenty?*; he asks, *Where are you?* Tom goes into his office, turns on the light, and gets the message slip from the top of his desk and calls Lexington.

He talks to Emerson Jones, who's the chief meteorologist. Emerson talks as if he takes his first name very seriously, Tom thinks.

"Chief, the situation is that this front is strong as hell, and it's been stalled north of us for three days. Every river above the Coollawassee is out of its banks already. Based on our records, Sheppard is facing a serious problem by tomorrow morning early. Have you seen the river?"

"Not this evening," he says. "I was out there this morning. But it comes up quick. We all know that. But it usually goes down just as quick. Some of the stuff that's real low around here always gets flooded. It's been happening for years. But the water hasn't been in the streets for decades."

"You'd better go look at things," says Emerson in his rotund voice. "Your man Ezekiel Watson has already called us three times. He says it's rising fast."

"Zeke's a good man," says Tom, and maybe he believes it. Maybe everybody's good. Maybe there's a reason for everything that happens. "We'll start filling up some sandbags. We got some standards of how far it rises how fast."

"Well done, Chief," says Emerson, and Tom wants to laugh. He hangs up and listens to the rain against the windows. It seems much harder now. He goes out of the office and down the stairs. Mayor Douglas Dickens is standing on the covered part of the front steps, smoking and shaking his head mournfully.

"It's ruining the flags," says Douglas. "And they never even got the bunting up. The merchants are going to howl about this." He pauses, as if trying to remember something. "A great howl will rise through the night about this."

"It's Sheppard Dollar Days," says Tom, adjusting his hat, "not the death of Lincoln." Douglas shrugs and nods; it's all over now, all those votes, he thinks. Sheppard Dollar Days was Douglas's idea.

Tom gets into the car and drives through town. It looks different through the windshield wipers tonight. The rain comes down so fast and hard it looks like harp strings or cell bars. Water in the gutters glows from the streetlights, goes foamy as it rushes into culverts. On the police radio he hears Leon calling Zeke Watson and saying to notify the civil defense volunteers and to be at the courthouse in an hour. Zeke says *Ten-four,* and then Leon says it, too.

Tom drives down Main Street, thinking of who lived where when he was a boy. They're all dead now. Miss Janie Fox taught piano. She taught piano to Tom, but it didn't take. That was what his father said, and everybody thought it was funny: *Tommy's piano lessons didn't take.* Everybody thought she'd live to be old, but she died of an aneurysm when she was fifty. Years ago.

He passes Sedge Bolt's place. Sedge was tall and deaf, a carpenter. He smoked roll-your-owns. Tom was in college when he found out Sedge had lung cancer. It took Sedge a long time to die, and they said you could hear him coughing all over town. Sedge built half the houses in Sheppard.

Tom sees lights on inside. Several young couples live on Main now. He thinks of being young, being old. Even Andy would be a middle-aged man now. He would have changed, looked like Patricia maybe, hair starting to go gray. That would be something. Sometimes when Tom watches a young couple in a restaurant or just walking in town, he feels an envy so deep he wants to run away. He could be in love. He's not too old for someone to love him. He's long since stopped thinking of it as sexual. He wants a harbor, safe arms to hold him and whisper that his fears are reasonable but cannot help anything. He wants eyes to follow his. He wants to live as if he had never been sheriff or a good man.

He drives down Main, takes a left, and goes the half mile to the cemetery. Lightning has begun to shred the sky. The thunder is various and powerful. He drives into the cemetery and parks. A strip of lightning rips the darkness away and thunder

*81*

follows with a finger-tingling crash. Tom takes his powerful flashlight and gets out. The wind is swirling, coming from nowhere, going nowhere.

The river's most dangerous flood plain is where it bends near the cemetery. No flood in history has reached the upper cemetery, and since it was built none has come close to the lower part. Tom walks through the stones, shining the flashlight and looking at the names. Some are familiar, but others died here as their families were all moving away. No one knows what they did. They have become their names. He finds the path and walks on it through the upper cemetery and goes down steps to the lower part. Past it a quarter mile away he can see the river in the lightning strokes.

He knows where he's going now, denies it, knows it's true. He wants to think he's on the business of Sheppard County, and he will be, but first he must check on his son. He turns left and goes straight for the spot, but instead of ANDREW MEADE he finds MARY MOSS who died in 1956. He looks around him: everything seems to have moved in this rain. He thinks of the stones subtly shifting in the night, orbiting around some invisible force, a power deep within the earth. Maybe God lives in those caves in Kentucky's limestone. Tom thinks he knows where he's taken the wrong turn, and he goes back, walks another hundred yards, but this time he finds LUKE MCDONALD, infant son of Mary and Jack McDonald.

Tom begins to jog slowly, shining the light on each stone. Rain pours off the brim of his hat. He sees a woman named Irene. He finds Sam Preston's father. They brought him back here and buried him after the suicide.

He turns again and moves against rain now; it hits him like pebbles or shrapnel. He stops, breathing hard, feeling choked and close. There it is. He's standing in the plot. He shines the light on the boy's stone and chokes back tears. He goes to it, touches it, and feels better. I'm old, he thinks, I'm getting so old. He shakes his head to clear the feelings and walks down the steps and on to the river bottom that extends between the cemetery and the Coollawassee. The city keeps this cut, and people walk and picnic here. Now, it feels spongy, unfirm. It takes Tom ten minutes to reach the riverside, but he hears it long before he's there.

Trees line the river here, beech and oak and elm. The rain and wind are fierce. He gets to the riverbank and can't quite believe what he sees as he shines the light upon it. The river is nearly to the top of its banks already, raging and whitecapped like sea waves.

"Mother of God," Tom says. Once it spills over its banks, it usually covers the meadow, then follows the contours. The worst flood Tom remembers was in '63, just after Kennedy was killed. It came to the lower part of Main Street. It took nine hours to rise that far. Tom turns and starts running back toward the higher ground of the cemetery. He steps in a hole and water gushes into it. He thinks he's hurt his foot, but he tests it, and it's fine.

He thinks he might never get back to the cemetery.


The car won't start. He tries and tries, but it's not going to turn over. Rain covers the glass, turns it opaque. Tom sits for several minutes not moving, barely breathing. He's useless. He couldn't save Andy. There never was hope, but he'd told himself as they dug that he could save them, that Andrew would make it.

Tom jerks. He's afraid. He reaches for the key and turns it, and the car starts immediately.

"Get ahold of yourself, Tommy," he says softly. "You just get ahold of yourself." He inhales sharply and puts the car in gear. Already he's thinking of what he must do next and how they might keep the river from rising into the streets. He might fail them. He must try.

Tom thinks of rivers, of water rising into the streets, then plunging to the center of the earth.

----

Zeke Watson's at the courthouse with his boy, Bowman. Zeke and Annie named him after her brother, who was killed in Italy during the war. Bowman was slow in school. Annie would tell everybody, *Well, Bowman's just fine, but he's a little slow in school.* He is, in fact, mildly retarded, and he made it through the eighth grade before they quietly took him out of school. Zeke owns a service station on Elm. He is wearing an orange raincoat and a frown. He and twenty other men stand in the interior hallway of the courthouse, and Tom can see them through the glass doors as he comes up the steps. Bowman stands close to his father and looks at him worshipfully. He's thirty now, but he might be nine. His mouth hangs open slightly, and his hair is tucked into an Atlanta Braves cap.

Tom opens the door, and Zeke rushes over to him. Leon is standing on the stairs that lead to the second floor with a few other deputies.

"Radar up in Indiana, northern part of the state's all red as the Fourth of July," says Zeke. "We saw it on the Weather Channel, didn't we, Champ?" Bowman smiles and nods. All these men have known Bowman for years, and they look after him. Tom looks at Bowman and then back at Zeke.

"I was just down at the river," Tom says. "I've never seen anything like this. I think it's going to come out in a big way. We might need to start thinking about getting people out of low areas and doing some sandbagging."

"Good Lord, Tom," says Douglas Dickens. "Do you know what this will be like? It'll be like chaos. It'll look to everybody like we don't have an evacuation plan." He laughs and lights a cigarette.

"We *don't* have an evacuation plan," says Tom.

"I been trying to bring it up at council for two years, but they won't let me," says Zeke hotly. Bowman's right hand comes up and he cups his ear and pats it twice. Some of the men agree, mumbling to each other.

"Well, this is just jumping the gun," says Douglas. "It's just jumping the danged gun. You're going to go and get all those people out of their houses for nothing at all. The old folks? You think about the old folks? Half of them are already in bed, Zeke. And we'll get them out and take them to the gym or something and the river will go back down just like it always has."

"Not according to the United States Commerce Department's National Weather Service!" bellows Zeke. He's short and gray, and his stomach bulges through the raincoat. He has moles on his face. "Now we have the CD team here ready to take action."

"Tom, talk to him," says Douglas weakly. "This is a big weekend for us. Talk to him."

"Okay," says Tom. "Zeke, you still got those empty bags stored at the work camp?"

"Ten-four," he says.

"Ten-four!" bellows Bowman.

"Then get them, and call Brad Smith and tell him to meet us as soon as he can down by the cemetery with a dump truck full of sand."

"Ten-four, hell. That sand's for the streets in winter!" cries Douglas. He looks at Bowman with disgust. "Are you taking responsibility for the wrecks around here when it's winter, Tom?"

"Would you all excuse us for a minute?" says Tom. He gets Douglas by the elbow and escorts him down the hall and around the corner by a water fountain. The lights aren't on back here, and they stand deep in the shadows.

"You don't have the authority," says Douglas. He's shaking his head.

"Douglas, you may be the mayor, but I've known you since you were a boy, and you were a jerk then, and you're a jerk now," says Tom. Douglas's jaw drops, and the cigarette, sticking to his lip, dangles briefly before Douglas closes his mouth and clamps around it once more.

———

"Tom Meade, you've never talked to me like this. This is serious."

"It is serious, Douglas," Tom says. "And if you ever look at Bowman Watson that way again or treat me like a fool, I'll kick your ass from here to Tennessee and back."

"This is, well, it's . . . it's . . . it's treason!" says Douglas darkly. "This is nothing less than treason!"

"It would be treason if you were the king or the president or even somebody who deserved some respect," says Tom, coming very close and towering over the mayor. "But since you are none of the above, and since you seem determined to put money over people, I have no choice but to tell you I'm going to be in charge tonight. You're screwing things up. I won't let you do it."

"You haven't heard the last of this, mister!" says Douglas, but his voice is so high, his face so pinched and red, that Tom finds him ridiculously funny and begins to laugh. Douglas storms back down the hall and Tom follows him. The men grow silent as Douglas nears them. He looks at them, then storms through the door and into the rain.

"Do I do what you said?" asks Zeke.

"Yes," says Tom. "Do it now. And since we need a special assistant, I want you to make sure that Bowman's right there to help."

Tom takes off his gold shield, steps forward, and pins it to Bowman's denim work shirt. Bowman looks down at it, then glances up and smiles broadly, then salutes. Tom salutes him back. Zeke grabs Tom's upper arm and squeezes it, not able to speak. Zeke, Bowman, and the men spill out the door.

"Bob, you and Allen go with them and make sure everything's okay," says Tom, and two deputies follow, leaving Tom and Leon alone in the hallway.

"What'd you tell His Excellency the mayor?" asks Leon.

"I told him that I disagreed with his management techniques," says Tom. Leon laughs a little and takes a toothpick from his breast pocket and picks at his teeth.

"He's sorta losing his grip, seems to me," says Leon. Then, "That was a classy thing you done for Bowman."

"I didn't do anything," says Tom.


Patricia's watching television when she hears the back door open. She can hear Tom taking off his raincoat and hat, hanging them up in the short hallway. It's a familiar sound, one she's heard hundreds of times, like a clock chiming the hour.

"You back to stay?" she asks as he comes into the den.

"No, I just came to say this might be an all-night thing, Pattie," Tom says. Her eyes almost smile. "What? What did I say?"

"You haven't called me Pattie in years," she says. "For a minute there, I thought I was young again or something." She turns and looks at the television. It's a sitcom and everybody's laughing like crazy. Patricia's eyes stay with the action, but she does not laugh.

"I don't know why I did that," he says. "It's the river. Coming up. The weather service says it could be bad before it's all over. I went and saw the river. It's churning and foaming like nothing you ever saw."

"Where'd you go, down by the cemetery?" she asks. She doesn't look at him. The sentence sounds to him like a flat line, as if a machine might have spoken it.

"Yes, dammit, I went down by the cemetery," he says. His voice is tense. He looks down and realizes that water is puddling at his feet on the dark blue carpet. "It's the easiest place to see the river."

"I didn't mean anything," she says.

"Yes, you did," he says quickly. "You meant everything. You meant it all."

"I don't know what you're talking about," she says, still not looking at him. "I just asked where you saw the river, and here you are getting all excited about it. I just asked. That was all I did."

"Forget it," says Tom. "I just came to tell you that I probably won't be back tonight. I thought you ought to know. Or something."

"You should be careful," she says. "Something could happen to you. You could get struck by lightning. There's a severe thunderstorm watch out. Don't overexert yourself."

"I'm not a child, Patricia," he says. "And it's my job. I just thought you'd like to know."

He turns and starts walking, and she wants to say something, to speak his name and ask him to call her Pattie again, but it sticks in her throat. By the time she can make a sound, he's gone out the door again.

Patricia puts her face in her hands and cries.

9

*Hermie hears voices.* When he was eight, he saw a spider descending down a shining thread as he lay before sleep in his room. Hand over hand, like a man climbing down a rope, the spider fell, and Hermie could hear it speaking to him. The voice was harsh and low, and it only sang his name over and over, two singsong syllables. The next day he listened, and he heard a fly humming a tune from a Walt Disney movie. His purpled lips would hang open as he listened. *Herman,* his mother would say, *what on earth are you thinking about?* and he'd say, *Nothing, Ma,* and it was a joke on him. His uncle Sy would finish answers for Hermie, saying, *Nothing, Ma,* then crack up. Uncle Sy had short fat fingers and a red nose. He smoked Chesterfields in a holder and quarter-folded the newspaper when he read it. He always wore a tie, even on Saturday when he wasn't working. He killed himself. He drank a bottle of Drano. At the funeral, when Hermie was fourteen, a voice came from the closed coffin: *Nothing, Ma,* then a burst of laughter. Hermie fled the services in terror.

Hermie hears voices now. Lying on his back in Sam Preston's small house in the hills of Kentucky for no good reason, he feels as if he's fallen down a well of milk. The world is inexpressibly white. He hears all the dead singing from graves below him. The world is hollow at its core. He's read that in science-fiction novels.

The voices are louder now, a singular laughter, someone talking, and Hermie blinks his eyes and sees those who have died before him leaning down. One is Clay, and the other is Bobby.

"Hermie?" says Clay. His voice is firm and insistent, perhaps even cruel, but not loud. "Hermie?"

Hermie blinks, feels his eyes roll into his skull, brings them back down, wonders why Clay has died, then remembers the gunshot. Hermie sits up sharply to find himself in a small room, lost. His eyes widen, hands wild.

"What?" he chokes. He coughs.

"Hermie, you pissed in your pants," says Clay.

"Oh God, he did," cries Misty. "I'm going back in the other room. Bobby, you're crazy. You're just crazy." Misty and Christiann head back for the front den, holding hands, trembling. Clay starts to laugh. A spreading dark circle covers the crotch of Hermie's baggy chinos. He sits up and feels himself. Mary Beth, still on the sofa, breasts half bared, feels as if she'll be sick, but she chokes it down.

The gunshot was a foot from Hermie's head, pounding a neat hole in the plastered wall, through the slats and into the rain. The smell hangs heavily in the room, and Mary Beth closes her eyes and cries. She thinks of daisies and asters, of annuals and the color they add to any garden in the warmer months.

Sam jumps at the gunshot, moves the chair in small hops. He shouts and curses, then goes silent. My God, what if he shot Mary Beth? He thinks of Ginger driving off, of her inevitable leaving, and he can't bear the thought of losing Mary Beth this way. He's only lately seen her through both eyes, differently, the way he always should have.

Almost immediately the chair tips again, and Sam's on the floor, the pressure from the ropes tighter than before. He begins to shout, "No! No! No! No!" and won't stop. It's a chant now, something from a medieval cloister.

In the other room, smoke clearing and Hermie sitting up to Clay's laughter, Bobby suddenly can't stand the sound of Sam's shouting. He closes his eyes and trembles. A thunderclap blows the top off the nearby hills, spills past them, rattling the windows again as Sam keeps shouting. Bobby's father would get into these deep depressions about working in the mines, and he'd start to scream and curse, and it would go on for hours, and Bobby would clap his hands over his ears and cry in bed. He feels that now.

Bobby pivots on one foot and heads back for the other room, and when he sees Sam lying there on the floor, Bobby thinks of his father in the coffin.

He'd begun to cough blood, at first small spots he tried to hide on a tissue, then choking gasps, his lips stained cherry red from it; towels, bedsheets, even the curtain in the kitchen where he'd been standing when an attack came on. His parents had a terrible argument much later. Bobby was in bed, but he heard his father saying, *If I don't go down they won't pay, and if they won't pay me, we cain't buy a damned thing for you and the boy. Onliest way I could give you any money is to die and get you insurance.* Bobby had awakened the next morning holding the knotted bedsheet in his fist, dry-eyed, determined to leave. But he saw his uncle Barney leaning over the bed, smelling of cigars and coffee, saying, *Come on and get up, Robert, your pa's passed.* And the first thing Bobby thought of was the money; how much was it, and when would it come? Bobby saw his father in the coffin later that day, in the house itself, and he looked waxy, white as cinders.

Bobby jerks back, shaking from his father's open coffin, and feels an explosion in his chest. His heart is about to collapse. He's had this idea for years that his head would explode. The doctor said his father's heart finally just blew out. Bobby thought at first that he'd said *blew up,* and the image never left him.

"Shut up!" screams Bobby.

"No! No! No! No!" chants Sam.

Clay wanders behind Bobby to see what's going on. Bobby drops the gun and sways like a drunken elephant. He cries, an unintelligible gargle, then steps into a vicious kick to Sam's face.

Bobby kicks Sam over and over in the head, on the face. Bobby groans and cries and screams for Sam to *shutup, shutup, just shutup!* Sam feels the stun of the blow, stars, galaxies. After three kicks he feels darkness; the blows seem less intense, nearly fading away. He seems to be falling, almost drifting down some endless hole.

It's two A.M., and Misty and Christiann are huddled together on Sam's bed, the sheet over them. The window's open, and occasional gusts of wet wind crawl across the bed. Clay's in the den applying a wet cloth to Sam's face. Sam's been unconscious for an hour. Hermie's asleep in a chair, and Bobby's disappeared onto the porch.

"Remember," says Misty, "when we learned how to shave under our arms? I cut myself, and then when I sprayed Right Guard on, it felt like I'd been stung by a whole nest of them hornet things." Christiann drowsily says she remembers. "And I thought, well, if this is what growing up means, I don't want *none* of it. You can't figure out who to trust."

"I never trusted mucha nobody," says Christiann.

"J.D. says he loves me, so I up and marry him," says Misty. "Then right off the bat he's hitting me like I was a punching bag or something."

"What you think he's doing now?" asks Christiann.

"He's prob'ly sitting around in his boxer shorts crying like a baby," says Misty, and the women both giggle a little.

"Misty, Bobby's so sad and scary," whispers Christiann. "He like to kicked that man's head in. I think he's half dead. You ask yourself how we wound up here?"

"Here's not no different from anywhere else," says Misty. "You ever seen any of them flying-carpet movies, Christiann? I always wanted just to snap my fingers or anything like that and be another person in a different life. Like getting up in the morning and going to the closet, and there's all these bodies to put on like new spring dresses. I had that dream. I have it all the time. And when one body don't fit no more, you go back to that closet and put on another one."

"You're crazy too, girl," says Christiann.

"Maybe I am, and so what," says Misty.

For two or three minutes they lie silently very close, touching along the legs and shoulders. Misty thinks it feels nice to be so close to Christiann. She loves her like a sister.

"You ever think about what's down there?" asks Misty finally.

"Down where?"

"Caves underneath the ground. I've done seen pictures before, and it's scary. There's spikes hanging down from the ceiling like a horror movie. Long fat things that would fall on you and bust you to pieces."

Christiann can't think of it. It's too frightening. So many things are like that.


"I can't stand this," says Bobby. One light's on in the den, and Hermie's deep snoring in the chair sounds pitiful to Clay.

"I know," says Clay.

The beer's nearly finished, and Clay can't keep his eyes open, so he slumps over on the sofa and begins to snore lightly. Bobby lights a Camel and walks through the house. It's dark. He'd untied Mary Beth's feet and covered her up on the small sofa in the library. Her hands are tied in front.

He looks in the door at her. She's finally fallen asleep, but she stirs in dreams, moans, talks. He thinks he hears something coming from the bedroom, where the girls have gone, and he listens, then hears nothing. Bobby watches Mary Beth. He'll have to kill her, too.

Sam's in the equipment room now. From the dim glow of the hall light, Bobby can see Sam propped in the chair, his face a mass of bruises and swollen tissue. He'll have to kill Misty and Christiann, too. It almost makes him sad to think about it.

Bobby's suddenly so tired he can't bear it. He walks down the silent hallway to the den and curls into a fetal ball on the floor. He looks at Hermie, asleep with his mouth open, and sees himself stealing there, sliding the barrel in his mouth, shaking it until Hermie's half out of sleep so Hermie will know, then waiting half a second more and pulling the trigger. Bobby can see Hermie's brains blown all over the wall.

Bobby's eyes roll upward. He begins to dream. He's back in Reidsville, in his narrow cot, handcuffed and shackled after the riot. They wouldn't let anyone move. He's on the cot, and then he realizes he's in the coal mines with his father, who's about to light a cigarette, and Bobby says, *Coal gas?* but his father just laughs. The old man's different down here. He's not trying to be Bobby's father. He's a hacking animal, burrowing through the earth like a worm in a blind fury, pledged to an early death. These are his adventures, tunnels and shafts, windless orchards of black stone to grind and load. Sometimes you'll run across a vein of another rock, something useless and shining, but no one cares. All the men are dumb and sweating, stripped to their waists, cursing, except for Bobby's daddy, who's lighting a cigarette.

"You're going to blow us up," says Bobby, who's a little boy again, same black hair but a different face, kinder and more afraid.

"Screw it," says his father, who never cussed in front of Bobby. Then all the men are stopping and lighting up, and there's a hissing of some giant fuse. But it's not a fuse: it's snakes, roiling up from some mined-out passageway, snakes, millions of them, reaching up from hell for their revenge, blind white snakes with fangs an inch long, bared and ready to strike. And the men don't run, but Bobby's scrambling toward the elevator.

"Run for your life!" screams Bobby to his father. The last thing he hears before he takes off is his father's pale laughter and the sound of death rising to them.


Sam awakens from the brutal kicking. The storm had abated, but it's back now. Sam lies flat for a moment, then sits up and tries to blink the room into his eye. He's mildly surprised to be alive, then wonders if he really is. He sits up, feeling his teeth with his tongue. Two are slightly loose on the left side, on top. He remembers Bobby kicking him now. He sits for a long time, listening and trying to remember. It's still night, but the house has never been so black; then he understands. *He's blind now.*

After ten minutes he knows from the steady rain and the silence of the house that everyone must be asleep. His hands are tied behind his back, but they unbound his feet when they laid him on a recliner. He stands shakily, getting his weight beneath him. He finds the window from the sound of the rain. He takes small steps and his feet hit a loop of rope, then he stops. He moves around it with baby steps. His face feels like raw, throbbing meat from the kicking and the cigarette burn. His neck hurts so bad he can scarcely turn it. He thinks of Mary Beth screaming and wonders if she's still alive. Perhaps they've gone. No. He can sense the others in his house, a collective breath or a breathing, a presence. He knows when he is not alone.

Sam comes into the hallway and stops and listens again. He tries to bring light into that eye, but there's only a profound blackness. The kitchen's down the hall, and he takes two steps. The floorboards creak, and he stops for a long time. A mockingbird begins to sing in a bush outside. The endless melody will awaken them all. But no one comes, and the bird finally flies away or falls into exhausted silence.

Sam's in the kitchen now, a crowded room on the back of the house, and he knows where the silverware drawer slides out. He backs up to it, pulls it gently behind his back, then turns. There's a stirring, a voice down the hall, and Sam freezes. He's motionless, not even breathing. He blends in with the darkness of the house. After a moment the only sound once more is rain. Sam tries to clear his head as he feels for a serrated steak knife in the drawer. He thinks of Mary Beth, of light. He blinks the good eye, but it feels swollen, not his face but the eyeball itself. He wonders if he will ever see again and how these men came to believe he was rich. He tries not to see some kind of justice or think of collapsing caves. Images come from nowhere: the deep green of a baseball field, emerald speleothems, a baptism, Mary Beth's smile, or her eyes when she had reached down and touched him. But they fail. He remembers the last thing he saw glancing up, that man's twisted face, his rage as he kicked.

Sam finds a knife standing backward at the drawer, but using it seems impossible. He remembers learning to drive, can't make the connection. He will move glacially. The only advantage he has is that slow silence. He finds the crack between the stove and the counter next to it and firmly wedges the knife into it, blade up. Then he slides the wrist ropes over the edge and begins to saw. The rope is nylon, will cut only slowly, not unravel like hemp.

Sam closes one eye, then the other. He thinks he can see something for a moment, but he realizes it's the wrong eye, and the image he sees is his bedroom in Richmond from childhood. He wants to stay there. He wants to get up from a Sunday afternoon nap knowing it's time to go to Baptist Training Union even though he hates it. He wants to get slim tracts and go toward the car with his mother, to feel the maternal grumbling of the Chevy. The smell of the church, the different way the sanctuary looks at night without daylight streaming through the stained-glass windows.

Sam closes that eye, opens the one Bobby Drake kicked in. This time he sees pictures from a PBS special on the planets, a speculative journey toward another spiral galaxy. Then, he glimpses his grandmother reaching out to him, smiling, saying something. She is soundless, and Sam realizes space is a vacuum and no sounds will travel over it.

Sam cuts faster now, and the ropes begin to fray and break. It does not take long, and it is not hard. In four minutes he is standing in his kitchen, unbound, listening to the wind. He could rescue Mary Beth, get her out while they're sleeping, but that's a dream, like his grandmother among the stars. If she is there, if she is alive, he'd never help her. The only thing he can do is get out of the house.

The back door, which leads from the kitchen to a porch, then into a overgrown yard and into rising hills, hangs badly on its hinges. Sam's planned to redrill the holes and replace the hinges. He walks with small steps toward it, feeling with his hands and feet for anything in the way. He stops. Can he hear soft voices? No. The sounds begin to clear themselves. They're whispers of wind, the way they will sometimes breathe between passageways deep in Blue Crystal Cave.


Hermie awakens. He sits upright in the chair and realizes Bobby and Clay are asleep, and that it's still raining very hard.

He realizes he can kill Bobby where he lies. So easy. Get his gun or Clay's and put a clean bullet in his brain. Hermie's mouth drops slightly at the thought in the lamplight. He sees it: slowly getting up, then getting the gun, and there's a sudden *wham!* and Bobby's gutshot, shocked, blood trickling from his mouth. But he'd have to kill Clay, too.

*Clay*, thinks Hermie. Now Hermie wants to cry. He's always loved Clay, even when they were boys. *He* could do anything, but he was stupid to get caught and sent to prison. Hermie wrote him once, twice a week. He started a sci-fi novel, sending Clay chapters until Clay told him to knock it off. Hermie would have to kill Clay if he kills Bobby.

There's another chance, though. He could get that woman while they slept. It would be so easy.

There's a crash from the back, and Bobby leaps to his full height, right in Hermie's face. Hermie can't believe it; like a demon rising from hell, wingless, eyes bulging from their sunken sockets. Bobby's pulling the gun out, ready to shoot, ready to do anything. Clay stirs, rolls over, looks up and says, *Bro?*

Bobby's slept hard, dreaming of the coal mines and his father's decision to blow it all to hell, and his face carries rug scars from the floor, angry pockmarks. His hair has flopped, askew.

In her room, Mary Beth sits up, feels the cool air from the window on her shirtless breasts. She's still alive. She wants to scream, even opens her mouth, but nothing comes out. Misty sits straight up, and Christiann's snoring like an old man next to her in the bed.

"What was that?" asks Misty. She shivers. Christiann groans and speaks nonsense syllables in her sleep. "What was that?"

Back in the den, Bobby turns from Hermie, thinking to kill him later, and starts to move down the hall, gun out, at first slowly, then at a stumbling, sleep-drunken trot. Before he gets to the kitchen he knows Sam's no longer in the house. Something's changed.

*  *  *

Sam bangs on his eyes as he moves into the backyard, and he realizes he can see a little, but things are constricted, distorted, out of focus, coming and going. Fantastic shapes appear before him. He trips over a log in the overgrown grass and falls heavily, only breaking the fall at the last minute. A slim strip of dead wood jams into his palm, cutting a diagonal line across it. He hears noises from inside. Sam gets up and moves away from the sounds, up the slope behind his house. The path is back here somewhere, the one run down by dogs and deer, winding up the hills straight to the sinkhole down to what's left of Blue Crystal Cave.

Sam's just to the treeline as Bobby comes to the back door screaming and screaming.

"I'll kill you!" Bobby sounds as if he's ready to kill anything that moves. He hears the breaking of a twig and raises the pistol and fires. Sam feels the swift whisper of the lead as it splashes past through the rain and hits an oak with a solid *thwock*. He runs. Ten feet ahead he hits a tree, falls backward, stunned, nearly addled. He scrambles back up and runs, talking to himself: *Get out of here, Sam, get out of here, get out of here.* Bobby fires again.

Inside, Mary Beth screams at the top of her lungs. Misty and Christiann are up suddenly, dressing, and Clay's rounding them up. Hermie runs into the room with Mary Beth, turns on the light and tells her to shut up. Her hands are reddened from the bonds. She's sitting on the couch and tries to pull the light blanket over herself.

Hermie's making guttural noises just as Clay strides into the room. Hermie barely has time to turn before Clay grabs him by the back of the neck and pulls him up. Mary Beth feels that lifting now. She's going to die. Her heart's about to quit beating. Her weight is nearly gone. She can see the stars come out in the ceiling of the room. Two more shouts outside sound like drumbeats in a well. She thinks of the Little Drummer Boy. That means she's dying. She barely hears Clay.

"Hermie, you're nothing but a fool," says Clay with soft disgust. Hermie smiles, a sickly grin, ready to shrug it off, when Clay's expression changes. He rocks back slightly and pushes Hermie through the window in a shattering of glass. The wooden frame splinters. Hermie screams, feels the sickening slice of glass along his face as he lands in the streaming yard. The yard is flowing off, taking him. He tastes his own blood in the corner of his mouth.

Mary Beth sees two women in the doorway looking scared. Clay glances at the window. Mary Beth wants to thank Clay, but why? Bobby comes storming back into the house. Misty and Christiann, still numb with sleep, glancing guiltily at each other, move away.

"He's got away!" cries Bobby. Mary Beth's lungs fill with light. "He's running up in the woods. Bring the women and let's go!"

"I about half killed Hermie," says Clay.

"Bring her, too," says Bobby, pointing at Mary Beth. "I'm leaving this place clean."

Mary Beth feels a sanctity now. She knows that she has gone into a biblical valley. Clay gets her up as Misty finds a T-shirt from a bedroom drawer to cover her nakedness. They untie her, slip on the shirt, and then retie her hands in front. Mary Beth thinks of rising, flying over a cliff's face into the setting sun.

# 10

*The earth* is round and solid. Sam's sitting in a fourth-grade classroom, listening to Miss Meredith as she points at the wall map. Everything is ordered, has its place. Even the air has its layers, each with a different job, but its life and works are invisible. That, says Miss Meredith, is one of God's graces to man. There is order, too, in the earth. Mankind is meant to progress toward new ideas, toward peace. The earth also has its seasons and layers. Miss Meredith shows them the crust of the earth, geological areas, and the descending stratigraphy below the crust down to the molten core. Sam thinks there's a sun inside the earth. He goes home and tells his mother that, and she gently says, *No, there's only one sun in our solar system; what's at the heart of the earth is liquid rock. Everything forms that way.*

Perhaps everything forms from liquid. If you dig deep enough, you'll find a sun in the center of the earth, he believes anyway. He can't shake that image, and later, when he found out about Little Jackie Moss, he would lie in bed and think, if he'd gone deeper, he'd have found the caves starting to become light.

Now, Sam Preston's lying flat on his stomach in a rain-slimy wash of drab hills behind his house. He hears them shouting, coming up toward him. *Miss Meredith, why am I thinking of you?* She died two years after she'd taught him. His mother went to the funeral and came home and said it was the most beautiful thing, there were so many flowers at the graveside.

Sam can't feel direction. He gets to his knees and listens, but they're veering off the wrong way, perhaps a hundred yards away. His head feels misshapen. What time is it? Sam stands and moves around quietly until he locates the slope and begins to walk up it. Everything leads upward here. The night trembles with thunder. Nothing seems familiar, or everything.


Hermie Baggett staggers inside, nose running, crying. He's holding his hand over the side of his face. He thinks his left hand is broken from the fall. They've left. He hears Bobby screaming in the rain as they ascend the slope behind the house. Hermie goes into the bathroom and turns on the light. It's weird. Aliens could live here. The power can't figure its level, and the lights glow brightly, then dim.

Hermie looks at himself in the mirror and says, *Oh Lord*, when he takes his hand away. There's a four-inch-long cut from the corner of the right ear to his mouth. His face is all blood. Blood's leaking into his mouth. Hermie gasps and cries harder.

"He cut my head off," says Hermie between sobs. He wipes it off, gets a towel and holds it to the slice, but blood bubbles up from the crevice. The white porcelain of the sink turns pink. Hermie looks at it then back at his face. "Ma, I brought you roses." His right hand is shaking. His left hand seems crooked, like a shepherd's staff, folded in as a paralytic old man's. Hermie's never seen so much blood before. Clay is his best friend, and he's cut Hermie so badly. All over that woman.

He keeps patting the slash until the blood slows, but it stings so badly. What do they do with your blood when you die? He'd asked his father that once, and the old man had slapped Hermie. *Herman, you always say things that make me sick,* he said, but Hermie just wanted to know. His grandpa had died, and he knew where his body was, but how about the blood? Where'd they put the blood?

Hermie feels the silence of the house and can't bear it.

"I'm coming, Clay," he says, and his voice is thick and clotted. "I'm coming."

Hermie goes down the hall through the kitchen, onto the back porch, and into the rain. He hears them far away now, cursing, talking. He wants to call to Clay and tell him he was right to cut his face. He should have cut me, thinks Hermie, and broke my hand, too.

"It's okay, Clay!" shouts Hermie. He wants to hug Clay. He wants to hold him close and say that all his brittle bones are Clay's to touch or break, as if they were his own.

Bobby hears a snap up the slope.

"That way!" he shouts, and he runs through the trees and brambles, nearly frenzied at the thought of Sam's escape.

Clay moves the women along. Christiann's soaked and starting to cry. What in the hell is she doing here? She says her friend's name over and over, tugging her damp sleeve, but Misty says nothing. They follow the beams: Sam's house seemed full of flashlights.

Mary Beth stumbles, falls, and Christiann helps her back up. Clay's moved ahead toward Bobby, who's making sounds of rage as he spills through the green darkness. Misty turns to say something to Christiann and sees Mary Beth running back from where they came.

"Hey!" cries Misty. "Where is she going?"

Clay turns sharply, ten feet ahead, and curses.

"Misty, for God's sake," says Christiann, who slumps against a tree.

"Bro!" cries Clay. "The woman's run off. I'm going after her. You head on."

"Dammit!" screams Bobby Drake in frustration. "Yeah." Bobby moves on and on, and Misty and Christiann, now swelling with the wet silence, move with him as Clay brushes past. Ten yards later, Clay sees a shadow to his left, lunges at it, and catches Hermie by the arm. Clay shines his flashlight in Hermie's face. Hermie doesn't have a light. His face is a mass of blood, swelling and caked, the mustache dripping.

"It's me!" cries Hermie. Clay looks at him without emotion then lets his arm go. He moves away, listening for Mary Beth's crashing down the hill. "Clay, it's me! I'm okay now!"

"No, you ain't, Hermie," says Clay quietly, then he moves on. Hermie watches the flashlight recede with Clay, feels the crushing weight on his shoulders again. He looks ahead, and far up there are more lights, so he moves on. He sips blood. It is warm and sour.

Sam Preston runs now, arms in front of his body, waving away trees, dreaming a path to the sinkhole. What if he gets there? Sam stops for two seconds, pounds his good eye, but it won't bring in the light. The cigarette burn on his cheek stings from the rain. If he's going to be shot, he'll take it like a man. He'll take this death as well as he can. He owes God a death, and he should have been a rich old man in Richmond, watching the shadows gather in his library. Now, he'll feel the bullet thud into his back, and it won't hurt. His breath will just go out like a candle, and he'll fall into darkness.

It's not far. Is it far? Sam wonders if he's turned around, if he's near the path: the land is leveling now. Thunder cracks, but Sam hasn't seen the lightning, and the shock makes him jump. Can he move more silently? He could swim to the sinkhole. He thrusts his arms out to swim, and his fingertips touch tree limbs. He swims and swims.

Bobby's gaining. He can't see Sam, but he hears his determined crashing, knows he can't get away. *You can't get away. You'll never get away.* Misty and Christiann can't keep up.

"He's crazy," gasps Christiann. "Misty, you know he's crazy. He's gonna kill all of us."

"He won't," says Misty excitedly. "You're just being silly about my Bobby."

"Let's get out of here," says Christiann. She grabs Misty and tries to square her up, but Misty shrugs the grasp off and keeps after Bobby. "Misty!"

"Go back, then" shouts Misty angrily. "But go back alone."

Christiann can't think of anything to say. She gets close to her friend again and fights through the weeds and trees. Her legs feel as if they're getting shorter. She ran in the cross-country run in high school and came in last.

"You smell that?" says Christiann. "Something's dead up here!" Misty inhales as she keeps moving. The rot of carrion rises to their nostrils. The whole mountain may be dying, for all she knows.


Mary Beth's almost to the yard, and she's wondering where her pocketbook is. The keys to the Cherokee are in it—or is she blocked in? She can be at Sheriff Meade's office in Sheppard in fifteen minutes. He will help them. She knows how much he likes to help. Then she thinks, *Sam.* She stops, turns to see where she might be, and Clay's there, a foot away, shining his flashlight into her face.

"Surprise," says Clay softly. Mary Beth screams. Far up the slope now, Sam stops for a moment, wrestles with his useless anger, moves on ahead. Mary Beth turns to run again, but

Clay's on her far too quickly. He takes her arm and spins her around. In lightning light she sees his eyes, and they are hooded and reptilian, cold and dead. He could be something rising from a swamp. "Come on or I'll have to hurt you."

"What kind of people are you?" cries Mary Beth. Clay laughs softly.

"Wind," he says. His grasp is suddenly much tighter on Mary Beth's arm.

"What?"

"Wind," says Clay. "Ice." His face is very close to hers now, and she think he's going to snarl like a dog and bite her throat, then he swings her close. It comes back. "Ice." He kisses her on the ear, and she feels a confusing impulse to kill or hug him. She can't stop trembling. Clay pulls back from the kiss, and he's laughing softly. She feels naked and beaten. She raises her tied hands to slap at him, claw, anything, but it's useless. He leads her back through the dense rainy underbrush toward the sounds up the hill. Mary Beth wonders what the world will be like without her. She wonders if she and Sam might have loved after all.

The rain comes and goes on gusts of wind.


Sam feels the land level now. He's breathing in great gasps. He'd cut the path when he and Ginger first moved here, but he's not on the path. He may be near it. Near a path isn't on it, he thinks, suddenly wondering if that might be important. He wants to laugh. He thinks of Ginger and turns toward a sound, turns again and runs squarely into a tree, goes down.

It's a Louisville Slugger in the head. The dull woody stun of an immovable object. Sam scrambles up, realizes the disorientation is complete; he can't tell standing up from sitting down. He swims forward again. They're gaining on him but gaining from the wrong direction. The wrong direction: thirty yards to the left, and Sam moves to the right. Yes. Here is where the geography changes, and the limestone underneath begins to buckle and fault, suck down streams of rainwater from the sky.

That other world begins here.

Sam listens for Mary Beth's screams, hears nothing. Maybe she's dead now. Things die in their season, only there's no season down there with the flowstone, the grottoes, the spongework. It's one unending death or life eternal. Sam's feet are kicking forward, and he thinks of life eternal, the world everlasting, then peace. He thinks of that story about Little Jackie Moss and the funeral, when the preacher said he'd gone from eternal darkness to light everlasting: Was that true? Where did a man without eyes find light?

Sam stops: the smell is familiar, the angles of the land embracing now. He walks slowly forward in the rain into whips. He swats them back, jumps, stops, knowing he's found the willow tree near the sinkhole. He wants to scream in triumph. He's never felt this strong.

He doesn't want to fall. He can't remember if this is what he planned, where he wanted to go. He hears them talking and shouting behind him, to one side. He stops, then realizes Bobby is closing the gap, striding through the bush, nearer and nearer.

"Damn," he says, and it's much louder than he'd thought it would be, a scream in fact, and Bobby's stopped, turning. Sam knows he's screwed up terribly.

"I got him!" yells Bobby Drake. "I got him!"

"Damn you to hell," says Sam. Bobby takes his gun out of his waistband and fires in Sam's direction, but he's off thirty degrees. Sam scrambles forward on hands and knees, finding pieces of rope, familiar debris from the sinkhole. It's twenty yards away, ten.

"He's crawling on his knees like an animal," says Bobby. He can see Sam now, has the flashlight on him, starts to laugh. Misty's caught up with Bobby and can't believe how exciting it is, like hunting possums. Christiann feels sick. She wants to feel something liquid and loving, not this. Clay's not far behind now with Mary Beth. The flashlights up ahead dance in the tree limbs. Just behind Clay, Hermie's calling his name over and over, and the cut on his face has broken wide open again. Hermie's trying to hold the blood in his head, but it's not working. If he could just get to Clay, everything would be okay.

"Don't shoot him!" cries Mary Beth. Sam's head jerks toward her. He wants to call her name, but he doesn't have to. She's alive, and they're after him. She's alive because he's alive.

"I'm here, Clay!" cries Hermie. He's caught up, and blood is flowing into his shirt. His nose is running. Misty shines her light on him and screams. Hermie's smiling at Clay, as if to say, *You're my hero, and you had to throw me through the window.* "I'm here."

"Shoot him," says Bobby to Clay. Clay looks at Bobby and thinks about it, but what's the point now?

"Ice," says Clay.

Bobby whips back around in time to see the earth swallow Sam Preston. He's sliding down its mouth like a worm in a fish gullet. Bobby feels a tremble of terror he hasn't known in years.

"Hey!" shouts Bobby, but he doesn't quite know what to say. He stumbles toward the sinkhole.

Sam holds the rope ladder and descends, hand over hand, not sure of the next grip but descending anyway. It's raining down the hole, but once he's at bottom and moves along the passageway it will be all cool and dry. It will be dark.


Bobby's at the edge of the sinkhole, shining his light down.

"He's going into the cave!" shouts Bobby. He fires twice into the sinkhole. Sam's at the bottom, feels bits of splintered stone and lead ricochet off the smooth surfaces. They spatter him as he moves down into Blue Crystal Cave, hands on the walls, reading it like Braille.

"Don't shoot him!" screams Mary Beth. She falls to her knees. Clay kneels with her. He doesn't feel anything. Misty is beside Bobby, peering down the hole.

"It's a cave hole!" squeals Misty. "Hon, is this that cave? The one that fell in?"

"He's dead," says Bobby.

"Well, that sure won't help nobody," says Misty, "if you shoot him."

Bobby turns on her. He is afraid to go down, but he's been lured. She's smiling at him. He can't bear it. He turns away slightly, then hits her in the mouth with such force she stumbles and falls at the edge of the hole. Christiann catches her friend's arm and holds her away from the edge.

Misty's not hurt badly, but she's crying and moaning. Mary Beth is suddenly dry-eyed. Sam's in the cave.

"I told you he's bad," whispers Christiann.

"How come you's to do that?" whines Misty. "All I ever done was try to love you."

"Is there more than one entrance to this thing?" Bobby asks Mary Beth. He's so close she can smell his breath, cigarettes and staleness. His flashlight beam is in his face, then hers. Misty is making choking noises. Hermie's hopping back and forth, holding his sliced face, saying soft, urgent things to Clay, peering into the hole then backing up. "Answer me."

"Let's just leave," says Christiann to Clay. She's at his side. "This is crazy as hell. Let's leave and go to California."

"Clay, I'm so sorry," says Hermie, who has started to cry. "I know you had to throw me through that window. I won't ever do that again. Scout's honor." Hermie begins to laugh. His head feels as if it weighs four ounces; maybe he's turning into an alien or something.

"I said answer me," Bobby says. He raises his hand. Mary Beth lifts her face to take the blow, but Bobby suddenly can't hit her. He waits a minute. "She'd of said no." He squints at her. "She'd of said no if there was another way out." Bobby nods, lowers the gun, and looks around. "He's trapped like a dog. I got him."

Suddenly it's so simple. Go down and pick him like a flower.

He'll be in there, huddling against the wall and waiting. Then he'll say where the money is, and that's it.

"You got him," says Clay.

"Clay, you guard it until it's light here," says Bobby, snapping his fingers. "The rest of you are coming back to the house with me."

"I want to stay with Clay," says Christiann.

"No," says Clay. Hermie says he'll stay with Clay, but nobody cares about Hermie anymore. Bobby looks at him and feels a brief thrill from the river of blood making channels down his face. "Clay stands alone."

Bobby turns and moves away from the sinkhole back through the brush until he finds the trail. It was there all along. There's always a trail, even to hell. The warden had told them that. It was a speech about trying to escape. He'd said, *Don't even think about it, because we have dogs that can trail you. You think you're smart, but you always leave a trail.*

Bobby gets Mary Beth by the arm and brings her along. She's never felt so tired. She's terrified for Sam. Clay might go down there and shoot him just for the fun of it. His lips were warm on her ear. She wants to kill him for making her feel that. The lies of the Serpent in the Garden.

In a few minutes Bobby and the women are back at Sam's house. The rain, which had slacked, suddenly slams back into the Kentucky hills with chilling force. They're inside, and Mary Beth wants to sleep. If she could sleep, she could die. She thinks that it's a switch you turn off in sleep. They said her grandpa died in his sleep. She couldn't get that phrase out of her mind for months.

"Take me to the bathroom," says Mary Beth softly.

"Misty, take her, bring her back out," says Bobby. Misty mumbles something, takes Mary Beth by the arm, and steers her toward the bathroom. Bobby gets Christiann's elbow and takes her down the hall to the den. They sit on the sofa. He puts his gun on the coffee table. Christiann yawns, looks warily at Bobby.

"We got him," says Bobby to the room. He's not talking to Christiann. "He thinks he's gonna escape. He's half blind. The money's probably in that cave with him."

"I don't think there's a damn penny here," says Christiann. "And there's more than money in the world; my momma told me that." Bobby coldly smiles at her. He thinks about the cave and shudders. She's wary of him, but he's teasing with her. She can't help it; she likes that.

"What else did she tell you?"

"Not to sleep with no man I didn't love," she says.

"So you love ol' Clay?" asks Bobby. He smiles, but it's mostly a grimace, hard and seeking a position.

"If I do, it's none a your beeswax," she says. "Me and Clay are going to California when we get this money. We're gonna live in Studio City. There's a town called Studio City, and I'm gonna be a actress."

"You're too fat and ugly to be an actress," says Bobby.

"I'm not talking no more to you," huffs Christiann. "You're just cruel and mean's all."

"Yeah?" says Bobby. "You think you know cruel? You ever see a man come up out of the coal mines after a twelve-hour shift?"

"What's that got to do with the price of beans in China?"

"They come up hacking black soot out of their lungs," he says. He stands and pushes his hair back and shudders, walking around the room. "They claw at it down there like animals, then they come up, and their skin is black, only underneath the dust it's white as a corpse's. And they're never gettin' outta the mines until they're dead. They're born to it, then they die from it up here or down there."

"Well, you're sure getting all worked up," says Christiann.

"The women all cry," says Bobby. He stops and looks out the window into the rainy darkness. "The place falls in down there, and the women get together at the mine, and they all cry."

"What d'ya think they'd do, have a picnic?" says Christiann. Bobby comes and sits beside her on the couch, and this

*111*

close, she feels something new, a hidden current that pulses between them. "Women always cry when their men . . ."

Christiann's words crumble. She can't think she's so tired. Women with tear-streaked faces blackened with coal dust walk in a solemn line through her mind.

"Is your daddy still alive?" asks Bobby softly. "You still got a daddy?"

"Sure, he and Momma run the store and . . ."

Bobby's mouth is suddenly very close to hers. Sounds come from the bathroom. Mary Beth and Misty might be finishing up. Christiann can't think. Sometimes she feels like a spider, wanting to grab anything that comes near. She saw that special on TV about spiders. They sit very still, then grab whatever comes near. She could love it.

Bobby suddenly kisses Christiann on the mouth, nearly crushing the breath out of her. She doesn't expect it, pushes back, then grabs his shoulders and pulls him forward. His tongue is all over hers, and he's lifting her breast as if weighing it. The door from the bathroom opens, and Bobby stands up and walks to the window and looks out as Misty and Mary Beth come down the hall to the den.

"Well, you look like the cat who ate the canary," says Misty to her friend.

"I don't know what you're talking about," says Christiann.

"Let me sleep," says Mary Beth. "Put me on the sofa in the library. I can't go anywhere."

"Take her," says Bobby to Misty.

"How come I have to?" whines Misty. Bobby's glance is bitterly cold. Misty makes a sigh of exasperation, takes Mary Beth back. Christiann is touching her lips and looking at Bobby. That feeling she has: you could climb on it, crawl down it across the room, all the way into Bobby Drake's arms.


Sam stops just before the ledge. A slip here, and he'll fly forty feet to the jagged stones below. The cave is soundless, and he is almost sightless. They aren't following him, but he's no better off now than he was before. He sits and leans against the cave wall and lightly rubs his right eye.

He starts to cry, but the tears burn, and he changes it to anger. He growls. He doesn't realize he's on his hands and knees until he's crawled ten feet and stopped. He suddenly realizes he can see. He can't see inside this cave. He can see other days, other shared moments, with his family, with Ginger. He sees himself standing and kissing Mary Beth with Lake Preston, that pitiful shallow puddle, there before them. He sees Miss Meredith in the fourth grade, hands tenderly on the globe, telling them of the perfection of the earth, above and below, the reasons for spheres.

Sam sits up. He won't crawl anymore. They aren't coming after him yet, but what good does this do? He's never been in such pain before, been so deeply tired. The cigarette burn is terrible. His mouth tastes of blood. A bat flutters behind him, closer to the sinkhole.

Suddenly he's suffocating. The cave has collapsed around him, come crashing right down. The other children are crying out to him. He stands and hits his head on the curved ledge of the cave ceiling, falls back to his knees. He can't get his breath. He can't run or he'll fall in a crevasse. He can't sit still or the cave will close up. They'll never get to him. He's already seen the newspaper headlines about himself and all the other children.

He lies down flat on his back and realizes this is death. Then it is comforting. The cave cradles him. He is held fast in its cool arms, and his grandmother whispers nicknames no one else could know. He's just been dreaming again. Or he's really here and death is a comfort, an expiation, the deep lull and lullaby he's always sought.

Sam sleeps. In that sleep, he finds he is dead after all. He spins around the equator of Miss Meredith's globe, and he's never seen such a light, as if God himself had lit this one pitiful universe among so many others. He hears a singing behind him, and he turns to see children with him, thousands, millions of singing children, a chorus of endless escape toward that light. He cannot understand why he's always been afraid of this. No one knows that the light beneath this small world is just as bright as what is above it.


Clay and Hermie are huddled beneath the willow tree at the entrance to the sinkhole. Clay sits calmly in the rain, holding his knees before him, but Hermie can't sit still. He's giddy from the loss of blood, and his cheek may be broken. Yes, he thinks, touching it, it's broken.

"You had to break my head," says Hermie. "It's like in *Dune*. There are tests. We're always going through tests, Clay. You did what you had to do." He smiles in the darkness. Hermie's waving his flashlight around. Clay keeps his eye fixed on the sinkhole.

"Bobby told you to keep your hands off her," says Clay. "You're lucky I just broke your head."

"Absolutely, I know that," nods Hermie. "But we're going to kill her anyway, aren't we? I figured we might as well get some good out of her. Aren't we going to kill her?"

"Yes," says Clay. "We're going to kill her."

"See," cries Hermie, "see? If Bobby's gonna kill her, how come I couldn't get a little of that?"

"First, you're a queer, Hermie," says Clay. "And second, we're going to kill you, too."

Hermie stops and begins to laugh. That Clay, he always could make Hermie laugh. Hermie takes his hand off the cut, and the blood begins again, this time into his mouth, and he realizes the thin tissue of cheek has broken clean through. He shines his light on Clay. His face drips rainwater.

"Kill me, too," laughs Hermie. "Like that makes any sense!"

"You ought to let *me* kill you," says Clay. "Bobby'll hurt you. I'll do it clean."

"Oh, right," laughs Hermie. "You'll do it clean. Like with

what, an electric chair or something?" Hermie's high-pitched laugh sounds like something cut by a thin blade.

"Hermie, you're already dead," says Clay. "You're just flopping around like a dead fish. Maybe you'll go into some other dimension or something."

"I'm not dead," protests Hermie. "I know you had to throw me through the window, Clay, but you don't have to, like, really kill me."

"You ought to pick your death while you can," says Clay. "Or somebody else'll pick it for you."

"Okay, okay, I'll make it up to you and Bobby," says Hermie. "You'll see. It's how come you came and got me to go with you."

"I got you because you had money and a license," says Clay. "Now, you're dead. You're already dead."

"I'm gonna catch that man for you," says Hermie, and it's suddenly so clear he can't believe it took this long to come. All he has to do is descend beneath the storm.

His new light will come up shining, far below the sound of rain.

## 11

*Clay doesn't say* a thing as Hermie moves through the rain toward the sinkhole with his flashlight. Hermie's never been in a cave before, doesn't feel very afraid of it. He can see this ending to his story: down there, finding the man huddled against a cool wall; pulling his arm tight behind his back and asking for the money; Hermie making them all rich. He'll make them all rich.

"You're gonna be sorry you said that about me," says Hermie. His nose is running, and there's a wild touch to his words. He's nearly lost control. "You had to like throw me through the window, but you didn't have to say that stuff about killing me. Once you're dead, you're dead. You know that, Clay?" Clay stares at him, unmoved.

"You're nothing now," says Clay, but Hermie's shaking his head.

"I'll prove you're wrong," says Hermie. "You got a hypothesis. That's all. That's a thesis. I got antithesis. Then we got synthesis, which is like I bring up the money, Clay. You'll see. I'm going to be your hero like you were mine, okay?" Clay says nothing. "Okay?"

Hermie knows he's not going to say a thing. He shines the flashlight on the rope ladder, which descends into the darkness. He can't hold the light and climb down with both hands, so he slides the light inside his wet shirt, and a dim glow comes from his chest. Ha, he thinks, just like E.T. He slowly descends the ladder, thinking about money, trying to look below then above, seeing nothing either place. I mean, how big can this cave be? Right? He's thinking of blood-sucking monsters when his left hand slips, and he's dangling dangerously for a moment before he gets it back. He groans, cries out for Clay. The ladder sways giddily.

He climbs down faster now, holding on, slipping, grasping it back. His feet hit the bottom before he expects it, and he falls with a terrified shout. He's falling now, down miles and miles, flat on his back like a parachutist. A monster's swallowing him. No. He's at the bottom. He sits up and laughs and laughs. There wasn't a thing to it! It's already nearly over! He wants to shout, *Clay! I made it!* but he knows Preston would hear him. Now, he must be silent. He takes the light from beneath his shirt.

This room isn't large, but it dazzles Hermie. A wash of rice crystal overhead looks like frost or a bed of diamonds. They're rich already! His light rakes a mottled drapery of flowstone. Stalactites hang heavily from the ceiling twelve feet above Hermie's head.

The cave's just ahead of his flashlight beam. It's not scary at all. A straight passageway with plenty of headroom. The air is cool and weird down here. At least it's not raining. Hermie's suddenly weak from his bleeding face, and he leans against the

117

wall and breathes. He remembers a sci-fi book he read a couple of years before, can't recall its name. There was a monster on the cover. The hero, whose name was Dac, had ten challenges, and one of them was killing a three-headed monster in a cave. He had to trick the monster somehow, but Hermie can't remember how he did it. The monster was named Zamran, he thinks. It lived on human flesh. Hermie reread that chapter a couple of times. He loved it when Dac tricked the monster. He was a hero! You had to have heroes or what was life?

Hermie pushes himself away from the wall and moves down the passageway. The ceiling begins to lower, and a hundred feet farther on it's only two feet above his head. He's careful to wave the light on the floor. He doesn't want to fall into something. He goes another hundred yards and there's a crossover, the meeting of two cave passages, and he stops. He'll keep moving straight now. He goes fifty yards, when he changes the flashlight to his left hand, only it slips out. His hands are bloody. The flashlight rolls, light over dark, over dark, over dark. Hermie falls to his knees and scrambles after it, but it rolls down a narrow crevasse. He puts his face down and sees the light fall, getting smaller and smaller until there's a dull crack, and Hermie's left in the profound, silent darkness of Blue Crystal Cave.

He laughs at first. It's not as bad as it looks. There's a switch somewhere, and it'll be thrown, and the cave will fill with light. A director will shout, *Cut!* Anything. Then he knows, marrow-wise, bone-certain, that this darkness is terminal. He is at the end of time here.

Hermie stands, can't find vertical, falls. He screams and screams. Far away, his voice comes back, distorted. When the sound dies away, he sits. *Try to clear your head*, he thinks. He stands back up. All you have to do is follow the cave back to the sinkhole. *Clay's there!* He'll be worried about Hermie, already be down the rope ladder and looking for him. That's all. Count your steps. That's what Dac did, count steps, and Hermie begins to count them out loud, *one, two, three, four, five, six*, slowly,

slowly. It's maybe a hundred steps back. He decides it's *exactly* a hundred steps back.

But after a hundred steps he's in a narrowing passageway, ceiling down to the top of his head, and Hermie knows he's somehow gone the wrong way. He'll have to go one hundred steps back the other way and start over. *Clay,* he says, and it's a whisper, then he says it again, a shout.


Sam Preston sits straight up. Someone's screamed, and it sounds like *day* or something. It's one of them. He knows the sound of a friendly voice. It's coming closer. He blinks, looks back down the passageway, but no hint of light spills to him. The darkness is not in this cave; it is in him.

Sam feels his way along the wall until he's at the edge of the precipice. He knows this place well: a small collapse chamber with a single unadorned column. He'd duck in here to work on the Prusik knots for his auto-belay. Caving alone, he'd make doubly sure.

Sam can't tell how far away the man is. He's closing. He seems to be talking to himself. Sam thinks of Mary Beth, and that anger rises to the surface, spills into his heart.


"Hon, I got to get some sleep," says Misty. She's whining, and Christiann, sitting across the room, can't take her eyes off Bobby.

"Then go sleep," says Bobby.

"I meant *us*," says Misty. "I'm so tired I could puke. Don't you ever sleep, hon?"

"Go lie down in the room with that woman," says Bobby. He says it like a command. Misty feels hurt, but she's yawning, too tired to think straight now. "You keep an eye on her."

"Will you come back with me?" she asks coyly. Bobby's cheek muscles work. He's thinking about the coal mines again.

"Just go back there," he says. He sighs. "I'll come back directly. It'll be light before long. Then we're going to get that Nobody."

"If he's not gone to get the law," says Misty.

"He can't get out," says Bobby. "I got that right."

"Right," shrugs Misty. She comes and kisses Bobby on the cheek, and he flinches, balls his fists, looks disgusted. It hurts her feelings, but she wanders off down the hall. Bobby and Christiann are across the room from each other.

"You treat her bad," says Christiann.

"I don't mean to," says Bobby. "Just stay out of it."

"It was wrong, what we did," whispers Christiann. "She's my best friend in the world." She looks at her fingernails. "I couldn't do that to Misty."

"Do what?"

"You know," says Christiann. She's grinning. "You want me, don't you?" Christiann licks her lips and arches her eyebrows. "That's how come you made Clay stay up at the cave, idn't it? And how come you sent Misty to bed."

"No," says Bobby. Christiann's face darkens. "It's because you want me. That's why you came. You want to be burned by something your momma told you was too hot to touch. I bet you always been that way."

"Like you know my momma," says Christiann.

"I know *you*," says Bobby. "I knowed a woman like you all my life. You'd sell the Holy Ghost for a chance somebody'd lie and say they loved you."

"That's a hurtful thing to say," whispers Christiann. Bobby comes and sits beside her on the couch. "That's such a hurtful thing for you to say."

"Hurtful," says Bobby. He puts his hand behind her head, and her heart is clattering, a train rocking north. She thinks he'll caress her, but he grabs her hair and pulls it lightly. She gasps, wants to cry out but doesn't. If she cries out, Misty will hear.

120

"Don't," is all she can manage, but Bobby's turned her head toward him, and suddenly his lips are on hers, and his tongue is lapping the breath out of her. Her arms are all over him. He pulls her hair harder, and she groans softly and tries to take his hand away. He's still kissing her. Maybe she could go to California with Bobby instead of Clay. He suddenly lets her hair go, and the relief, the absence of pain, fills her spine with expectant voltage.

He's helping her take off the T-shirt, and Christiann's looking down the hall where Misty went. This is bad, but she can't help it. It's nothing she can do a thing about. She unhooks her bra, and the heavy breasts fall free in the cool air of the room. A breeze lifts the curtains.

She can't believe this is happening. Maybe he's wanted her all along. He's in love with her. Maybe he's been thinking about her the whole time, saying to himself, *Christiann Mizelle is the prettiest thing! When she's outta my sight, I can't hardly wait to see that pretty thing again!* She can't worry about Misty. What happens happens.

"The light?" asks Christiann. Her breath is ragged. She doesn't sound like herself. Bobby doesn't answer. His hand rubs her left knee for a moment then plunges upward. She's kissing his neck. She rubs his back, reaches around with one smooth arch and lets her hand come to his zipper.

Bobby suddenly stands and takes off his shirt, unzips his pants, pulls them down.

She looks at Bobby's face now, and it's set in a hard frown, looking past her. That's when she hears the scream.


Clay's pacing back and forth in the rain in front of the cave. He can't get used to the wide-open spaces. In prison, you knew where the walls stopped. There were rules. And you made your own bonds that kept the walls from you: *ice, air, steel, blade, water.* Here, there is nothing.

He and Bobby had suffered through Reidsville together. Some men came out beaten down and soft. Halfway through their sentences they might become girl-boys. They'd trail their men around. Nobody cared. You made your own rules, or you followed the prison's rules, or you had none at all. There were limits.

The lightning is the limit here. You can see the sky and know where it goes, up and up and up. They'd watched the *Challenger* blow up. All of the cons, even the hardest of them, became restive, upset. A few cried. Bobby had cursed and sat on his bunk for a long time. Clay thought of that schoolteacher trying to get free of gravity. It made him so mad he wanted to choke somebody from NASA. Everybody in Reidsville understood dying while running away from this earth.

Clay feels the sky opening before him. It's too much. He needs walls. He could feel them in the car. He could make walls with Bobby's words. He could walk to the corners and look up and see the concertina wire and think, *Yes, these are the boundaries of a life. I may go beyond this only at my peril.*

Crazy thing to find out, thinks Clay, from stealing a car. Now, he wants to see stars. He wants to start rushing faster and faster into the sky, then be blown toward some lost elliptical orbit. That was the worst part of the *Challenger*, that it fell back to earth. Better it had been blown toward the heavens, except there were no heavens. Just endless, clotted darkness.

Clay rubs his hair back from his eyes and goes under the dripping fronds of the willow tree and lights a cigarette. It tastes harsh and foul, just right. The rain has slowed again, but the willow is still weeping. Clay thinks about Camels. He hadn't even smoked when he met Bobby. They'd been talking one night, and Bobby'd said that smoking an unfiltered cigarette was like screwing death. Clay couldn't get the image out of his head. Two, three days later he smoked one. Within six months he was up to a pack a day. Each puff was an act of defiance.

Clay shines his flashlight back toward the sinkhole. Hermie has gone down there, and there's been no sound or word in forty minutes. Maybe he is dead by now. Clay thinks of Hermie dead and feels nothing at all. He thinks of himself dead and feels nothing at all. He'd always said he was in prison because of a bad break. He wasn't the kind of kid who stole cars. His high school test scores were through the roof. He could have been a doctor. That counselor, Miss Markham, said he could be whatever he wanted to be. Clay just couldn't think of a thing he wanted to be.

He smokes the cigarette down to his fingers, drops it in the foul-smelling mud and leaves it there. He shines the light into the willow branches. They go everywhere. They are channels, paths up and outward to nothing at all. He puts the gun in his waistband and turns the flashlight off and thrusts it inside his shirt. There is no light. He feels for the first branch and begins to ascend into the tree.

A wind comes up, but the rain does not. The rain spatters him, then stops completely. The wind is hot and damp, from the Gulf. Reidsville was in south Georgia, and not halfway through your work detail, the men stank from stale sweat and hopelessness. You could never forget that smell. The branches blow, tremble, shake off their water like a dog as Clay climbs higher.

He goes as high as the smallest limbs. He wants to take a swan dive. They had a ten-foot board at the pool when he was a kid, and Clay did the most beautiful swan dive. Girls loved seeing his muscular body pump upward off the board, spread out with an elegant wingspread, and come down into the blue water. He could do that now. He could hold his arms out for balance, let them come slowly to his side, kick upward once, and dive into the earth. He would break the surface with his forehead and come through into that cave. He would drown in darkness.


Hermie's back on his feet blundering along. He stumbles, talking. He's sure creatures with pods on their feet live in here. He should have a thread to follow out. He's read that story but he can't remember anybody's name. The monster was half bull. That was funny. Hermie laughs.

"Bull for a monster," he says. His hands are on the walls. He's trying not to be afraid. Waves of terror wash over him. He'll never find his way out of here. The cave seems to be breathing.

Twenty yards ahead, Sam hears Hermie moving, knows at once who it is. This makes no sense. Why would *he* be the first? Sam blinks, bangs his fingers on his good eye, but there's no light.

Hermie stops for a moment when he remembers he's got a box of matches in his pocket. Matches! He's saved.

"Oh God," says Hermie. He has to keep spitting blood now. Hermie reaches in his pocket, and it's there, and he takes it out. He drops the first match, curses, falls to his knees and tries to find it. Sam listens to the muttering. Hermie can't find the match, so he stands and takes out another. He strikes it, and the cave does not look as he'd thought. It's full of twisted shapes, old men hunched over, pointing at him. Hermie gasps. It's one thing to read about a violent wizard flinging spells; it's another to have fallen into his cold heart.

Hermie swings his match hand around as he turns in a circle. He stumbles. His feet feel heavier than he thought possible: Perhaps it's another planet, with different gravity. It's another world altogether, one of childhood terror and delight. He could be in a Saturday serial. Hermie Baggett could be the hero! Hermie thinks of himself as the hero, but the match goes out so fast, he thinks the cave's sucked away the light. He lights another from the dying flame, realizes soon they'll all be gone and then the darkness will close in on him. He starts to run, hunched over, crablike.

Sam hears him coming and braces. His hands are out, and he's braced. Sam hears his footsteps coming nearer, and a great throbbing rush of adrenaline begins to strengthen him. He becomes so tall the cave can't hold him. His arm muscles thicken.

Hermie lights the third match. He looks at his fingernails and sees they're bitten down to the moons. That's never bothered him before; now, he wonders if the movie audience will notice. They'll wonder how he became a hero if he bites his fingernails. He decides to stop it. He's thinking of fingers, movies, caves, when the passageway turns slightly southwest.

Hermie's trying to get his breath. That's when he runs straight into Sam. His breath goes out like a flame. He hears himself scream at the monster's face: swollen, misshapen even, its claws coming up for him.

Hermie doesn't have time to plan or think. He drops the match just as the monster's arm encircles his neck.

"Lord, Lord," whines Hermie. "Oh Lord." It's a cry from something forgotten. Hermie suddenly wants to scream, but the monster's arm is around his neck, dragging him, and he can't breathe at all. He decides to make peace with the creature, but he doesn't know what to say. He feels a light coming up from somewhere. It's the most brilliant light of his life.

Sam cannot imagine his own torque. He's as strong as earthquakes, dragging Hermie the twenty feet toward the crevasse. He feels nothing but the man's blood on his arms and shoulders, hears the silly gasping sounds. Sam counts the steps. He's been here a thousand times. He can see it without seeing it.

Sam stops and gives Hermie a fierce shove. Hermie feels the monster's clutch relax, is filled with such gratitude, such relief, that he half turns to say something, when the cave's floor comes out from under his feet. He turns into a dream. He's part of his own dream, falling, and when he hits bottom he'll be on the floor, and his daddy will come into the room and say, *Herman, were you having bad dreams again?*

Halfway down, Hermie's head hits a slick outcropping of rock with a sickening thud. It breaks his neck. He falls forty feet limp as a cloth doll and lands in a dusty, flat chamber that leads nowhere. He's dead before he gets there.

_____

Sam leans against the cave wall and listens for Hermie, for others. He hears nothing at all. There's no sound from down there. He'll be there forever now. Sam throws his head back and howls and screams, falls to his knees and cries. He's shaking so badly that every sob is rattled. He wants something to count, something to bring him away from the night.

Mary Beth sits up, listening to the screaming in the front room. She's alone. She's been in a deep, ragged sleep. She couldn't bear it. Without looking around or feeling afraid, she gets up and walks down the hall into the kitchen, gets a knife from the silver drawer, and walks out the back door. They're going crazy in there. She can't imagine what the brawl is about. Women are screaming. Somebody could be tearing hair out in a minute. She's seen girls fight at school. Women fighting scares men half to death; they don't have a clue what to do next.

Suddenly she realizes that she's no longer in the house, no longer with them at all. She's in the damp, dark greenery of the backyard. She goes a hundred yards and stops and tries to use the knife to loosen her tied-up wrists, but it's no good. She keeps moving now.

She stumbles out on the road, but she can't walk here. It's the first place they'll look for her. She crosses it and sits in a dripping grove and tries to think. Sheppard is due south. If she simply walks south, she'll eventually get to somebody's house near town.

The earth is indistinct and soggy. This is how it was that year her husband died. It had been raining all that week, and every-one thought Charles had hydroplaned, but there were no skid marks. He'd simply driven off a cliff sometime in the morning. There was no evidence he'd braked at all. Mary Beth would lie awake in bed fingering a lump of lapis lazuli and wondering if he'd just had enough or gone to sleep.

She knew Sam better already. And they'd been so close to

126

making love. She wishes they had. She thinks of herself lying after it, snuggled to him, naked in his arms, dozing, then awakening to the joy and wonder of it all.

But now Sam might be dead. He could have slipped anywhere down in the cave and fallen, fallen, fallen. He could have dropped from exhaustion and drowned in the shallow splendor of Lake Preston.

Mary Beth realizes suddenly that her bonds are loosening. The rope on her wrists is somehow starting to get weak and loopy. She walks in the wooded glen, sets the knife down, and tears at the coils, and her fingers feel nearly numb. The rope humps up like an awakening snake and falls into the underbrush. She can't quite believe it's happened or understand why. Lightning sparks, but it's not close. She feels as if God has taken the ropes off just as he rolled the stone away. She starts to cry.

Where does she go now? The trees are women: bent and cackling, waiting for some mistrustful pilgrim to stumble among them and beg for help they will never give. They won't help anyone. They'll say, *You believe in certain things you know to be untrue. That is why it is belief instead of knowledge. We believe only in soil, air, and water. We will not help those who believe without knowing.*

Mary Beth's certain she's lost now. She looks around. It goes on and on. There are no landmarks, no stars or moon to steer by. The coils of briar are like rising waves. She feels her way forward, moving where the growth is thinnest, letting the forest guide her toward its sodden heart. She stops and looks back and listens. They'll be after her, or will they? They were screaming, women were screaming. Maybe that man was hurting them. He might have been killing one of them while the others watched.

She moves on, thinking of going south but following the easiest line. She bursts out into a clearing of woods. The air is filled with the snickering and croaking of frogs, counterpoint of vague bird sounds. There's an overarching terror to this place,

127

a magic. What if she found a cliff here: would she hydroplane in a dream and find herself flying off it, downward in a wet slope?

She's thinking of that flight, but the canopy is so dense the slight rain doesn't penetrate far, and there's little underbrush now. She understands: the forest floor is thin where light can't wedge. Rocks peek up from earth like monsters' noses taking a sniff of fresh air. She can see them imprisoned below her.

A tremendous crack terrifies her. A rotten limb, weakened by rain, collapses and falls. She turns away from the sound and goes down a slope, no longer sure which direction this is. She could be heading back toward Sam's house for all she knows. She's thinking of Sam, of his arms, his aroma, the sound of his breathing on her neck, when her foot sinks into the earth and turns at an impossible angle.

Mary Beth screams and falls. The ankle is set afire. The pain spreads up through her knee, into her thigh. She pulls the leg out and sits, feeling it and sobbing. The pain is monstrous. It comes in swollen waves and makes her nauseous. Fern fronds crowd her, brush her cheeks.

They'll be coming for her soon. They'll hear her breathing here, lost in the woods. She wants to tear God's features from his face. She lies back on the forest floor and waits. The wind could be speaking her name. It could happen anytime.

Bobby's putting on his pants and cursing. Misty and the still-naked Christiann are fighting on the floor, pinching and biting and slapping. The sound makes Bobby nearly sick. He wants to kick both of them until they don't move. That's what happens when you lie with a woman. It's always that way. You think it's going to be wonderful, then it turns into this hideous thing. Misty's shrieks sound like his mother's when she was dying. She'd scream and be sick in a bedside bowl, loud groaning vomiting between her cries.

Bobby goes down the hall, feeling as if his brains might leak out his ears from the pressure. That's when he feels this door swing away beneath him, and he knows the price. He rushes into the library, then all the other rooms. The woman is gone.

He knew it, could almost see it. He feels the walls of the house very close, holding his breath heavily in lungs that would break.

# 12

*B*owman *Watson's badge* shines as he holds up a burlap sack and his father shovels in the sand. They're at Sheppard Park, and the dump truck's unloaded a mound of white sand just off the baseball field near the concession stand. When each spade of sand hits the bottom, Bowman emits a small grunt. More men have come out, dozens of them, and the lights from the ball field cast a dull glow. To Tom, it seems barely real.

Already they've taken a hundred sandbags to the river and stacked them along the lowest part below the cemetery. The water is rising, and Zeke thinks it could come over the banks in an hour. Mary McClain from the *Sheppard Tribune* is taking pictures and talking to the men. The rain comes straight down.

---

The men barely talk, and a rough silence has settled over them. Tom hears them coughing, speaking in soft slow words, just doing the job. He sees Leon walking up from a long way off and waits for him. Leon's looking around as if he can't believe the rain.

"How's it looking down there?" asks Tom.

"The water looks mighty angry," says Leon. "Barney and the boys from the fire department are working their rears off. I can't say it's gonna do much good."

"Well, keep at it," says Tom.

"We will, boss," says Leon. "I came to tell you that Sheriff Ireland of Woodley County? He called and said all hell's broke loose up there and water's in the courthouse itself. It's like the weatherman said, coming right on up. I think we ought to start thinking about getting the people along lower Main out now."

"I agree," says Tom. "Tell Allen and Bob to call Dick Miller and see if we can use the gym at the high school. We need to get some doughnuts and coffee and cold drinks, too. Blankets and pillows. Get us a bus from the shop at the school. Wait, get Miller to get us a driver with insurance. I'll be along directly and talk to some of them while we're taking them out. They know me. Maybe they won't be afraid."

"Right," says Leon.

He turns and walks quickly back toward his car. Tom goes to Zeke and tells them to carry on, that they're doing a fine job. He's going to the river to check. Zeke and Bowman both tell him *ten-four*.

Even on high, Tom Meade's windshield wipers can't keep the road from blurring.

Barney Timmons has set up two large floodlights on the river-bank so the men can see where to put the sandbags. Barney's a tall man who doesn't say much. He runs the volunteer fire department and is also manager of a poultry plant just out-

---

131

side town. The lights show the men stacking bags.

Tom parks his car and walks to the men. Several are leaning on the bags in exhaustion. The Coollawassee makes a grinding roar now, and Tom knows these sandbags won't hold, but they have to try anyway. Barney sees him and comes over. The men have stripped their cumbersome rain gear and are soaked to the skin.

"Tom," says Barney, nodding. "It's coming up fast. I've never seen it like this. The boys are working hard, but we're up against a tough thing here. This isn't something men can stop. Maybe the rain will slack and we'll get out of it all right."

"I don't know," says Tom. He looks at the distance between the river and the lower part of the cemetery. A quarter mile, perhaps. He looks at the men, then realizes an absence, a hollowness. "Is Sam Preston here?"

"We called Sam twice, but the line's dead," says Barney. "It must be the lightning. Nobody's had time to go up there. It all happened so fast."

"He'd want to be here," says Tom. "He's a good boy. He'd want to be in here pitching."

"I know," says Barney. "If we sent somebody after him, we'd lose a man we need here. I'd be glad for you to go after him."

"I don't have the time either," Tom says with a sigh. "I just wish he was here, that's all."

"Dickens was sniffing around half an hour ago," says Barney. "He's about to go crazy because Len Wilson called—you know, his brother-in-law who owns Sweet Sally? Len told him that water was starting to back up in the cave."

"Water's in Sweet Sally?" says Tom. "God, I've been here my whole life and never heard of that. I don't see where this is going to end."

"Barney!" a man shouts. "You better get over here!"

Barney walks to the edge of the river, Tom a step behind. The river has come up two feet in the past five minutes, and the men, exhausted, are staring at it with disbelief. Barney shakes his head and wipes his mouth with both hands, looks around, as if someone will give him an answer. The men are waiting, but Barney seems overwhelmed, unsure what to say next.

"We can't stop it here," says Tom. He's surprised at the strength and volume of his voice. The men turn to him. Tom wheels and looks at the soaked landscape. "Look. Over there where the low spot touches the road. If we start bagging there, maybe at worst we can make a waterfall that will slow it down until the rain quits. Also, it shortens our line of supply by half a mile."

"But if we do that, it might back up into the cemetery," says a man whose name Tom can't recall. "That would divert the whole thing into the cemetery."

"Then we'll bag at the wall of the cemetery, too," says Tom. "That will form a wedge and push the water straight down the street. It will flood the lower part but it might slow it just enough."

The men look back and forth from the street to the cemetery. The rain is suddenly harder. Lightning forks. The thunder is barely two seconds behind, rattling the hills around Sheppard.

"It'll work," says Barney. "By God, I think that might work."

"I think it will, too," says Fred Hill, who teaches math at Sheppard High School. "We could sandbag that ridge up there, too, and we'd almost make a lake in here, covering this whole bottom."

"I see it," says Barney. "Tom, do you think we need to clear this with Zeke?"

"I'll tell him what's going on," says Tom.

"We got to get these lights out of here!" a man cries. "Look!"

They can't talk anymore. The river is now at the edge of its banks, spilling angrily, popping and fizzing. A man who fell into

---

this might be found miles downstream. Tom thinks of the Casey girl. She'd been walking along the river after a fight with her parents. In the seventies, he thinks. They'd had a storm, and she slipped and fell in. They found her nine miles downstream, tangled in a tree. Wanda Casey.

Barney orders the men to haul the floodlights off on their wheeled bases, and suddenly they're moving quickly, everywhere. Tom walks to his car back near the street and radios Leon. It takes Leon a minute to get to the car. Tom tells him to bring all the bags they have right now, that the river's coming out and they've got to make a fallback position where the bottom touches lower Main Street.

"What about the cemetery?" asks Leon.

"We're bagging it, too," says Tom.

"Okay," says Leon. Tom's already turned the engine on before he realizes that Leon did not say *ten-four*.


Tom stands on the porch with Leon. It's a small frame house that's neatly bordered with daisies, hostas, and ferns. When Tom shifts his weight the porch sags slightly, like a board crossing a creek. They've been knocking on the door for nearly a minute. The doormat says WELCOME, NEIGHBOR! Leon's about to hit the door again when the porch light comes on. Tom hears a dead bolt going back, then a nightlatch. The door cracks back, and Harry Stone peers at them, trying to adjust his thick glasses. Harry's eighty, owned a five-and-dime on North Main for fifty years before he sold out two years before. They turned it into a boutique. Sometimes he'll come downtown, stop wistfully in front of the building, and read it as a blind man reads Braille, touching the brick, shaking his head. He's only five feet tall, wiry and pleasant.

"Yes?" he says, struggling with the glasses. "Yes? What is it? Tom? What are you doing here? Elmira and I were asleep."

"Harry, it's the river," says Tom. "We're in for a big flood, and we're having to get out everybody around here. This

134

whole area could be underwater within an hour unless we're lucky."

"Got to get out of here," says Leon.

"And leave my home?" he says. "There could be looters. I wouldn't leave the house."

"Got to," says Leon. "It's an emergency civil defense management order."

"What the hell is that?" cried Harry. "You can't order a man out of his home. I'll die here first."

"Harry, can I come in?" says Tom softly. "Leon, you stay here." Harry sighs and backs up and lets Tom in, turning on a lamp. The den is small and cozy, perfect, Tom thinks, for two old folks. Tom sits on the edge of the sofa. Harry cinches his bathrobe and stares at Tom and waits.

"Harry, this isn't a precaution or anything," says Tom. "You remember back in '57, the fire?"

"I hope I never live to forget it," says Harry. "It took half the downtown. My store, too."

"Well, at first it looked like they were going to keep it down on Jefferson, and they quit with the water," says Tom. "Do you remember that?"

"I do, now that you mention it, Tom."

"They stopped because they thought the fire was out, but they didn't check well enough," says Tom. "I was part of the fire department, Harry."

"I disremembered that," he says.

"Now this river's coming out of its banks," says Tom. "I can't let you and Miss Elmira stay here and get hurt. It's my job to take care of folks, you understand. And you're not the only ones. We're getting maybe fifty, sixty families out along here and taking them to the high school. We'll have a nice place for everybody and food. Everybody in town's starting to pitch in and help."

"I guess they can reschedule Dollar Days," says Harry sadly. "I was looking forward to that."

"You get Miss Elmira, and y'all dress as quick as you can,"

says Tom. "We got a school bus out here that'll take everybody to the high school gym. It's safe over there."

"Okay," he says. "I been here half a century and never saw the river get this high."

"Maybe there's a reason for it, Harry," says Tom. "You believe in God, don't you?"

"Of course I believe in God," says Harry testily. "At my age, I'd be a fool not to."


Tom drives around the town, stopping to tell people at convenience stores what's happening. He goes in a restaurant and tells everyone to finish and get home. He finds it strange that not a person raises an objection. They all look into his eyes and nod. All along lower Main they're getting people out, taking them in loads to the high school. He drives to the sandbagging. The river's out of its banks now, boiling into the swale but not yet to the street and only halfway to the cemetery. The lower wall of the cemetery is slowly rising, now up two layers of sandbags. He goes north of town to the fissure he'd seen earlier in the day, and though the water's not out of these steep banks, the cave is covered. He thinks to drive up to Sam's house and get him. Sam will be sorry he wasn't there to help. But that's too far, and one less man won't make a difference against the river. Anyway, Tom cannot bear the thought of Sam being hurt. If Patricia would listen, he might say that Sam Preston was like a son to him. He might say that. Sam could have been here tonight, and they could have worked side by side. Tom might have deputized him.

No. Tom can't take the time. He drives back through town, and the streets seem deserted except for the odd car passing through town on its way north or south. He parks in front of the courthouse just as a fierce slash of lightning strikes something nearby and all the lights blink once then go out. Tom curses, gets out, and comes into the courthouse and goes up the steps to the second floor two at a time. He's surprised: He feels light

136

on his feet. His footsteps are so light he could nearly fly. He turns on his flashlight and goes into his office. He's never seen a darkness like this in the courthouse. Sometimes, when he can't sleep, he'll come back at night and sit in his office with the lights out, brooding over his life and wondering what he could do to get Patricia to love him once more. But it's always in the ambient light of the streetlamps. Now, only the flashlight beam shows him the objects of his life.

He sits at the desk and dials the emergency number for Sheppard Electric. The phone rolls to Paul Rusk's house, and his husky voice comes on. Tom tells him what's happened, and Paul thanks him, says he'll get right on it. Tom hangs up, cataloging what must yet be done in the night. Instead, he starts to listen to the rain against the window, feel the storm around him. He turns off the flashlight.

Tom suddenly seems more tired than ever before in his life. He closes his eyes, then opens them just before another lightning flash. The room looks like a painting, everything losing its third dimension. Then, darkness once more. He could be in a cave now, going down, downward in Blue Crystal Cave. He could be falling.

He sleeps, awakens, finds himself on the floor next to his desk. He sits up and touches his own arms. He feels the desk, wondering if this is Sam. Dreams. Lightning illuminates the room once more. Tom slides up against the desk and cries softly for a minute. He nearly had the boy in his arms. If he could only dream Andrew back for a minute, a single minute. He cannot bear it. He gets up, wipes the tears away, gets his flashlight. Out the door and down the steps, he goes into the storm, gets into the car, and drives. He feels calmer now. The worlds above and below never really meet. He knows that, but sometimes it is so very hard.


Bowman Watson is sitting in the dugout of the ball field eating a Snickers and watching the men out there fill bags full of sand.

Tom comes in with him and sits down. Bowman never seems surprised by anything. You could come up behind him in a dark hallway at night and touch his shoulder, and he'd turn around and say hello very softly. People in Sheppard feel so badly for Bowman and like him very much. They help him, make him feel special. Bowman is happy to see the sheriff.

"It's a big rain," says Bowman. He eats the candy with his mouth open, not caring how it looks. His teeth are dark with chocolate and caramel. "Bad men go into the rain."

"Bad men?" asks Tom. He looks at the badge and decides to let Bowman keep it. "The men out here are good, Bowman. They're all better than I am."

"Oh!" says Bowman, and he puts his hand on Tom's shoulder and shakes him gently and grins. "Oh! That's a thing!"

"You think there's bad men out there?" Tom asks.

"Good men," says Bowman. "Bad men. Birds go sit in trees when the rain. You see birds when the rain."

"When the rain what?"

"Daddy's a scarecrow," he says. "Look at him." Tom looks at Zeke, moving slowly now, filling bags and talking to the men. There must be a hundred out there now, filling bags, working like ants. "He's out in the field."

"He's like a scarecrow?" says Tom.

"Bad men," says Bowman darkly. "From the river, they just keep coming up and up. Daddy could be out there when the blackbirds start coming in. You know that?"

"Yes," says Tom.

"Oh!" cries Bowman. He doubles up with laughter. "You should see this!" He can't stop laughing, then he's choking on the candy bar, and Tom hits him on the back, and Bowman stops choking and laughing.

"You okay, Bowman?" Tom asks. Bowman nods.

"Okeydokey," he says. "My daddy." He gets up and walks out of the dugout, loose-limbed, heading for his father in the rain.

Patricia washes her face and looks at herself in the mirror. The power was off, but it's come back on. She wears a light cotton gown. Her hair is down now, and she turns back and forth looking at the gray; Tom has asked her about tinting it, but she won't. She wants to look old because that's how she feels. She wants to look like a mummy. She could be something in the *National Geographic* that they found in Egypt, a desiccated sexless shape that they will invent stories for. But what she feels is not deathful: it is anger, something pure and unyielding, a thing beyond which she cannot voyage. Anger is the only thing that keeps the fear beyond the edges of the light. On some nights, when she thinks she might soften for Tom, the fear comes from its hiding place and touches her around the throat. It knows her name. And so she brings the anger back, and the fear recedes. She must keep them in balance or they will destroy her. She must watch for anything that will push one beyond the other.

She turns out the light and goes into the bedroom, which is comfortably cluttered. Tom listens to Cincinnati Reds games on the bedside radio at night and sometimes tells her the scores. She doesn't care who wins. She pulls the spread back and lies on the clean white sheet. She washes the sheets twice a week so they stay crisp and clean. A single lamp is on.

She says her prayers before bed, but doesn't say them out loud. She doesn't know what they are about, just scattered thoughts, the name of Jesus popping up from time to time. Her prayers can go on for a long time, with detours into memories of who was on Oprah that afternoon or something she must do for the church Ladies' Auxiliary. She begins her prayers, then stops them.

"I can't," she says quietly. "I can't do this."

She's not quite sure what she means, but she whispers it again and puts her hands down by her side. She could be dead, in her coffin, lying like this in her gown. He's a good man, and he's tried to reach out to her, but he's wrong to live in the past. She's told him that over and over. He never was the same after the thing. He always calls it the thing, as if that changes it, *but we know it doesn't. He would start to talk about taking a vacation or visiting friends, and he'll manufacture a reason to stay and work. All he's done is work! He forgot how to love me! He did love me, and he thinks he still does, and maybe he does, but what he loves are shapes and words no one can make or say anymore! He won't look at me and see that I am not what I was but I am still here.*

"I am not an old woman!" she cries out loud. Tears run down the sides of her face. "I can't do this! I can't!"

She gets up and goes into the darkened formal living room and sits in a wing chair, curling her feet beneath her hips. Her own father was not very good to her. She's missed him, though. She misses every moment in her life that has already passed. She's done so many things wrong. She was not a good mother. No, that isn't true, just something she told herself after *the thing.* She was a good mother. *Sheriff and Mrs. Tom Meade announce the birth of a son, Andrew Henry. The maternal grandparents are . . .* Patricia rocks and sings a song, something you'd do for a baby.

The storm is fierce now. Tom's out there somewhere. He's trying to do his job the best way he knows how. He will die out there on the job. She can't stand the thought of losing him, and the anger shifts back and the fear moves forward. She needs a Darvocet, and she goes to the medicine cabinet in the bathroom and stands before the mirror, holding a cup in one hand, the pill in the other. She needs this Darvocet to calm her down and get things back in balance.

Patricia Henry Meade looks at herself in the mirror again.


Tom can't quite believe how high the water is now. The area between the cemetery and the river is full and the water is not forty yards now from the sandbags on the street. But they've made a levee twelve feet tall and four bags thick, and weary men stagger through the rain, refusing to quit.

Women are out here now, bringing them food and hot coffee. Some of the stronger women are helping put bags on the wall. Older men carry messages back and forth. Tom stands in the rain and feels himself grow with a deep sense of belonging to this place, a pride.

He's simply standing there when he sees Douglas Dickens scuttling toward him like a crab.

"I hope you're happy with all this," he says angrily. "All those people out of their houses for nothing. You can threaten me all you want to, Tom, but you'll have to answer to these people. You're an elected official of Sheppard County too, you know."

"Not anymore," says Tom.

"Huh?" says Douglas.

Tom walks away, leaving the mayor standing there. Barney intercepts him before he can get to the wall of sandbags.

"Tom, we got a problem we didn't anticipate," says Barney.

"Yeah?"

"If we let the water get to the top of this wall, we'll spare all the houses below us, but it might go over the lower part of the cemetery. They're way behind on that wall over there."

Tom nods and walks a few paces away and stops. If anything, he thinks, the rain is harder.

# 13

*T*hen *Bobby thinks* of the money: piles of
bills, snapped with rubber bands, thick chunks of twenties and
fifties. His mother had read him the story of the woman who
spun straw into gold. He can't recall her name. She'd be in this
room night after night, turning a spoked wheel, feeding it straw
and watching slender slivers of gold spin out. Bobby would lie
in bed and think of a room filled with golden straws. Preston
may have that kind of money down there: bound stacks, piles
of gold and silver. They could be in Chicago before anyone
knew a thing.

*The onliest ones who have money don't need none of it.* That was
what his daddy'd say before going to work, sick and coughing
as if his heart would blow up. *You don't go down there and do the*

*job, and the Man'll find somebody who will.* He'd also say, *A workin' man ain't got half a chaince in this world, Robbie.*

Bobby jumps: he can see the man's face in the room with him now, hear his last-night rattled breathing. Until then, his mother kept saying over and over, *He'll pull on through this one, too.* Then she said, *I think Daddy's going on a long journey, son. Oh Lordy, Lordy, he's aimed for that long journey.*

"Leave me alone," says Bobby, turning sharply. His father isn't really there. Or is that the smell of Prince Albert burning first thing in the morning? "Get away from me!" His daddy would righteously whip Bobby, beat him with his belt until blisters rose along his hips and legs.

Bobby shakes the old man from his head. The women are still fighting in the other room, Christiann screaming hideously. They're cursing, slapping, biting. Bobby's had enough of this, grimly storms down the hall and goes into the den, and pulls them apart. The naked Christiann is covered with red blotches, bite marks, scratches that drip blood.

"Let me go!" screams Misty, and she struggles to break from him. "I'm gone kill that bitch! I orta kill you, too!"

"You couldn't keep him, that's not hardly my fault!" yells Christiann back. "You couldn't even keep that husband happy!"

"Damn you!" screams Misty. "I'm gone kill you!"

Bobby pushes Misty to the sofa, where she falls, then pops up. She starts for Christiann when Bobby takes the pistol from his waistband and points it straight at Misty's face. She sees the barrel and Bobby's eyes at the same time. She groans, backs up.

"Don't kill me," says Misty. "Hon, put the gun down. Hon? Hon?"

"Don't shoot her!" says Christiann. She slips into her panties, jeans, and shirt, saying over and over, *Don't shoot Misty, Don't you think about shooting Misty.*

"I ought to shoot both of you!" he shouts. "You let her get away!"

They stop suddenly. Misty's got a dark red cheek from Christiann's slap. Their faces look cat-scratched, as if from a gym fight in high school. Misty looks at Christiann, and they seem to know, suddenly, that this is much worse than infidelity. Bobby just might shoot them for this.

"Go get her, hon," says Misty, suddenly in a higher, southern-belle drawl. "We'll wait."

"*You* find her," says Bobby. His lips barely move as he talks.

"Me find her?" cries Misty. "You don't mean I got to go find her!"

"You're going to find her, and I'm taking Christiann up to the cave, and we're going down to get Preston and his money. You find the woman and bring her up there."

"*Me?*" gasps Christiann. "I thought you wanted me, Bobby."

"What if she don't want to come back?" whines Misty. "I mean, it's not like I got a court order or nothing."

"You could bitch at her until she comes back," snarls Christiann, and they're about to go at it again, when Bobby cocks the hammer of the pistol and they both stop, frozen to their spots.

"I'm tired a both a you," he says so softly Christiann has to lean to hear. "Misty, you go find her and bring her back to the cave. You understand?"

"I understand," says Misty. Her mouth is dry. "But I need a gun, Bobby. I can't just ask her to come with me, you know."

Bobby thinks about it. He's naked without his gun, can't imagine going down inside some damned cave without it.

"Get a knife from the kitchen," says Bobby. He takes Christiann roughly by the elbow, and they go down the hall toward the kitchen and the back door. Misty's bouncing around, shivering.

"Hon, I never cut nobody in my life," she says. "She could be from here to Timbuktu by now. Why don't you let me and Christiann go up to the cave and wait while you get her? We won't hurt one another. I'll swear a blood oath."

144

"Misty, you say another word, I'll hit you," says Bobby, his lips barely moving.

She stops in the kitchen as Bobby and Christiann go outside. Christiann turns and looks confused, then angry, then afraid as they leave. The silence of the house settles around Misty, and she could just cry. She looks in drawer after drawer until she finds a sharp, serrated meat-cutting knife. She gets a flashlight from the pile on the back porch and goes out into the darkness, walks around the house and stands in the road.

She could just leave. Serve Christiann right to get shot! Misty's scratched face hurts. How do you find someone? Misty's never had to find anyone before. She can't think of how to start, where to go. She walks off down the road slowly. It's not raining now. A whippoorwill cries.

Misty fears the dark. She's always slept with a night light, and she has this recurring dream: It's night, a deep still night, and she awakens and walks into the kitchen, and the light won't work. Then she's going in every room, and the lights won't come on. Then the window blinds won't come up, and the doors won't open. She always wakes up gasping. When she was seven, her father locked her in a closet for cussing. She stayed in that closet all night. They'd been drinking and forgot she was in there.

Misty can't see farther than the end of the flashlight beam. How should she call this woman? *Lady? Woman?* Misty walks down the road, shining her light left and right. If she sees anyone, she will die of fright.

Misty is terrified that she will find that woman or that she won't.


Sam can't seem to tell if he's asleep or awake. In the dark, every sound could be part of a dream. He wants to howl with rage. He thinks of Hermie falling, and it makes Sam feel deeply good. He is afraid of that feeling.

---

Now, he moves past the steep ledge, holding on to the smooth flowstone with his strong fingers.

He thinks he may be near Lake Preston now, but he's not sure. If he turns away from the main channel, he could be burrowing into a deep grave. He stops and listens. Nothing, no rumble.

His breath, that's all.

Clay's still in the willow tree, feeling the wind wet his hair. The rain keeps starting and stopping. Nothing matters, but he wants a thing to happen, some broken arch of light to come. At Reidsville, his nights were terrifying. He slept poorly, always had, until he met Bobby. They'd stay up late, whispering after the lights were out. Their cells were next to each other, and they'd hold out mirrors to see the other's face. Later, near the end of their sentences, they moved into a dorm area.

When one was crazy, the other would grasp his arm and say *ice* or *blade*. Now, Clay says nothing as he sits in the limbs. When he was ten, he took a nap one Sunday afternoon and dreamed he could fly. When he awakened, it seemed so logical, so real, that he jumped from the corner of the roof, flapping his arms. He fell straight down and broke his ankle. You couldn't trust a dream.

Clay hears sounds coming up the hill, knows it's Bobby heading back up. He doesn't know why, doesn't think to care. He swings down, limb by limb, until he's at a low limb, dangling by his arms. He drops to his feet. You can't fly. The ground is so sodden it's like walking on a sponge.

"Clay! You there?" Bobby shouts.

"Here!" says Clay. Bobby's following his flashlight beam, Christiann at his side. They've brought lanterns, rope, matches, all from Sam's storeroom. It's not raining. They set it down on the shaking earth. Christiann feels guilty just looking at Clay's face, but what happened happened. There wasn't a thing she could do about it.

146

Bobby and Christiann come up the last of the slope and stand by Clay.

"Misty was guarding that woman and let her escape," says Bobby with disgust. "I sent her after her." He cups his hands and lights a Camel, shares the light with Clay. "Maybe they'll both fall down a hole or something." Bobby's laughter is hard and clear.

"So now what?" asks Clay. Christiann watches them suck on the cigarettes as they stand next to each other. The twin glow looks like the violent stare of some creature with wide-spaced eyes. "Get out of here?"

"Get Preston," says Bobby. "It's light in a few hours. There's no house right near here." Clay shines his light in Christiann's face, and she tries to smile.

"What happened to her?" asks Clay. Her face has two long scratches down one side.

"I was making it with her, and Misty found us," says Bobby.

"Bobby!" cries Christiann. She takes a step back, wonders what might happen now. "Clay, sweetie, that's not right! I slipped on that back step and fell down's all. Bobby, you orta be ashamed."

"She good?" asks Clay.

"No," says Bobby. "Not worth a damn. You want her back?"

"I never wanted her at all, bro," says Clay. Christiann feels choked. "She just hitched on, like a tick."

"Well, poop on you, I'm not no tick," says Christiann.

"She and Misty like to've killed one another," says Bobby. "Too bad they didn't. Clay, let's go get this money and get the hell out of here."

"Where's that Hermie thing?" asks Christiann.

"Down there," says Clay.

"Down?" asks Christiann. Bobby flinches, nods.

They get the gear, walk to the ladder, shine down it. Bobby tries to master the shiver, saying *ice* to himself over and over.

In Reidsville, Clay told him stories, how all stories were lies.

When Clay had said that, Bobby first felt something true and terrible resonate in his bones.

"I'm not going down into no cave in the dark," says Christiann. "God didn't mean man to go runnin' around under the world like that."

"You ain't a man, and there ain't a God," says Bobby. "Either you go down, or I'll hit you."

"Bobby!" cries Christiann. She lowers her voice and puts her mouth close to his ear. "After what we done?"

"We didn't do nothing," says Bobby. It sounds so purely mean that Christiann almost wants to laugh. She's trying to think of a funny saying. Everybody in her family always said Christiann could come up with the funniest sayings! She hears a cricket, turns to see that Clay has thumbed back the hammer on his gun. He's pointing it at her and looking at Bobby.

"Bobby!" she squeaks. "Clay, baby, put that thing down! I'm coming down with you! Put that thing down."

"She does anything dumb, tie her up," says Bobby.

"Okay, bro," says Clay.

Deep in the cave, bats are starting to settle on Hermie's face, picking off sightless bugs that skate on the drying film of his open eyes.


Mary Beth's ankle feels swollen, throbs. She can't say she knows where she is or where she's going. The road winds down south toward Sheppard, but she's no longer on the road or sure she's going south. She's cried herself out. The storm seems to be a county off for now. She tries to walk a few yards, but the least pressure on her ankle is terribly painful. She finds an old limb, breaks it down to staff size, hobbles along.

She realizes they're probably gone now.

"Gone," she says out loud. "I got away, and they had to leave. They're probably on the road to Nashville or something by now." An owl cries, inhuman and startling. She gasps, leans against an oak. Bird, she thinks, almost laughs. "Owl. They're gone, so I could go back to the house and call. Sam's okay. They wouldn't go down there and get him. I'll call the sheriff in Sheppard, and they'll come and get us. It'll be in the papers."

She moves ten steps, gets tangled in a coil of briars, and falls. She stands painfully and listens for a sign. Nothing human lives here. Her mother read her stories of fantastic forests with hidden gnomes and monsters, and someone was always passing through, fearful. She thinks of those stories now, bags of gold, gnarled trees. The wind lifts the tips of her wet hair, blows the clouds briefly from the face of the moon. In a clearing, she stops and looks up. The Man in the Moon is grinning: All these worlds pass before him, and he's indifferent. He's seen all this before, terror, aches, the sense of being lost with no hope of discovery.

Mary Beth moves more slowly, even slower, until she's on the side of a hill out of the forest. She looks around. The clouds cover the moon, then blow away once more: it's gibbous, nearly full but misshapen, littered with rocky smiles. She falls to her knees and tries to remember why this place is so familiar.

Mary Beth hobbles across the clearing as the moon dodges clouds. The air is hot and sticky. More storms are just over the hills. Thunder trumpets their presence. She gets to the crest of the clearing and looks around and sees nothing she recognizes at all. She could wander out here for days, even after the sun comes up. She could starve to death.

She wants to fall to her knees and say, *God help me* or something, wants to see her flowers. She thinks of the flowers, marigolds, clematis vines, celosia, and columbine.

"Sam's dead," she says out loud, and then she weeps, hot tears that pour down her smooth cheeks. At the angle of sorrow, though, she suddenly knows he is alive. He is breathing. She can feel his breath coming up from somewhere below. She can almost pretend that he is just below the surface, hands pushing up to hold her footsteps, each one in its sweet stride.

149

Clay goes down first.

He's mastered many of his fears long before, including dying. He'd made friends with a con named Oswin who was in Reidsville before his appeals ran out and they sent him to Jackson for the chair. Oswin knew they'd electrocute him sooner or later, and he was right. He'd choked his wife to death with a fishing stringer because she hadn't washed his clothes for work one morning. They lived in a trailer. Oswin told Clay it wasn't the dirty clothes. It was the filth. Oswin couldn't stand filth. He said he'd come home and the trailer was swimming in filth. His appeals lasted nine years. Clay asked him if he wasn't scared of being electrocuted. Oswin said he was more afraid of *not* being electrocuted. They said he was humming some song when they threw the switch. Nobody quite caught the tune. Clay thought, *The man who masters his fears can rule the universe.* Maybe he read that somewhere.

Now, he descends unafraid. He gets to the bottom, shines his light around, lights a lantern. The cave entrance is high and easy.

"Come on down now," he calls up. "It's not much."

"Get your gun out and ready to catch Preston," says Bobby. He and Christiann are looking down at Clay below them.

"I don't want to go into no hole, sweetheart," says Christiann.

"Two choices," says Bobby. "Go down or I shoot you here."

"Bob-eeee," singsongs Christiann. She tries to laugh, but he is still. She exhales. She was crazy to have let him get into her pants. She should have listened to her mother. Now Misty is mad at her. Misty may be lost out there somewhere; God knows where she is.

Christiann closes her eyes and climbs down the ladder. She's not strong enough, feels as if she'll fall. Her hands are shaking, and she stops and clings.

"I can't go no farther!" she cries. "I can't go up nor down!

Somebody help me!" At the bottom, Clay looks up and shrugs. He doesn't care if she does fall.

"Shoot her," says Bobby. Christiann starts to cry, then comes on down the ladder to the bottom of the sinkhole. It's cool down here, almost cold.

"I'm here," she says. "Don't shoot me."

They look around in the beam of Bobby's flashlight. He feels a deep chill. His daddy had told him to look up at the light that day he'd taken him into the mines. *You won't see it for a right smart spell, Robbie,* he said. Bobby had looked up at the light, and it got smaller until it was a dot, then it was gone. The top of the elevator was open. It needed air or something. It's brighter now. Bobby climbs down and sees the switchbox on the wall, goes to it, flips up the lever.

The cave just beyond where they stand is suddenly filled with a glorious light. They walk slowly through the large room. Lights circle the wall. Against one wall are ropes, more lanterns, steel buckles. Clay looks up, and ten feet above them the ceiling is studded with speleothems, stalactites still dripping, pointing down. The floor has knobby stalagmites, smooth as cypress knees. Just off center, a large column seems to hold up the ceiling with its rippled magnificence.

The walls are covered with names and dates. Bobby sees 1926 and thinks, That's the year my daddy was borned. Christiann feels the chilled air sink to the marrow.

"It's freezing under here!" she says. "My friend Lacy went to the Mammoth Cave once, and she said it was cold as a icebox. Bobby, sweetie, how come it's so cold under here?"

"The devil's down there froze in ice," says Bobby. He's barely paying attention to her. Clay walks along the wall, touching the flowstone, marveling at its texture and color. "Right, Clay? Remember that?"

"Right, bro," says Clay. He'd told Bobby about the *Inferno,* how Satan howls in the center, frozen in a lake of ice. Bobby couldn't get it out of his head.

They finally see the passageway leading out of the room. It's lighted for a short distance. Bobby takes his gun out and looks into the tunnel. It's only seven feet high, but the floor is worn smooth by water or time.

"Where you think Hermie is?" asks Bobby.

"Lost down there," says Clay. Bobby shivers. He leans against the wall of the large room.

"He's got his money in here," says Bobby. He doesn't seem to be talking to them. Christiann looks at his eyes and feels a deeper chill: he's not of blood and bone or human warmth of any kind. "He's got tons of money, maybe jewels, too. He's done put it all in here 'cause he thinks won't nobody come down here and get it. I bet the son of a bitch is sitting on top of it right now. It's all piled up. We won't never have to work again."

"I never seen you work *before*," says Christiann. She's fiddling with a broken fingernail, just tosses the sentence off. It's nothing. She doesn't even see Bobby coming until he's right next to her. She's starting to smile when he hits her in the mouth with the back of his right hand. The force of the blow knocks her flat on the cave floor. All she can do at first is gasp. She holds her cheek, can't get the breath back. She's going to cry, and tears fill her eyes, but then she's afraid they'll kill her if she says a word. She sits up. Her head is turning in wild circles. The room swims. She swims with it, waving her arms for balance. She's not sure she's breathing anymore.

"I never seen you dead, but I could," says Bobby.

"Bro, let's kill her now," says Clay. "She's nothing we need. You and me don't need anything."

"Don't you kill me!" cries Christiann. "Please don't kill me. I'll help you. I got me a driver's license. I can help you. Bobby, sweetie, don't do this."

"Not yet," says Bobby, and she's elated, until she thinks of that yet part. She'll be good. They'll see.

"We going on in there or what?" asks Clay. "You think Misty's gonna bring that bitch back?"

"She don't, I'm going to hurt Christiann," says Bobby.

"Then let's go get him and the money," says Clay.

Bobby looks back at the room once more, then leads them into the passageway. The tube recedes into complete blackness. Bobby walks very slowly. He hears them breathing as they walk. Christiann's in back. Bobby's put the gun back in his waistband, and he holds a lantern in his left hand, a flashlight in his right. Christiann remembers she read something about saltpeter being found in caves. The girls had laughed about that in high school. She can't laugh now. She can't remember what saltpeter is, anyway. Her face stings. She can't believe she let Bobby have her. It was almost an accident or something.

"Where you think the blue crystal is, bro?" asks Clay softly.

"Halfway to hell," says Bobby.

Bobby thinks of getting lost down here. He thinks of it as a burial, the lid slammed shut, then no way out.


Misty's singing softly in the darkness, looking around. The flashlight's in her left hand, the knife in her right. She feels sick, afraid but giddy too. She should have known that Bobby would turn out to be no good.

She's singing "She'll Be Coming 'Round the Mountain," but very slowly, like a dirge. Her daddy sings it that way. He can't carry a tune, and neither can Misty. It takes him forever to get through *six white horses,* and her mother gets redder and redder in the face the whole time. Her father is slow at everything. Misty didn't really notice it until she was fifteen, then it drove her crazy. They'd be in the car heading for the grocery store, and he'd go back inside for something and never come out. Misty would go inside, and he'd be down in the workshop holding his keys in one hand and a screwdriver in the other. That was the family joke. Now, Misty wants things to go that slowly. She wants the rain to come down in slow, sticky strands. She wants each of her steps to take an hour.

*153*

The biggest fight they'd ever had was when they were seniors. Christiann had been sleeping around, and Misty called her trash. Something about the word sent Christiann into a rage. They had a fistfight at school. Misty's lip was busted. The boys all seemed to love it, but what could you expect from them? Christiann had even more dates after that.

"You *are* trash," says Misty. She wants to say, *And so am I,* but she starts singing slowly again. She's been walking down the road, and now she's stopped. The mountains spread out before her. The moon's come out, but angry clouds keep flying past it. It's like a scenic overlook. They'd stopped at a scenic overlook in Tennessee, and Bobby'd peed over the edge in broad daylight. Hermie thought it was the funniest thing he'd ever seen. Where would she go if she were this woman she's supposed to find? "I don't give a damn." But she'd better. She has no money, no place to go. What will she tell them?

There's a gentle slope down this scenic overlook, and she goes over the edge and down the hill. She could die out here. The moon's suddenly out completely, and the landscape looks bombed, terrifying. Water is running down a hillside near her. It sounds like her daddy gargling. Misty sits. She just can't go any farther.

She hasn't slept, and the urge to lie down is as strong as gravity. She tries to get comfortable on the slope, but there's not much use. Everything's wet. The world's soaked.

She throws the knife as far down the slope as she can and starts to cry. She should be having babies. Maybe Christiann would get Bobby's baby now. There is not a thing to do. A strand of blue black clouds covers the moon, casting Misty into blackness, but then the moon's out again.

She can't believe the sight: coming toward her, straight up the hill, is a shape, a figure, something human or close to it.

# 14

*B*obby *Drake's breathing* fills the passageway as they follow the flashlight beams. Christiann's been hit by a man before, but this hurts worse than those times: sharp red, pulsing, swelling. Her right nostril has closed. When she touches the bridge of her nose lightly a string of pain fists up between her eyebrows, down to the corner of her mouth.

The cave is grotesque to her: bent fingers spilling slow drips from the ceiling, periodic rocky rubble. She wants Clay and Bobby to talk, to call out warnings, but so far they've said little.

Bobby knows what to call this: a vein. His daddy would come home and announce they were reopening the northwest vein, and his mother would nearly cry. There'd been an explosion there a few years back. Bobby had barely remembered it.

"Stop," says Bobby. He holds up his hand. They've reached the crossover passageway. "Clay, you think we ought to call out after Hermie? No telling where he is."

"No," says Clay. "We got to sneak up on him, bro. He's probably asleep down here."

"Yeah," says Bobby, shivering. "Which way we ought to go, you reckon?" Bobby's whispering and isn't sure why. Christiann's right behind Clay and wants to touch him on the shoulder. They could kill Bobby. Nobody would ever know! They could kill him down here and get away to Hollywood, California!

"Keep it straight," says Clay.

"How come?" asks Bobby.

"I don't know," says Clay. They're close. Bobby can see right through his friend's eyes, through the pupils into the darkness of Clay's head. Bobby stares; they're tunnels into the brain. He can't shake the image. "You okay, bro?"

"Right," says Bobby. "Let's go straight."

The cave ceiling and floor rise and fall as they walk past the crossover. Christiann touches both sides of the cave, tracing layers of limestone laid down on a shallow seabed millions of years ago. The cave gets smaller, and they have to bend over to walk, and Bobby can't get a deep breath.

Just as he's thinking of turning back, the cave widens slightly, then opens into an echoing corridor.

"There's a hole over there," says Clay. They shine their flashlights to the left, hold up their lanterns, see the ledge and the black pit disappearing downward. Bobby starts to take baby steps. His legs are shaking now. He can barely stand it. They move together, a few steps at a time, until they're at the edge.

"Oh God," says Christiann. She sniffs, and the pain goes from her chin to the hairline. She takes a step back. Bobby shines his flashlight around the edge of the pit. It's no more than twenty feet across. The ledge around it may be six feet wide; it looks like a monster's thin lip. Slip, be swallowed.

Bobby and Clay shine their lights downward. They lean out a little. Christiann hangs back, but she wants to see. She imagines the red-hot center of the earth at the bottom, a red eye a thousand miles down. She suddenly wants to see that red eye.

"Well, that's that," says Clay.

"Dammit," says Bobby.

"What is it?" asks Christiann. She moves to Bobby's right, holds his arm and peers downward along the flashlight beam. Below them, Hermie lies with one arm twisted impossibly behind his neck. His eyes are open fully. The eyebrows are arched upward in fright; the mouth is an O below the mustache.

Bats flutter off his face. A small bat emerges from his mouth and bangs against the cave wall in the sudden light.

Christiann falls backward and screams. That scream is torn from her heart, everywhere. She scrambles up and keeps screaming. Bobby and Clay rush her, lights going up and down, everywhere in the cave.

"Get her!" shouts Bobby. "Shut her up!"

Clay grabs her, wraps Christiann in his arms, clamps his hand over her mouth. She can't breathe. His strength is terrifying. He easily drags her over to the pit. She wants to scream, but even when Clay takes his hand away nothing comes out. He pushes her down to the cave floor. He grabs her ankles and suddenly lifts her upside down. He swings her out over the pit. Clay's a lifter. He spent all his spare time at Reidsville in the weight room, and this living weight is nothing, one forty, maybe. Clay holds her feet with his arms crossed over his chest. Christiann is screaming. Clay bangs her on the pit wall, and she feels the breath go out of her. She goes black.

She's back awake. Bobby's next to them, and it sounds as if he may be crying. He's waving the flashlight down there on Hermie's dead face. Christiann looks down into it. She faints again. She reawakens. She sees her own death now, nobody missing her, wondering where she went. They'll still think she's alive in, like, Omaha, Nebraska, or something. She'll be dead. *I'm dead.*

She wants to stop her heart from beating before Clay drops her.

The moon comes and goes. Misty sees the figure coming up the slope. It's hobbling. A crippled old man. He's evil. She can see that right off, and he's coming to kill her. What is she doing here, anyway? She wants to hear the wind blowing through stiff clothes on the line, that laundered smell. She'd settle for being touched by J.D.'s dirty fingernails. When his hand would creep under her gown in bed, she'd think of those always-dirty nails, and it would nearly make her sick. If she fought it, he'd beat her. A freshening wind rakes her wet hair.

Misty wishes she hadn't thrown the knife away. She couldn't cut that old man, though. She saw a stabbing once, remembers it now: She was fifteen, at Virginia Beach. A skinny boy stabbed another skinny boy.

Misty stands up and takes a couple of steps back. She's about to turn and run, go anywhere, even home, when the clouds blow away from the moon's face once more, and she sees it's Mary Beth. Bobby would love me for this, she thinks. Then, He's gonna kill Christiann.

She has to catch Mary Beth. Misty gets an idea. She's amazed.

Mary Beth doesn't see Misty until they're ten feet apart. Mary Beth feels so tired. She can't hobble much more, doesn't have a clue where she is. She should crawl under a tree and nap until morning, but you don't go near trees when there are storms about. The moon's cleared brightly, and Misty is suddenly just there. Mary Beth inhales sharply and simply stops. The fear chokes her. She gasps, groans, shakes. She drops the walking stick and holds her arms over her chest, as if that might do any good.

"Oh my God, it's her," says Misty.

"What do you want?" asks Mary Beth. Her voice is ridiculously high, she thinks. She sounds like a cartoon elf. She sees now that it's Misty, and that she's alone. Misty shines her flashlight on Mary Beth's face, then moves it away, shines it down.

"I can't believe it's you," says Misty. "My God." She catches her breath. "I guess I've done come for you."

"I think my ankle's broken," says Mary Beth, who wonders why she said it.

"It is?" asks Misty. "How'd you do that, hon?"

"I stepped in a hole," says Mary Beth. Misty walks slowly toward her. She stops when they're a few feet apart. "What are you doing out here? Are you going to kill me?"

"I ain't even got a knife," says Misty. "I had one but I throwed it away. Hon, you got to come on back, or Bobby's gonna kill your husband and Christiann, too. He's done took her up to the cave."

"He's not my husband," says Mary Beth. "He's just my friend." It's not over, then. Mary Beth feels terribly sick to her stomach.

"You got to come on back, hon," says Misty. "It's just awful."

"What are you doing with them?" asks Mary Beth. Misty thinks about it, looks at the moon. A night bird cries for rain. She makes small circles of light on the ground with the flashlight beam. "You're not like them."

"Maybe I am, and maybe I ain't," she whispers. "Maybe don't nobody know what he's like when push comes to shove, you know what I mean?"

"No," says Mary Beth.

"I mean sometimes, one bad thing's better than another one," she says.

"No, it isn't," says Mary Beth. A sodden glow of sheet lightning flares to the south. There's no thunder with it. "You make the good things happen."

"Maybe rich folks do," says Misty. "You poor long enough, don't nothing matter, you know?"

"No, I don't know," says Mary Beth.

———

"Anyway, Bobby's got a bad mean side, and I think he's gone kill your friend with the one eye down in that cave if you don't come back, and I know he'll kill Christiann," says Misty.

"She's your friend?" asks Mary Beth.

"I hate her guts," says Misty petulantly. She makes the flashlight beam dance, small circles on the wet soil. "I caught her and Bobby doing it on the couch." Mary Beth wants to smile, feels it coming on, but her face turns it down. This world is heaving beneath her. Would he kill Sam? Yes. He would blow the head off an old lady.

"Then I'm sorry," says Mary Beth. "I need help."

"Oh, I'm sorry, hon," says Misty. She comes to Mary Beth and puts her arm under her shoulder, around her back. "Come on now. You walk like this here?"

They move about ten feet, and Mary Beth nods, yes, this is fine. Mary Beth can smell Misty, body odor, stale hair, cigarette smoke, something else, electricity, musk. Lightning flares behind them, and ten seconds later, thunder grumbles along the lower ridges down near Sheppard.

Mary Beth thinks of her garden, wonders if it has been beaten down, drowned from too much water.

Christiann wriggles at the end of Clay's hands, trying to touch the side of the deep hole, get any fingerhold. He swings her back and forth as if she weighs two pounds. He wants to let go, but he looks at Bobby, who is grinning grimly. Bobby shines the light down on Hermie's face so Christiann can see it.

"Shut up or he's dropping you!" cries Bobby. Christiann's mouth goes numb. This is how it is to be dead. They were going to kill her. Why hadn't she seen that before? Anybody with a brain would scream at that. She looks down at Hermie. The bats are all gone. He won't get any deader.

"Okay, honey bear," chokes Christiann. "I'm sorry. Please Jesus Mary God don't drop me. Please don't. I don't want to die."

"You don't want to die?" says Bobby. His voice is quiet and intense, each word seemingly unconnected to the one before or after it. "You think if we pull you out of there you're gonna live?"

Bobby trembles. He can't stop thinking of his father. The man's in here somewhere, he's sure of it. He can nearly hear his voice, smell cigarettes and coffee, see white skin beneath the sooty cloak of coal dust.

"I won't scream again," says Christiann. She closes her eyes. She won't be ready when she falls. She will land on Hermie. She'll lie on top of him forever. She wants to throw up. "Please don't kill me."

Clay looks at Bobby. The cave is full of their own shadows. Bobby hears something.

"Hush," says Bobby. He turns sharply to fix the sound. "Get her out of there." Clay swings Christiann back, lets her drop heavily to the cave floor, where she curls into a fetal ball and cries without making a sound. She's never been more scared or relieved in her life. "I heard something." Clay comes next to him. Bobby turns off his flashlight while still holding the lantern. He takes the gun from his waistband.

Sam's moving straight toward them. He's mumbling, but he doesn't know it. He can't hear the scream anymore. They've killed that woman. He's mumbling about Jackie and monsters and blue crystals. Nobody's ever seen the blue crystal, but it's supposed to be in there.

Bobby and Clay move back down the passageway silently. Christiann gets up and follows them, moves past them. She can't quite believe she's alive.

"He's coming right to us!" hisses Bobby. "Get ready."

Sam stops just before the pit. He knows his steps. He's been here a thousand times. A sudden calm descends: he's no longer afraid of this place or its long night. He doesn't need to see. He believes he hears a word, but he can't be sure. If they're in the cave at all, they'll be back at the beginning. The acoustics are unpredictable here. Sam comes along the edge, hands up against the wall. That man's broken body is down there. Sam stops and listens to hear a moan, breathing. There is nothing there. Sam knows how many steps. He feels his power over this sunken world growing.

He crosses the ledge, reading the stories of wall stone with his fingers. They speak of limestone geology, warm and shallow seas that rose, bringing vertical faults. They whisper directions, his name. Past the ledge, he walks swiftly, expecting nothing in this darkness but the sound of his feet.

He comes right to them. Bobby Drake jumps behind him and sticks the gun behind his left ear. Clay's in his face. Christiann scrambles up, farther back down the cave from them toward the beginning.

"Happy birthday," says Bobby triumphantly. Sam bucks and struggles, then feels the barrel on his occipital lobe.

"Don't think about fighting," says Clay. "We'll make it hurt worse."

Sam's heart is hummingbird fast but heavy with gravity. His heart could be anywhere in his chest. He looks back and forth at them, realizes he can see a slight wash of light now from his kicked-in eye; no shapes or lines, just a bare smudge of light. He feels terrified, almost exultant. They hear steps, and Christiann's running back toward the cave opening. They look.

"Don't worry about her," says Bobby. "She's not going nowhere."

"Don't hurt her," says Sam, not sure who it is. Bobby laughs, a high-pitched, snickering giggle.

"It ain't your girl," says Bobby. "She'll be here soon."

"You aced Hermie," says Clay. He looks at Sam, who's lean and muscled from days of climbing. "Bet you didn't think you could."

"I pushed him," says Sam. "I just pushed him." Bobby starts to feel the walls coming down like shades. He looks around. Even though it's always fifty-four degrees in here, Bobby's sweating.

———

"You did us a favor," says Clay. "You did Hermie a favor mostly. He's probably having more fun dead. Maybe you will, too."

"The money," says Bobby. He tightens his grip. The gun is hard against Sam's head. Sam can feel the small circle of death. He can nearly smell gunpowder, even see the bullet drilling a shaft through the soft stone of his brain.

"I told you there's no money," says Sam. What could he make up to satisfy them? How can he string this out? They still have Mary Beth. But who's watching her? Sam tries to think. The smear of light taunts him. Firefly that shuts off when he looks for it.

"I know better," says Bobby. "I knew there wasn't no other way out of here. I figured that out for myself. Pure mind." Clay whispers *mind*. Sam wonders if they're at all sane. "And I know you got money in here. Hell, everybody knows it. Everybody."

"I'm not everybody," says Sam. "I never had any money. My father has money from this cave, and he inherited it from his father. It's in banks back in Richmond."

"I don't have time for this," says Bobby, looking at Clay, then at the walls around them. "Bring him back to the room up front. Maybe he doesn't care about pain. I guess that depends on who's hurting."

Bobby can't wait to get out. Clay swings around him and grasps Sam in a choke-and-hammer lock. Bobby puts his gun back in his pants, retrieves the flashlight, and moves on by battery and lamplight, shadow-wise along the slim corridors of Blue Crystal Cave.

They get to the crossover, and Sam can smell the draft. He can't believe how well he sees this place now. He's never needed his eyes. He feels a small slip in Clay's grasp.

"Awnnnn," says Sam with a deep, shuddering groan. Bobby's already a turn ahead, and when Clay relaxes his hold, Sam elbows him in the ribs as hard as his arm will move. The point catches Clay in the stomach. He doubles over but doesn't

---

completely release Sam's neck. Sam swings his fist over his shoulder backward and smacks Clay in the forehead. Clay falls flat down, stunned. Sam's off up the crossover tunnel.

"Shit!" Clay shouts after the stun has slipped his eyes. Bobby, hearing, turns, goes back. He can't bear this cave. He feels it may fall soon. Clay's getting up, taking his gun out just as Bobby returns. Sam's gone.

"Where in the hell is he?" screams Bobby. His voice creaks and echoes everywhere. A thousand Bobby Drakes rage. Clay has this foolish look on his face. He turns around and around.

"He sorta got the drop on me, bro," says Clay. For the first time since Bobby's known him, Clay looks foolish. "He's gone up that way." He points toward the crossover. It's even smaller and more cramped than the main trail, littered with breakdown, swelling to wild chambers, a grotto half a mile in.

"He got the *drop* on you?" shouts Bobby. The echoes litter the cave floor. "He got the drop on you?" Bobby's face is twisted. Clay looks down and shakes his head. Bobby wants to hit Clay, wants to hit him so badly he's shaking. Bobby glances up the crossover cave trail. He feels a clammy sweat streaking his temples, even though it's so cool here. Clay feels stupid. "Then you go after him. I'm going back to stop Christiann leaving. Bring him back, you understand me?"

"Ice," says Clay hopefully.

"Oh, hell," says Bobby. "Just get him back."

Clay wants to say another thing, but Bobby's gone already. Clay knows he can't wait until Sam's gone far. He walks slowly up the crossover trail along the breakdown rubble. He shines his light. Flowstone draperies shroud the cave ceiling. He listens for footfall, hears a faint sound, far away now. He follows the cave. The path isn't level. With each step he's going higher. He might have to kill Mr. Nobody when he finds him. He could tell Bobby Drake damned near anything.

The lights are still on in Sam's house. Mary Beth and Misty walk up the road toward it, Misty still holding Mary Beth up. The lightning is coming quickly toward them with its sheets of thunder. Even the barest pressure hurts Mary Beth's ankle terribly. When she sees the house she starts to cry. She'd wanted Sam so much. He might be dead now. It had all happened because she loved him. Whatever she loved died or went away. It had always been like that.

"Hon, you gone be all right," says Misty. "Just tell that feller to give Bobby the money, and we'll be gone."

"There's not any damned money," says Mary Beth. The edge in her voice shakes with tears. "You're just going to keep on believing something that's not true. You heard it, and that makes it true to you all. Just hearing a thing doesn't mean it's true. It's just a story. It never was true."

"Well, poopy, then somebody sure got it wrong," says Misty. She thinks of Christiann. "I'm gone kill that girl. I cain't believe she was letting Bobby have her."

Mary Beth wants to ignore it all. The rain starts to pelt them, but she can't hurry. They're almost to the house. Maybe they're all back by now anyway. A long snake's tongue of flame splits the northern sky. The thunder slams them. Misty emits a small cry and jumps.

They get to the house, and the cars are still there, door open on the stolen Taurus. They come up on the porch, go inside. The rain lets go.

"You need to tinkle, hon?" asks Misty.

"Yes," says Mary Beth.

"Well, me too, but you can go first," says Misty. "You got any chips or nothing in the kitchen?"

"I don't live here," says Mary Beth. Misty shrugs and walks to the kitchen while Mary Beth goes in the bathroom, closes the door. She's gasping and crying now. She looks at herself in the mirror, feels a shaking horror at her image. She might have driven off a cliff to look this bad. She washes her face with warm water. It feels so good she can't believe it. The eye makeup is smeared down her cheeks. She almost never wears makeup, but she'd put some on in the afternoon when she came to see Sam. She wanted him to think she was pretty.

She tries to think of anything to do. She could find her keys, jump out the window, and drive to Sheppard. They might really kill Sam. They might be up there now waiting on her. She'll have to go. She sits on the closed toilet lid and pulls up the leg of her slacks. The ankle is already swollen three times its size, all shades of blue and purple. It throbs. She believes it's broken. All these years, and she's never had a broken bone. She uses the toilet and then comes into the hall, walks to the kitchen. Misty's in there, eating a piece of cheese.

"Feelin' better, hon?" asks Misty. "Let me winkie, and we'll be on our way." Misty walks to the bathroom. She doesn't close the door. Mary Beth looks at the clock above the stove. It's nearly three now. Once Sam had joked that, down below, it was always Central Cave Time, always midnight. Mary Beth hears Misty stand, zip, and flush. That woman doesn't even know this is wrong. She doesn't even know how much it will always, always hurt.

Everything hurts, she thinks, and it will never end.

Misty comes out, and they're off, out the back door into the wind, up the slope.

"I never seen such weather," says Misty. "Down home . . ." But she stops, can't really focus on it. Was it ever her home, anyway? Was J.D. ever her husband? She always knew she'd leave him and that he wouldn't come after her. He wouldn't cross the street to rescue her from a lion. He seemed motionless, and she liked that for a while. She thought he was strong because he said so little. Then she found out he was silent but weak. He'd say he was thinking things over, but he'd never do anything. Misty wanted to go dancing. *Anything*. He'd say, *Let me think on it,* and twenty minutes later he'd be asleep on the sofa. The man was not worth much. She never could tell when he'd start coming for her.

"We get rain," says Mary Beth. She can't imagine why she said it. Except she's a gardener and loves to sit on rainy days in her bookshop. You measure rain in tenths of an inch. Even that much can be important. Instead of rain, she's thinking of Sam now, trying to reach into her feelings to see if he's alive. He could be alive. She has a sudden thought: What if he does have money down there? If he were rich, where else would he put it? She hadn't thought he might be rich.

Living alone, no one will come after you. Wealth is freedom. Or it's a noose. She's read so many things. Some of them stick in the wrong sentences, making lies of the homilies some white-bearded sage sang in New England a century ago. Early to bed, early to rise.

The sound of rain is the sound of singing. She was a young girl, and her aunt May told her each raindrop was an angel who sang just for Mary Beth. The next night, a flood had drowned two girls in a town five miles away. Some angels had horns. Go down deep enough, and you'll find the devil.

They come up the path. Mary Beth knows she has to follow Misty, who walks with extreme fatigue. Rain comes again through the trees, a few shots then a sheet. They're soaked, and Mary Beth feels a deep shiver shake her arms. It doesn't take long before they see lights coming out of the earth.

"Well, would you looka there," says Misty, wiping the rain from her face. "It's like the ground ate a big ol' Christmas tree or somethin'. Bobby! Bobby!" Her shout makes Mary Beth jump. "I got her, Bobby! We're coming, hon!"

Christiann hears her friend, wants to leap up and embrace her. Bobby's not there, and neither is Clay. She's been sitting alone in the large room at the cave mouth, not daring to leave, knowing Bobby or Clay would find her. She thinks of dangling over the hole, over the dead Hermie. She thinks of bats coming out of his mouth and gags. She says, *Misty,* but it's soft. Her throat's almost closed with fear.

Misty and Mary Beth get to the ladder, and Mary Beth feels as if she's lived here forever. She's scared to look down. Maybe Sam's down there dead. She loves him. She's in love with him. And now he's dead. She wants to take flying lessons.

"Bobby, hon?" says Misty, less sure as they reach the hole. Misty looks down. The hole is full of light. She sees the ladder going down. It doesn't seem so far. This is nothing to fear. Christiann's face is suddenly below her, looking up.

"Misty!" shouts Christiann. "Oh, Misty!"

"I got her!" says Misty triumphantly. "I went and found old Nobody's wife. You okay, Christiann?"

"No," she says, waving her hands around her face. "That man's done killed Hermie, and Clay liked to killed me."

*That man's done killed Hermie.* Mary Beth feels a tremendous pulse. Cool air rises from the cave mouth, and she thinks, That can't be; cool air sinks, hot air rises. But the cool breath comes up anyway. Sam's killed one of them. He's still alive.

"Hermie's dead?" says Misty. She feels shocked, then wonders why. "I mean, no great loss or nothing, but he killed him?"

"He's dead at the bottom of a pit, with his eyes open and bats on his face," says Christiann. She looks back down the cave, and all Misty can see is the top of her head. "They're bound to kill us all, Misty. You don't know what they're like. I seen it in Bobby's eyes." Her voice is a whisper, monotone line. She sounds sunken in terror. "They done caught him, too. They done caught that man and are bringing him back from this cave. They gone kill all of us."

"Oh, pooh," says Misty. "A man'll get rough time to time, but they ain't gone kill us, or they wouldn't of brought us along." That sounds right to Misty.

She swings her first foot on the rope ladder. To think of her Bobby and her Clay killing them! Misty could almost laugh out loud.

# 15

*Sweat blossoms* along Clay García's forehead. He's gone up the crossover passageway now, walking deliberately over the breakdown. Your foot could slide between the slipped stones, crack an ankle or a leg. You'd have to crawl out. Clay thinks, I've never crawled for any man, but that's not true. He's been crawling for Bobby for a long time now, and he can't quite understand it.

The ceiling has cracks and fissures that rise up into darkness. He glances around as he walks. He walks with his gun in one hand, a flashlight in the other. The spot of light seems feeble against this heavy darkness. Water's dripping somewhere.

Clay can't decide whether he'll kill Sam when he finds him or just beat the life half out of him. He made Clay look foolish in front of Bobby. Clay wants to think of what he's become. He can't do that. *Concentrate*. He swings the light back and forth, tries to make as little sound as possible. He stops.

Footsteps pass away far ahead of him. He can move swiftly toward the rear of a sound. He hears a terrible wheeze, realizes it's his breathing. He can't stop thinking of Hermie's face down there, bats in his mouth. Hermie hadn't been such a bad guy. He'd taught Clay about books. A pool of anger stirs in Clay's chest.

He jogs over the breakdown karst, light on his feet. He leaps from sheet to sheet. Feet of Clay. That was a joke they made in high school because he was on the track team his junior year. He got kicked off as a senior. They found the pills in his locker. Now, he's light once more: he goes one hundred, two hundred yards and stops. Preston won't believe he's come so far so swiftly.

Clay listens. A scrambling walk not far ahead. He thinks of where he is, the immensity of the earth above him, like the sky on an autumn night. Stars are special in prison. He clicks off the flashlight, and the swollen silent darkness overwhelms him at first with unseen horror, unimaginable fears. Then, he thinks he might see stars. He begins to move ahead slowly. He tries each step, takes another, stops and listens. He can hear the man's unguarded stride up there.

He thinks of killing Sam, and the feeling rises from his fingertips to his heart and head: a deep sensation of revenge that will etch its words on his heart.

Sam Preston touches the walls and walks on. He's been in here many times, but he can't recall each rock. He thinks he hears someone behind him, but maybe not. They'll never catch him in here. But what good is going deeper and deeper in Blue Crystal Cave now? He can hope they'll give up and leave. He'll climb up the sinkhole in a day or two and find they're long gone.

He barely believes that. A man will trail you like guilt, inexorable and with fearful permanence. Sam feels the wall begin to recede, and he's come to a small grotto on the cave's right wall. He brought a picnic in here once. He goes on in. It's forty feet wide, thirty feet long, and nine feet high. He's measured that. Sometimes Sam pretends science calls him. He'll map trails, measure speleothems, take mineral samples from the floors. He'll take the barometric pressure, photograph flow grooves for no good reason. He'll retrieve baby food jars of dusty guano. But it was never science.

He moves to the back wall of the grotto and slides down to his seat. He has a sour taste in his mouth, and his injuries throb terribly. He has a headache. He could sleep for days. He feels so sleepy. He can't tell if he's awake or asleep. He talks to himself underground but not now. He wonders if the real blue crystal might be lodged in here somewhere.

Sam touches his face. The cigarette burn is lost in the swollen mass of tissue. Then he hears the slow creeping down there, one step every three seconds. He listens for the next one, then the next.


"Here's Bobby," says Misty. She tries to straighten her hair and look pretty for him. He blinks at the light as he comes into the big room near the sinkhole. Christiann and Mary Beth sit against the wall. Misty licks her teeth and smiles. She knows she needs a bath, but so does everybody else. "Hon, where's Clay and that man?"

Bobby feels shaky. He wants to choke something. He can't even trust Clay anymore. When he was sent off for killing Elijah Morton with a tire tool, he decided he'd never trust a man again. Then he got to know Clay. But now he sees that Clay is just like the rest of them. He's weak, stupid. Bobby can look ahead. His mother had it, the gift of foresight, a creepy vision of the future. She would be sitting in her rocker, reading the Bible,

171

and her mouth would gap half open, and a faraway look would spill into her eyes. Bobby would wait for her to tell what was to come. Most of the time she was wrong, but that wasn't her fault. Things changed.

"Leave me alone," says Bobby. He brushes past Misty and stops in front of Mary Beth and Christiann. Mary Beth's ankle hurts so bad now she can't ignore it.

"I got her, hon!" chirps Misty. "I done gone out and caught this woman, just like you said! Ain't you impressed with me?" Bobby squints at Mary Beth, as if trying to decide something. "I said ain't you impressed?"

"Misty, shut up," he says.

"Well that's a fine how-de-do for nearly gettin' killed out there in the dark findin' this woman," says Misty petulantly. "See if I ever do a favor for you again." She sniffs and looks at her nails. They're dirty. She'll get a real manicure when she gets to California.

"Misty, for God's sake, he's gonna kill us!" says Christiann. "Can't you see a thing when it hits you in the face?"

Bobby squats in front of Christiann and Mary Beth. A thin smile curls his lips slightly upward. Christiann's face is broken down nearly to tears. Bobby's already betrayed her. The scratches from her fight with Misty hurt. She feels as if death might be better than this.

"Christiann, you're the biggest dope sometimes," says Misty. She laughs girlishly. "We just get his money, and we're all on our way down the road, idn't that right, Bobby?"

"I can't believe this," says Christiann. She lifts her hands to her face and holds them there. She mumbles into them, but the words aren't clear.

"Maybe you'd like to tell me where it is so we can get this over with," says Bobby to Mary Beth. His voice is reedy but steady, a soft, unwavering line. "I'm so tired." He looks back around the cave room. "I just want to go ahead and get this over with."

172

"Then get it over with," says Mary Beth, looking straight at him. Christiann drops her hands and glances at Mary Beth.

"Do you wanna get shot?" she chokes. "He's gonna shoot us. Don't y'all understand that?"

"I know he's going to kill us," says Mary Beth.

"Well, if y'all ain't the biggest weenies I ever seen in my life," says Misty. She half dances around the room, rocking, hands in her pockets. "I think it's this cave. I'm starting to like it down here. It ain't nothing bad to me. I mean, it ain't a grave or nothing."

"Everything's a grave," says Bobby. He's sweating madly. "You think you're getting out of a vein, and it blows up." He sits in front of Mary Beth and Christiann. "You ever seen a coal mine?" Neither says anything.

"A coal mine?" says Misty. "What in the tippy-toe does that have to do with the price of eggs in China?" She laughs, as if she's invented some hilarious joke. She feels great. Bobby made love to her. He's gonna take her to California. Or Clay will. There's hardly a way she can lose. Bobby ignores her.

"It's so hot that it makes your breath blow out," he says. He's whispering. "You grind up the coal to get it out and breathe in that dust. It turns your lungs into charcoal. Back home they cut up this man who died, and his lungs was little and black and hard like charcoal from a grill."

"Charcoal?" squeals Misty.

"You try to get a breath, and all you breathe is blood, then you spit it back out," says Bobby. "Your lungs get full of blood and coal dust. You drown in your own blood. That's what a coal mine is."

"Where's Clay and that man?" asks Christiann. She's afraid she knows the answer.

"Clay let him get away," says Bobby. "He's gone after him. They might come back." He takes the gun from his waistband. "They might come back, they might not come back. Maybe they're down there breathing up blood."

―――

173

"Oh God," says Christiann. She pulls her knees up to her chest and rocks. Mary Beth wants to scream. She thought she'd die an old woman, listless and sweet, addled in her bed. She would be like her Granny Brinkley, losing track of everything so leaving meant less. This is not a way to die.

Christiann screams now. The sound echoes along the wall, goes down into the cave. Misty stops pacing. She sees the blind-snake tattoo on Bobby's arm, the gun arm. It seems to be writhing up a rope of muscle, heading straight for Mary Beth's eyes.

After a dozen paces, Clay turns the flashlight back on, and now he's following the beam over fantastic breakdown. Boulders the size of Volkswagens have cracked off, fallen. His slick finger frets the trigger. That part's easy, but what will a gunshot do here? He saw a movie once where a man fired a gun, it was in the Himalayas or somewhere, and an avalanche buried him. Retribution.

Clay's thinking of moral lessons when he comes to a widened part of the cave. There's a scalloped recession to the right. He steps slowly to it, shines the light in. Sam's in there. Clay sees him just as Sam hears those slow footsteps. Clay shines the light in his eyes, but Sam can barely see a thing. He hears soft footsteps, the click of the gun hammer going back. Sam jerks upright, swings his head back and forth, trying to see anything.

He'd dozed off. He can't find the line between sleep and awakening down here. He wants to call something out. No words come to mind.

"Kiss your ass goodbye," says Clay. He knows he'll kill him now. He won't feel anything.

"I'll take you to the money," says Sam. "Don't shoot. It's close to half a million dollars. You can just take it and get out. I don't want it anyway. I never wanted it."

Sam listens to his own words. They are disembodied. He

waits for the whack of the bullet. He probably won't hear the gun's explosion. There won't be much pain. He'll die quickly. He keeps trying to see the man, but there's no light for Sam.

"You made me look stupid," says Clay. "Nobody does that." He wants to go right back down the cave and put the gun down Bobby's throat and pull the trigger.

"I was saving my life," whispers Sam. "I wanted to get out of here alive."

"Being dead's nothing," says Clay. He waits.

"It's untraceable," says Sam. "It's cash. My father left it here after the place caved in. I can take you to it."

"Come on, then," says Clay. Sam stands and walks toward his voice over the stones. "Can you get back?" Clay looks at Sam's smashed face and cannot believe he's still a man.

"I got nowhere to go," says Sam. "This section stops not far ahead. I can follow the wall back to the crossover."

"I'm behind, and if you try to leave me, I'm going to shoot you in the back," says Clay. Sam nods. They move back down the cave. Clay thinks of bats in Hermie's mouth.

Sam gets to the crossover, turns right down the smooth cave floor, heading steadily for the big room. He can't think of what to do next. They'll shoot him soon if he doesn't change his story. He read something about a man subtly changing his story, lies, then half-truths, then a profound truth, then a half-lie. No one could tell which story was real, which trail to follow. He might confuse them a while longer. He is suddenly more tired than he's ever been in his life.


"Sam!" Mary Beth sees him stumbling into the room, puts her hand on her mouth, and cries for joy. Tears swell into her eyes, then spill over her cheeks.

"Mary Beth?" he says. His voice is cracked, froggy. He turns toward her voice. Bobby angrily swings toward him. Clay slides to the side, pushing his hair back and trying to think.

"Sam, I'm here," she cries. "I'm here." He starts to smile, steps toward her just as Bobby gathers torque, the gun coming up over his head. He brings it down on Sam's head just as he begins to shout.

"Son of a bitch!" cries Bobby. The blow is terrible, above Sam's left ear. Sam collapses on the floor, and Mary Beth screams, jumps up, and starts for Sam. Christiann holds her back.

"Hi, hon," says Misty hopefully, coming toward Clay. "Have trouble catching that old thing?" She smiles. Clay looks at her teeth. They aren't clean. He can't stand a man or a woman who doesn't brush. She turns. "Bobby, hon, you're gonna break him."

"Where is the money?" screams Bobby. The gun is pointing at Sam. He's lying on the cave floor. His head is throbbing. Galaxies surround him in a stately swirl.

"He's got it, bro," says Clay. "He told me. It's half a million dollars."

Bobby's face falls. He's planned to shoot Clay, but this changes things. He looks at Clay. Sam's bleeding. Blood streams from a cut over his ear. The blood is dark red.

"He's got it?" shouts Bobby. "He's got the money?"

"He's got it," nods Clay.

"Leave him alone!" screams Mary Beth. She's crying. Her nose is running. Christiann holds on to her.

"I'll be in Hollywood, California, before the weekend!" squeals Misty. "Well, how's about them apples?" She touches Bobby on the shoulder and tries to smile. She can see herself sitting in this big mansion, and maybe somebody will even do her fingernails! They do their toenails out there, too!

When Bobby turns, she sees that his eyes are all black. They're all pupil. Enormous black pits.

Bobby reaches out for her, placing his left hand behind her neck. She smiles until she feels the pressure. She sees the gun coming up. She thinks she hears thunder. His hand slides around her neck until the thick fingers grasp her throat, and he squeezes her slowly, like a constrictor coiling up.

"Hon," she chokes. Her hands come up to his, but his strength is overpowering. Her breath is almost cut off. Her body shakes, and she tries to pull away, but she can't get loose. Bobby pokes the gun in her stomach at solar plexus level. Christiann and Mary Beth hold each other. Sam tries to sit, then falls over; his center of balance is gone. Clay watches Bobby and doesn't care what will happen next; there's no meaning in life or death, and so it cannot matter. It has never mattered. Bobby pushes the gun hard into Misty's stomach as he chokes her. He decides to kill her, and so he thumbs the hammer back, and she hears it and looks down. She's choking now, strangling, fighting hopelessly and struggling. Her eyes are wild, and her mouth is open, sucking hard for any air, but she gets none. Bobby looks into her mouth, and he feels a horror beyond description, mines, veins, his mother, women, birth.

Bobby swiftly raises the gun and thrusts the barrel in his own mouth. His face is an inch from Misty's now, and he releases the grip enough for her to take a sip of air. His eyes are feral, loosened from anything human.

He begins to suck on the barrel. The hammer is back. Bobby sucks on the gun barrel. He taunts her as he sucks the blued barrel.

His eyes turn up in a half smile. Christiann can't stand it and looks down as Mary Beth wants to scramble to Sam. He's bleeding and broken. Bobby starts to smile broadly now, and his mouth corners turn up. He relaxes his grip on Misty and takes the gun out slowly and lets the barrel drip spit. He holds it by her face.

"Scared the shit out of you, didn't I?" he whispers. He lets her go, and she staggers backward two steps. She's not going to California. She's going to hell if she doesn't get out of here. She runs across and falls down beside Christiann, who reaches out for her.

177

"I told you," cries Christiann. Her voice is harsh and loud.

"He like to killed me," says Misty. Her face is ashen, her eyes unfocused, level and weak. "I can't hardly believe he like to killed me."

"Ice, bro," says Clay. They're looking at Sam. Bobby tries to think. It's not the same with Clay anymore. It will never be the same anymore. "Ice, bro." Clay looks hopefully at Bobby.

"Screw this," says Bobby Drake. "I need a smoke. I got to think. Get Misty and Christiann against this wall." He points to his left. They're across the room, and Christiann begins to whine and curse. Clay walks to them and holds his gun out and makes a compact gesture with it. Christiann wishes he'd just shoot her and get it over with.

"You heard the man," says Clay. Misty and Christiann help each other up and move without speaking. They're holding each other tight. They're trembling. Mary Beth sits up straight. She just wishes she could touch Sam one more time. Misty and Christiann sit down. Bobby lights a cigarette and runs his hand through his hair. "What about her?"

"I'm thinking," says Bobby angrily.

Sam gets to his hands and knees and starts to crawl toward the sound of Mary Beth. Blood drips from his ear around his face and off his nose. She cries. Sam crawls now, and Bobby watches him. Clay watches Bobby for a sign, but Bobby's face is impassive, as if Sam were a wasp that might be heading for an open window.

"Bro?" says Clay.

"Blade," chokes Bobby.

"Blade," whispers Clay.

Sam doesn't care. He raises his head, keeps his face toward Mary Beth, realizes suddenly that his head has cleared. He crawls, and she gets to her knees and reaches out for him. The gunfire could erupt any second. If she could touch him it wouldn't matter. Sam turns his face back and forth.

"Mary Beth?" he whispers.

"Here," she says. "I'm here." He subtly shifts his course and moves straight for her. He tries to smile. Clay thinks Mary Beth is very beautiful now. Bobby watches them, not knowing what to feel. Maybe if Nobody gets his bearings again, he'll take them to the money. Bobby can't think.

Sam gets to her and she tugs on his arm, and he sits next to her. She cradles him in her arms, crying, holding his face on her chest. She touches his hair, his face. She kisses his hairline. She's never loved anyone this much before. He raises his face to her, and she tenderly kisses his cracked lips.

"It's okay, it's okay," she chants. "Sam. I love you, Sam."

He puts his lips to her ear, and she knows what he'll say: something undying, a phrase that will last after their imminent deaths.

"Tell me when they're turned away," whispers Sam Preston. A cool thrill spills along her arms.

"Yes," she says.

Sam tries to gauge the distances. He knows it's not far. Against the north wall of the room, he's not far. He widens his good eye, but he can barely see light. He wipes moisture from it, thinks of summer sun.

"I'm going to get the lights," Sam says softly. His lips on her ear carry a cool sexual voltage. "Then I'll take your hand. Follow me."

"Yes," she says.

Clay and Bobby have moved back toward Misty and Christiann.

"Bye, Misty," says Christiann. They're both crying.

"Bobby," gasps Misty. "Bobby, you ain't gone hurt us, are you? I mean, you done loved both us, ain't you? Clay, hon, talk him into seeing this right."

"Bye, Misty," says Christiann.

"We never shoulda brought you women," says Bobby. He's holding the gun down at arm's length. "Just the way it is. I'm gone do you in the head. You won't feel nothing."

---

*179*

Clay can't believe he's going to kill them, but he can't say anything. He's lost his standing with Bobby. Just like at Reidsville. You only gain respect through silence. You can lift weights and keep your mouth shut.

"Bobby, Bobby, hon, don't shoot us," says Misty. Her voice wobbles, wet and trembling. "We don't have to go to California. We could get the money and go to, like, Canada or East Dakota, something."

"Too late," says Bobby. "It's just too late."

"Now," whispers Mary Beth.


Sam flies. On his feet, he feels the cave floor nearly liquid beneath him, and he holds out his blind hands. It's not far, he reckons. He waits for the gunfire, but he's swift, faster than light now, and he senses that he is invisible, that his footfall makes hardly a sound.

Bobby has the gun up. He's decided to kill Misty first because of her mouth. Maybe there's a reason for this; maybe not. He feels the world dying in his heart. He can't bear eyes. He sees her eyes follow Sam before he hears Sam's steps. Clay whirls around. Bobby spins, too, raises the gun, and nearly shoots before he knows he'll never see the money if he kills Sam. He turns back to Misty. Where does he think he's going? He can kill Misty now.

Sam gets to the switchbox for the lights, but it's moved. He slaps the wall wildly, cursing. Christiann's never seen a thing in this world more horrible. The box isn't where it should be, and he moves five feet, seven, and it's still not there. Then his hands hit it. Clay realizes what he's up to now.

"Shit," he says. He starts running, gun out. Bobby looks at Clay just as Sam turns out the lights. Misty screams.

There has never been on this earth such blackness before: a complete death of light that stops them. Sam doesn't notice a difference. He scrambles back down the wall, gets to Mary Beth, and whispers, *It's me.* She gets up with him, grasps his hand so tightly it hurts. He's running, leading her. She barely feels the pain in her ankle.

"Son of a bitch!" screams Bobby. He starts whirling and firing. Orange flames lick the barrel. The shots miss Misty and Christiann by yards now, but the lead splinters and spills through the room, and a shard strikes Clay in the thick lump of his deltoid muscle. It feels like a lit match thrust into the cleft of his shoulder. He touches it and feels blood. Bobby stops firing. "Clay! Get the lights! Clay!"

"Come on, Misty," says Christiann. She gets her friend's hand, and they run along the wall. Misty follows but is so fearful her feet barely reach the floor.

"I'm shot," he says. "I'm hit, bro."

"Get the lights!" Bobby is frantic. He hears footsteps all around him and wants to shoot, but he suddenly knows a secret: *one of them is his father.* He's been in here before. It's the northwest vein. They've just opened it back up, and it could cave in again. He's afraid of killing his own father. Then he remembers what his mother said the night he died. They had stood at the foot of his bed. A bedpan lay next to it where he'd spit up black foamy blood all night, and the room was dark because she kept the curtains pulled. His daddy couldn't stand too much light. She said, *Robbie, he worked that job for you, so you'd have good things. He did this for you.* And Bobby couldn't stand the thought. He'd died from breathing coal dust so Bobby could live in a miserable shack where the air itself was black. His breathing was like a chain being pulled across metal.

"I don't know where it is," says Clay. "Was it on the wall?"

"Then find a damned flashlight!" screams Bobby. He can't believe the cave now: it's a deep world beyond pain. Clay gets to his hands and knees and scrambles around.

Sam and Mary Beth come to the passageway silently, move out down the passageway into Blue Crystal Cave. He leads. She holds his hand. The sounds begin to seem weaker behind them.

Mary Beth's eyes are dry, and she tries to see where they are going, but there's only a profound emptiness.

Misty and Christiann miss the passageway and come back around the room, and halfway around Christiann knows it and stops.

"Keep on going," whispers Misty.

"We've done gone too far," says Christiann.

Bobby hears them and fires a round that way, and the bullet splits the air between them in an orange-blue flash. They scream, and the sounds of explosion and scream echo in the cave terribly. The room smells heavily of gun smoke. Bobby fires again, but the gun's empty. He has shells in his pocket, but when he tries to get a couple out, he drops them. He curses, falls straight down and feels the floor, but they're gone.

"Clay, get the light!" cries Bobby.

Christiann finds the passageway now, and they move along it, hearing Bobby's curses and screams behind them. Twenty yards down, Christiann stumbles over a knob of stalagmite, and they both fall. Misty thinks she's falling down to land on Hermie, and she wants to scream, but when she opens her mouth, nothing comes out. She thinks of a bat coming out of her mouth. They get back up and keep moving.

Bobby works his way around the wall until he gets to the switchbox and turns the lights on. The room is flooded with noon. The light makes Clay lose his balance, and he falls to his seat. For thirty seconds they're both blinded, but shapes come back, and Clay sees the blood leaking from his shoulder. The wound is serious.

"I'm hit, bro," says Clay softly.

"They're gone," says Bobby. He whirls. "They're all gone." He runs to the rope ladder and looks up it.

"I think they're gone down the cave," says Clay. "I don't think they got out."

"Shoulda shot everybody," says Bobby. He feels as if he's alone now. They're making fun of him. They're all making fun of him.

"I'm bleeding," says Clay helplessly.

"Well say *ice*, you pussy, and maybe it'll stop," says Bobby.

Clay checks his gun and walks slowly to Bobby. He must look strong now. He wipes blood on his jeans. He knows now that people will die, more than just Hermie. Bobby's breathing like a boxer at the last bell.


In the hills, new streams form beneath the cover of lightning, start to pour into the limestone formations all over south central Kentucky. The river at the bottom of Mammoth Cave will rise a level.

Sinkholes will fill, new rivers rush into dry caves. At first, a trickle breaks from a roof fissure, then it's a small stream. Pressure blasts it open: rainwater rises and chokes the smallest caves until they're underwater. The largest ones sometimes get ankle-deep, and the floor loses its permanence.

Cavers say it's a fearful sound, where you mostly find the night and the silence.

A front's stalled up there. The sky is full of white-hot tongues. Already Lake Preston is rising and soon may spill backward into the passageways.

183

# 16

*It's four-thirty* and still the rain comes straight down. The sandbags at lower Main Street are holding. Bowman Watson's asleep on the backseat of Zeke's car, holding a small tattered blanket. Zeke is too tired to continue, so he sits in a dugout at the ball field, watching a fresh group of men fill bags with sand. Word goes back and forth from the river to the park, ebbing and flowing; first, they say it's going to hold and everything will be fine. Then they say it's giving way and the flood could break at any moment.

Tom Meade has not slept, but he feels a strength growing, an alertness he did not know he possessed. He's been all over the town, helping old folks out of their threatened homes, speaking to the National Weather Service and the governor's staff. He has personally placed ten or more bags on the growing levee. He has checked on coffee at the high school and ordered them to start cooking breakfast by five. He got Bill Vinings to open the Winn-Dixie so he could buy hundreds of cups for coffee. Each group in town has felt that Tom Meade has a special interest in it. Just after three, he went house by house along the endangered area collecting pets, taking them across town to the Sheppard Animal Shelter.

Men nod at him with respect as he passes them at the park. He can hear them speak his name. He makes sure enough fresh men are there to fill sandbags, then he drives down Main to the towering wall of sandbags, which holds back a lake now. If it breaks, the men behind it stacking will be in serious danger; they will be swept away. Tom parks well up Main and walks down to them. He will share their danger. Barney Timmons is striding back and forth with a walkie-talkie, looking at the bags in the floodlights.

"Tom, it's holding!" he shouts. His voice sounds hoarse and ragged, as if he were getting over a serious cold. "We got it forty high and ten thick now. We had a small leak a while back, but I think we got that stopped."

"Incredible job, Barney," says Tom. "Keep at it. Everything here'd be underwater if it gets loose."

"I've sent some men over to the cemetery," Barney says, "but I don't know. It's near the top of that wall. The problem is that if it gets over there, it can spill back down behind here. Could happen. You heard from the weather bureau?"

"It's starting to move south," says Tom. "Should be stopping in half an hour. You know how it is with this river. It'll go down quick once the rain stops, take maybe ten hours to get back in the banks, but we'd be safe, I think."

"It may be over the bags at the cemetery in half an hour," says Barney. "You might ought to go over there. Probably do the men good to see you there."

185

"Okay," he says. "Did, uh, Sam Preston . . . Did you ever get hold of him?"

"Never did, but we haven't had time," says Barney. "Odd. Normally, he'd be right in the middle of this. You know how he is."

"I'm sure he's fine," says Tom, but as he walks away, he has a deeply troubled feeling about Sam. It's a familiar feeling, something he can't shake.

Patricia starts her car and sits in it for a moment and listens to it idle. Tom has a police scanner at home, and she's been listening to it. She could not sleep. From time to time his deep voice would come on, strong and certain. She's in the garage with the car running.

When she was a little girl, she was terribly afraid of storms. Thunder would start to rumble in the distance, and she would get close to her father and stay with him. He was never afraid of anything. Even when he got lung cancer and began to drown in his own fluids, he never lowered his head for any man or asked for pity or mercy. He took the pain. Patricia learned from him, but she could never stand her own losses. She could surround them with gentle lies. She could pretend that her life was no different from anyone else's. But that wasn't so. She had always been afraid, and now she's afraid of becoming one of those dried bodies in the *National Geographic*. Tom told her that her love had dried up, and she had cried and cried and said it wasn't true, but when he touched her, in the kitchen or in the night, she would turn away from him. She knew that her love was there, but she was terrified to show it. What little she had left could be swept away in a single hug or kiss or a word of kindness and joy. She would hold that final ounce of love until she was dying.

She puts the car in reverse and backs into the rain, dressed in old slacks, a flannel shirt and raincoat, her gardening boots.

The tires crackle over the gravel and small fallen tree limbs. Lightning comes, but it's distant, and she can't hear any thunder. This storm seems to be failing finally, wearing itself out as all storms do. She backs completely out of the driveway and puts the car in gear and goes up the street. She knows the way. She'll go there without driving around or killing time. They're talking about it on the police band, that they need more people, and she can do anything. She can help.

She drives through town, and it seems different. She feels something hopeful growing in her. The limp flags hang down the utility poles in the slackening rain. She sees lights on in the courthouse, where her husband spends most of his time. In an hour or so it will be getting light.


Tom's back at the park now, and men can't believe how he seems to be everywhere in the storm. Zeke's too tired to work and too proud to leave, and he leans, exhausted, against his truck.

"I'm slap out of energy, Tom," says Zeke, smiling.

"You want me to take Bowman home for you?" asks Tom. "His momma probably wants him back anyway."

"You can't get the boy awake," laughs Zeke. "It takes an atom bomb to wake him. It's something about . . ." Zeke looks at the men and nods, as if searching for some word he mustn't speak. "It's something about the disorder. He can't shift back and forth between asleep and awake like a normal person."

"He is a normal person, Zeke," says Tom. "He's normal for Bowman."

"You can give it a try," says Zeke. "His momma'd be glad to see him. Tom, aren't you getting tired by now?"

"I'm fine," he says.

"Barney and them? How they doing?" Zeke asks. "I heard there's a problem with the cemetery."

"No problem," says Tom. "They got it all under control, the

young men do. Good thing they're not all as old as me."

Tom pulls up next to Zeke's car. Bowman is sleeping in the backseat, curled up, knees to his chest. He's still wearing the cap. Tom opens the door and shakes him and softly calls his name. Bowman doesn't stir at all.

"Bowman?" says Tom, touching his shoulder. "Come on, son. Wake up. Your daddy said I could carry you home."

He hardly seems to be breathing. Then he groans and turns a little, and his eyelids rise a little, see Tom, and Bowman smiles and falls back asleep.

"Okay, son," says Tom. "Here we go."

He leans into the car and puts his arms under Bowman and pulls him out of the car, then lifts him. Bowman's arms come around Tom's neck. He's too heavy for Tom to lift, but he does it anyway, carrying him in the light rain to his car ten feet away. Tom puts him in the front seat, and Bowman falls over and curls up again. Tom comes around, breathing hard, and gets in and drives off. He waves to Zeke as he passes.

Tom thinks of his dream, of the child inside the blue crystal, of the slate of his own losses. Is it possible, he wonders, to reach a point where you can never lose a thing again? Could a man awaken one morning and know that his next loss could be years away, and it might then only be his own tenuous hold on life? He rests his hand on Bowman's shoulder as he drives.

The Watsons live on the south side of town, across the river. Tom drives over the Highway 40 bridge, which is high over the river. Only some biblical flood could make it come this high. He doesn't look for it as he drives. Tom tries to touch the fatigue but it slips his shoulders like a raindrop: why is he not tired anymore? He feels as if he may never be tired again. He seems light. That's what they say death is like for those who have been good on this earth, but he's spent his life mourning and what good is that? He's seen evil up close, men who would kill you for ten dollars or simple violence, shooting a man over a game of billiards. He's also seen men working all night in storms to hold back things more powerful than any life.

———

Tom gets to the Watson house down a shady street in one of Sheppard's nicer subdivisions. The front porch light is on. The yard is perfect, boxwoods and azaleas, well ordered and clean. He knocks on the door, and it opens almost immediately. White-haired Annie Watson opens the door in her bathrobe.

"Hey, Tom," she says. "Zeke called me on the CB. Is he awake enough to come in by himself?" She looks through the drizzle toward the car.

"I'm going to bring him in, Annie," says Tom. "Where should I lay him down?"

"Oh, the sofa here in the living room, I guess," she says. Tom says okay and goes to the car, opens the passenger door, and lifts Bowman out and starts toward the house. Bowman sleepily holds on to Tom's neck. Tom comes up the stairs, into the living room, and lowers him to the couch. Almost instantly, Annie covers Bowman with a blanket, throwing it up and over him with the flourish of a matador. Bowman's quickly back asleep.

"Well," says Tom.

"Did he have a badge on his shirt?" she asks. "I thought I saw a badge on his shirt."

"I gave it to him," says Tom. "He can keep it. When he wakes up, tell him that he's a deputy now."

"It'll mean a lot to him," she says.

"Take care of him," says Tom. The voice feels as if it's coming from another man, not from his throat; someone else could be looking at this young man, this boy, this child, and saying those words.

"I will," she whispers. "You take care, too, Tom Meade."

He's halfway back to town before he notices that it's raining steadily again, but this time it's benevolent, the kind that makes lawns stay green for days.


Tom stops the car in the old part of the cemetery high on the ridge above the river. Floodlights spill over the people down there still piling bags at the lower level. Before them is a lake, stirring angrily. Tom stands in the rain. He hears them down there, but not much. They aren't saying much, just taking sand-bags from the truck and stacking them up, higher and higher.

Tom walks past the graves of Sheppard's founders, granite stones with names and dates, perhaps a fragment of Scripture. The word *blessed* is on several. He wonders if they know what is happening here. Tom wonders if he does. Something of ma-jestic power has swept into the country, but he doesn't know its name. He comes down the slope through the plots and grass. Do they feel the rain?

Tom's got his hands in his pockets and wonders if he'll just collapse when this is over, but for now he feels strong, will give these people some support. He can do that. For all the things he cannot do, has never been, he can make them feel that special way; he can radiate strength. He wonders if he is merely a conduit of some kind.

He walks down the stairs to the lower cemetery and doesn't look at Andrew's stone as he passes. He wants to live his life in another time, in what is to come. He gets near the sandbags, which are ten feet high now and growing.

"Good work!" he shouts. They look at him and smile wea-rily. The water's high on the bags. It's dangerous here, but with the rain slackening, an undercurrent of victory moves among them. Tom looks around, making eye contact and nodding. Down there, toward the end of the sandbag wall, he sees Pa-tricia.

She's wearing her gardening clothes, her green gloves. She's been leaning over and helping retie a bag that's broken loose. She stands up straight when she sees him. He wants to move toward her, but fatigue suddenly overwhelms him. Or perhaps it is some great weight trying to grind him down. He can't imagine that she is before him. She is home in bed. In this light, her hair tied back, in this rain, her face wet, she looks young, as young as a girl out playing in a summer shower.

They move toward each other. He's close to her now. Invisible hands choke him.

"You must be exhausted," she says.

"Pattie," he says. "Pattie Meade."

"Tom," she whispers. "I just thought you could use some extra hands out here. I heard it on your radio. I didn't want it to break down here."

"You didn't need to come out here," he says. "I don't want you to get hurt. You shouldn't be here."

"It's where you are," she says. "So it's where I ought to be."

He raises his arms, and she steps into them, puts her head on his chest. He holds her. A few nearby move away a few feet and keep working. Tom strokes her hair and kisses her on the cheek. She is afraid to let him go now, wants to hold him through the rest of this night, all the next day and the next night, every minute for the rest of this life.

"We're going to get through this thing," he whispers to her.

"I touched him, Tom," she says. She cries a little. "I went straight to the plot and I stood there, and I felt him all around me, and I touched him." Tom chokes back most of the tears. Somebody says that the wall is holding.

"Yes," he says.

"I touched him, and he didn't say anything, but he held me, and then he let me go, and I didn't feel afraid or too bad," she says. "I don't know what I'm talking about. I'm not scared. I'm not mad at you. I never was mad at you."

"Sssssshhhhhh," he says. He rocks her gently. He kisses her on the temple and stands back a step.

"We're going to get through it," she says.

Leon James comes down from the cemetery's higher part toward them.

"Tom?" he says. "I don't want to interrupt nothing, but I just called the weather service in Lexington, and they said it'll quit raining here within the hour. It hit fast, and it's leaving fast. According to what the Coollawassee's done in the past,

---

*191*

they think it shouldn't rise more than another foot or so. I was just across the way, and Barney and them have it knocked. It's not going to come through on Main. I'd say from the looks of things, we're going to make it here, too."

"Thank God," says Tom. "Lord Jesus."

"Yes," says Patricia. Leon touches the brim of his hat.

"Ma'am," he says, and then he moves away. He's gone ten feet when he turns around. "Oh. Douglas Dickens is over there driving Barney crazy. You might oughta go over there and do something."

"Great," says Tom with disgust. Leon moves away in the misting rain. Patricia steps close to her husband once more and hugs him.

"I'm so tired," she says.

"I know," says Tom. He kisses her on the lips and hugs her. "I'll go see what's happening with our good mayor. Why don't you go on home?"

"Not while I can help here," she says. "I'll see you at home for breakfast in a little while, okay?"

"Okay," he says.

Driving back around toward lower Main, Tom thinks of her when they first met, of beginnings.

When he gets back to the sandbags at lower Main, Douglas Dickens and Barney Timmons are standing toe to toe shouting at each other. Exhausted men lean against the bags and watch. The mayor's face is red. Tom gets out of the car and walks toward them. He realizes that he isn't tired, that he's never felt so energetic in his life. He could climb upon those bags and swim in the lake they've made.

"Sheriff, the fire chief's insubordination is something I will not tolerate!" shouts Douglas. "This is intolerable!"

"He wants us to move everybody uptown to start sweeping the gutters!" screams Barney. "He's lost his damned mind!"

"You say that to my face!" shouts Douglas.

"I would if you were a man!" screams Barney. Tom takes

192

Douglas Dickens by the arm and pulls him away from the men and tells Barney to get them back to work. He also tells him that the river will be going down soon. A few men applaud, but more are too tired to do anything but mutter their exhausted joy. Douglas talks almost incoherently. Tom escorts him to the car and puts him in, then comes around and gets behind the wheel.

"Are we going somewhere?" asks Douglas. His voice is shaking he's so angry.

"Yes," says Tom.

"Would you mind telling me where?" asks the mayor.

"I'm going to take you home," says Tom.

"I'm not going home," he says. "My car's at the courthouse. I won't have any way to get back."

"That's crossed my mind," says Tom.

"You can't do this," he says, fuming. "You can't interfere with the mayor of a town."

"Sure I can," says Tom. "And what's more, as I've already told you tonight, I can and will kick your ass. Your judgment is terrible, and you're in the way. You need to get some sleep."

"God . . . I'm . . . Well, I never thought I'd . . ."

Douglas can't find much to say now. He seems to shrink in the seat. He looks at Tom Meade and knows. He's always known what he sees in others' eyes.

"First thing tomorrow, I'd think about apologizing to some folks," says Tom.

"What's wrong with me?" asks Douglas. "I just wish some-body'd say out loud what's so bad about me."

"Okay," says Tom. "Douglas, you're a horse's ass. How's that?"

"More direct than I would have liked," he says. He doesn't say anything else until Tom drops him off at his house on the other side of town, and even then he says nothing.

Driving back to the men, Tom thinks of Andrew but he isn't

angry or sad. He thinks of Little Jackie Moss and the others whose time ran out that day. He thinks of Patricia and what she said and what it means.

And he still wonders why Sam didn't come to help.

# 17

*Mary Beth's ankle* still hurts, but she hobbles with Sam, holding his hand, stopping every few feet to listen. They hear something behind them, can't stop until they're far down into the cave.

"Don't let me fall," whispers Mary Beth. Sam stops, and she nearly runs into him as he turns and takes her into his arms. She sobs and puts her face in the curve of his neck and shoulder, trembling, holding him.

"I know this place better in the dark than I thought I did," he says softly. "We can get to the lake. Battery-powered lights in there. Just stay with me."

His bruised lips brush hers, and she presses her face into his briefly, tasting his mouth on hers. He turns away, holding her hand tightly as they move past the crossover trail, toward the pit where Hermie lies.

Three hundred yards back, Christiann and Misty stumble along, falling, crying softly, trying to find a wall, a light, anything. The sound of gunfire has barely stopped behind them, and Misty can't stop thinking of Bobby sucking on the gun barrel; what kind of man would do a thing like that?

"Wait, wait, I'm scared," says Misty. They stop. Misty thinks she hears sounds before them and behind them, too, and she has a stiff pain swelling behind her sternum. Her mouth is dry, and her tongue is thick, maybe swollen. "I'm scared."

"Me, too," says Christiann.

"Maybe if we go back Bobby won't hurt neither of us," says Misty. "He's just mad, that's all, and maybe he's—"

"Misty, stop it!" says Christiann with a barely audible violence. She takes Misty by her shoulders and shakes her. "You know he was going to kill us! If the lights hadn't gone out, we'd both be dead right now, and you know it! We shouldn't never have gone with them, and you know it! If we could catch up with that Preston we might find a way to get out of here."

"We ain't never gone get outta here," chokes Misty.

She knew she'd never get to California, that she was cold doomed to die in the South. She could be happy for hours, days at a time, hanging out the laundry and singing to herself, talking to her momma on the telephone about nothing in particular. The smell of fresh laundry made her happy. J.D. was slow and thick, but sometimes he loved her, and you could get a lot less in this world, that's what her granny told her. *A man really loves you, take him quicker than a jaybird, hon.*

"They can't keep us down like this forever," says Christiann.

"Oh yes they can," says Misty.

They start moving forward again, touching things, feeling

196

the absence of cave walls, their presence, the passageways that go steadily downward.

Bobby's in a tortured stride around the room, pushing his hair back and stopping to slap his own face. He looks at the opening of the passageway, sees it lead away in darkness and can't decide to go down there. He can't think. Clay sits against the wall, holding his shoulder with a bare hand, trying to stop the blood; it's a trickle now but steady, and the luminous pain throbs through all his upper body. His teeth even hurt, and he can't stop a buzzing that screams and churns in his left ear. A twisted lump of lead lies buried in the clench of his shoulder. He can feel it in there, feel facets from its shearing on the cave where Bobby shot. It's a ricochet, thinks Clay, but it's still a bullet, and it's sunk in my flesh. His gun lies on the cave floor. He tries not to breathe so hard, but he's not doing it; his body is, of its own volition, trying to pump air into his lungs. Clay feels sleepier than he ever has. He thinks that if he sleeps, Bobby will shoot him in the head, and he doesn't care. There's nothing past this wall of life. There are no moral lessons or moral acts, only days that spill away toward a blank and final death.

"I can't hardly stand it," says Bobby. "I just can't hardly stand it. I'll be back."

"Where you going, bro?" asks Clay softly.

"Up for some air," says Bobby. "Then I'm coming down and getting this over with. I got to make an end to things. They just keep going on and on, and I got to make an end to it."

*Yes,* Clay somehow knows, *let's just make an end to it all, blue crystals, cash, rain, blind men, bats flowing from the tongues of dead men, let's just make it all end.*

"Okay, bro," says Clay.

Bobby goes to the rope ladder, sticks his gun in the waistband of his pants. He gets halfway up the ladder and looks back down at the bleeding Clay.

*197*

"I wasn't never your brother," says Bobby. He sees Clay's eyes, the sadness, the sudden falling, and it gives Bobby confidence and power; that hurt gives Bobby Drake power. He gets to the top and climbs into the wet air, where it is still dark. Light is not far away now, nearly five-thirty, but the rain is steady, and the trees bow and dip on a cool wind. Rainwater sprinkles on his face from the trees. Bobby thinks of his mother ironing: she had a Coca-Cola bottle with a corked stopper on the end of it, and when she'd sprinkle water on the clothes, the sound was like nothing else. She washed his daddy's pants, and Bobby could never understand why.

Bobby walks a hundred feet from the mouth of the sinkhole and stops, looking around. He doesn't know where he is or how far it is to a town or to food or a bed or the arms of a woman he must have but cannot know. He cries. He breaks down.


Sam knows they're at the ledge now, and he stops Mary Beth with sudden urgency.

"What is it?" she whispers.

"This is the pit," he says. She knows Hermie's down there with his eyes and mouth open. She remembers how he was going to sodomize her and feels glad that he is dead, then guilty.

"Are we going on past the pit?" she asks.

"We can't stop," he says.

He doesn't give her a chance to fear, taking her hand and moving tightly against the wall with the pit at their backs. A single loose stone falls, bounding down the walls, sound disappearing. Mary Beth says, *Help me, Jesus*, very softly, but in less than forty steps they're past it.

She tries to concentrate on his grip, on the path, the walls, but she feels pinned to a dream, the clear fact that this may not be happening at all. She feels stupidly elated: the way she felt briefly, for a day or two after she was baptized, as if there were nothing more to fear, but that was not true.

"You okay?" asks Sam.

"I'm fine," she says.

"We're almost there," says Sam. "We can rest for a minute. It gets a little harder, but it goes on and on from here. We could get so far in this cave they'd never find us." Mary Beth wants to say, *Then what?* but she just whispers, *Okay,* and the only sound is their steady footfall.

In a minute or two they stop. Sam listens for footsteps behind them, hears nothing at all. He moves to his left. The batteries are not strong, but he thinks the lights will come back on, and he finds the switch easily.

"Close your eyes," he says. "I'm going to turn on the lights. You have to keep your eyes closed for at least thirty seconds. Try to start seeing the light through your eyelids. If you see the light when it comes on, it could blind you. Ready?"

"Yes," she says.

Sam lifts the switch, and the light swells like an organ note. Still holding her hand, he sits with her, back to the cave wall. He moves his arm around her shoulder and pulls her to him. He tries to see light through the lid of his kicked-in eye, thinks he might see a bare smudge. They do not speak for nearly a minute.

"Look down into your lap and just barely peek," he says, and she does it, and the light seems angelic, overwhelming. She looks up, blinking like a Christmas child come downstairs to yawning tree bulbs. "See anything?"

She looks up and blinks, can't quite understand what has gone wrong. As she looks, Sam hears it for the first time, the splashing of water, something he's never heard around four-inch-deep Lake Preston.

"My God, it's all over the place," she says. "Sam, the water's out and spilling everywhere. It's running into cracks. It's coming out of the walls." She closes her eyes tightly then opens them again, but she sees the same thing. "It's coming out of the walls!"

"Rain," says Sam, his voice unsure. "My God, it's the rain. The sinkholes are like funnels when it rains enough. Every year somebody around here drowns in a dry cave after a heavy rain. But I've been in here during heavy rain, and the lake never rose."

"It's rising now," she says. "I'm scared."

She holds on to him, and he takes her face and presses it to his neck and feels her trembling.

"I won't let you get hurt," says Sam. "Just rest for a minute, and we'll go on. Sshhhhhhh. Don't cry."

Sam holds her close and rocks. She feels the tears subside, feels her own lips on the skin of his neck, kisses him softly once, loves the smells of him. Her ankle is a steady hive of pain now, but its familiarity is somehow almost comforting, a close pain that she can touch.

"I'm okay," she says. The tears nearly stop. If they died right now, she could stand it. She pulls away from him and takes his tortured face in her hands. "But I want to tell you something right now, Sam, before it's too late. Will you please listen to me now?"

"Yes."

"I love you, Sam," she says.

He feels water coming in the heel of his boot.


Misty and Christiann have taken the wrong path at the cross-over cave, scrambled over the breakdown for a few hundred yards until they get to the grotto and sit. They both know they've gone the wrong way and gotten lost but neither will say it.

They hold hands, hip to hip.

Misty suddenly feels the fear and uncertainty that have swept her for so many years. She isn't sure she even wants to have Christiann sitting next to her, so she stands and feels the walls again, as if she could see. She takes a deep breath.

"What's wrong?" whispers Christiann.

"I'm gone go back," says Misty. "I'm gone go back there. I was wrong. My Bobby wouldn't shoot me. He was just like playacting because he was mad. Nor Clay, neither. They wouldn't kill nobody. They was just riled."

"Misty, Jesus," says Christiann. Misty's always been like this, changing her mind three times in two minutes.

"No, I'm gone go back now," says Misty, and the words give her confidence. "I'm gone apologize to Bobby, and it'll be all right. You coming, hon?"

"No," says Christiann.

"Well, poo on you," says Misty. "You sit here and die, but I'm goin' back." She starts to walk away, then stops and turns back. "You're really comin', ain't you?"

"I'm really staying," says Christiann. The silence between them lasts nearly a full minute before Misty turns and moves back toward Bobby and Clay. She stops once to listen: something's rubbing the inside of the cave walls, bubbling like coffee in a kettle.

Bobby Drake walks back and forth, waving his arms, looking up at the sky. Something's out there. His daddy had tried to explain about Jesus to Bobby that time. Bobby was eight, and his daddy had walked with him into the rocky soil of their backyard in West Virginia and pointed up at the clouds and said, *That's where God lives. You done orta give yore heart to Jesus.* Bobby had looked up and tried to imagine a bearded man sitting on a cloud. Much later, after his daddy had died, Bobby argued violently with his mother, who said it was God's will that his father died groaning up coal dust and bile. Bobby had told her there was no God, and she'd wept, touched his face, and said, *Well, something's out there.*

For most of his life, Bobby had thought nothing was out there, but now he wasn't so sure. He felt eyes following him.

They slid silently behind trees when he approached. They would grow on the walls of the mess hall, in the shower area. Some con's girl-boy would flirt with him, and those eyes would burn him. Clay was wrong; the earth *did* have a meaning, and it was cruel and vindictive and surgically clean. The eyes are on him now, but it isn't a single pair; thousands, millions of raindrops still come straight down, and each raindrop is an eye, a globe with pupils turning to him.

He swats them away. They come right back.

"Get away from me," he mutters. He wants light. The glow from the sinkhole dimly lights the predawn sky. That glow is a monstrous eye, the eye of God in the earth, looking upward at him. The eyes all want his death. "Leave me alone!" He screams it, and his words are dark red, arterial blood. He'd seen it when he hit Elijah Morton with the tire tool.

"I can't stand this no more," he says. He runs back and forth, crying, pushing his wet, dirty hair back. He's soaked. He looks into the faceless sky. "Why are you doing this to me? What are you doing to me? All the eyes!"

He has to run away. When the eyes found him, he'd run away. They'd taken him to Atlanta for tests once after he'd run headlong into a wall thirty times in a row, knocking himself into a bloody mess. Just after that, Clay came. Clay would say *ice*, and the eyes would blink and disappear. Now, millions of them stare at him, waiting for him to die.

He sees the willow tree. Bobby runs toward it with all the traction he can gather in the mud, puts his head down and hits it full force with the crown. He falls down in a puddle of faint circling stars. He gets to his knees and coughs a few times, and tastes blood. He runs back to the sinkhole entrance, to the light, and touches his mouth, and blood comes away on his flickering fingers. He hears a sigh and looks back toward the tree, and his father is there, wearing his coal-stained overalls, grinning, a Lucky Strike hanging out of his mouth, shrugging his shoulders. *Sooner or later, you'll go down in these mines and come up coughing blood.*

"Daddy! Daddy!" Bobby screams. He knows now that he must get to the car, leave these people and get away. This is more than any man can bear. He runs for the trail, gets halfway to the house before he hears something in the tall branches of the trees. It's laughter. They're laughing. He stops and whirls. Below each pair of eyes is a mouth, and now they're all laughing because he can't control three women and a blind man. He can't control a thing.

He turns and slogs back up the hill. He can't bear the sound of the laughter. Before he gets back to the sinkhole, he's made up his mind.


Clay's wound won't stop bleeding. He's compressed it, but he can only sit and watch his life slowly leak out, down his chest and onto his pants. It's enough to kill him.

Clay can't think straight. His feelings tell him that he must kill Bobby, his best friend. He should simply shoot him and then get Misty and Christiann and go north, maybe to Canada. They could hide out until things cooled down. Clay would go to the prison library and look at pictures of Canada. It had mountains and tall trees, deep crags and rivers, plains and ice lakes. Anything you wanted was there. Best, it had miles of country where no man ever went. You could go up there and be the King of Canada. From the walls of Reidsville, Canada seemed close enough to heaven.

But he'll never make it to Canada like this. He knows how it goes. He'll get light-headed, start talking gibberish, think he's in another country already. The cave's ceiling will be stars. The floor will become a great plain, swept with storms and swarming locusts. For a while, he'll feel an ecstasy too deep to believe, then it will all come back, the black slate of this poor hole. He'll shiver into terror. He'll die huddled against the wall like a beast.

"I'm going away," says Clay. He's been sitting, and now he stands and feels faint and weak, and it frightens him. He takes a deep breath, and his head clears instantly. He pulls his hand away to see that the blood is clotting now, down to a drizzle. He can see the lump of lead knotted blackly beneath the muscle. It looks like a blueberry trying to burst out. He's thinking of berries when he hears Bobby coming back down the ladder. Thank God, he thinks, now we can start this thing moving again.

He was afraid Bobby might never come back.


"How could it be coming up?" asks Mary Beth. Sam's felt the water in his boot, and her eyes make the story plain to him. "I thought the level of the water here never changed."

"I've never been here with this much rain," says Sam. "But if my little lake is coming up, then water will be backing up everywhere in the cave. I've got to think." He holds her close. "Is the water getting around the batteries?"

The batteries are near the cave wall by the entrance where it is still nearly dry, and she tells him, but the water is lapping that way.

"It won't get there for a few minutes, I don't think," she says. Sam listens and begins to stroke her hair. She looks into his face and wants to cry. The swelling is terrible, and the burn from the cigarette is angry and festered. "Can we go farther this way?"

"It's probably too dangerous by now," he says. "There are tubes and crawlways that go forever. Once I thought the blue crystal might be back in there, you know. I got stuck and thought I'd never get out. It nearly scared me to death."

"So what can we do now?" she asks.

"Try not to drown or get shot," Sam says. "Other than that, I'm open to ideas."

She laughs against his thick chest. She could almost feel content here if she erased her memory. She can't remember ever being happier in a man's arms or more afraid. He still strokes her hair. He can hear the water lapping, coming up steadily. The rain could stop now, and the water might not fall for hours. Every motion has its natural delay.

"I love you so much," she whispers.

He kisses the top of her head and tries to plan some move. Nothing much presents itself. He blinks his good eye and sees the shapes of the cave through a teary blur, and then the eye clears more, and he can see her hair.

"Hey, I can see again," he says. She leans back and looks at his eye as if searching for her own image in a mirror. He squints and looks at her. "You sure look like hell."

"You ought to see yourself," she laughs, and then she starts to cry, heaving tears, a groaning she can't stop though he shushes her, holds her close. She turns her face up, and they kiss deeply now, just as the lights flicker once.

They turn toward the batteries. This isn't possible, but they see it at once: the water is rising rapidly now, so fast that it's coming over their feet. They hear it spilling.

Sam thinks of blood running through veins.


Misty's feeling her way along the breakdown of the crossover tunnel, singing and whistling. She just can't ever get a thing right. That dumb ol' Christiann! To think Bobby'd actually really and truly kill them! Well, poo on her!

Misty thinks of Bobby making love to her. That means he's in love with her, but so is Clay. She could almost have her pick.

"Leastways I ain't going back to North Carolina," she says out loud. Her voice gives her courage. "Christiann'll come wanderin' out of there and find out we done gone to New York City or something, that we done got the money. And she'll find out I done got both them men. Her daddy'll have to come get her; boy'll he be mad!"

Misty thinks of Mr. Mizelle, a dour, tall man with a hearing aid and fat poodle. It always looks like it might blow up any minute. Mrs. Mizelle paints its nails pale pink. It tips around the linoleum.

Misty laughs at herself for being afraid, for thinking she will never get out of the cave. How do things like that get into people's heads? Soon, she'll find the tunnel back to the sink-hole. They'll be back there waiting on her. Bobby will be look-ing at his watch, and saying, *I didn't think you'd ever get back! Come on, honey, we got the money from old Preston, and we're head-ing off! Let's get us some breakfast and sleep.*

Misty smiles in the darkness. When they get to the motel, she can sleep with either one of them. They both need her so much.

# 18

*Bobby thinks* light may be swelling from the east, but the rain still falls like harp strings, straight as strands of glass. Soon, someone will stumble upon the house and find all gone or a neighbor will phone Sam. It must happen quickly now. Bobby puts the gun in his loose waistband and goes down the sinkhole rope ladder without hesitation. His legs tremble. He is soaked, and the cool uprush of cave air chills his teeth and bone. As he descends he stares at the blind snake on his forearm. It is crawling again. It blinks once, opens its eyes, and turns toward Bobby. He always knew that it would.

When he gets to the bottom, he sees Clay sitting against the wall in a pool of light. Blood smears his shoulder. His shirt is red, then a pale pink, as if the blood were mixed with water.

The bleeding has stopped below the blueberry-dark lump of lead in Clay's shoulder. The wound is on fire. Bobby's knees won't lock as he walks toward Clay. He listens and stops.

"The hell is that?" asks Bobby. Clay stands and leans against the cave wall.

"Water," says Clay. "It's like it's flowing in the walls or something."

"Time to make an end to this," says Bobby.

"I'm hurt bad, bro," says Clay. He watches Bobby hopefully and sees only his blank eyes, his soaked clothes. He is some species of predator, made for tearing and killing.

"Look, just hold on, Clay," says Bobby. "I'm going after that son of a bitch and get this over with. I'm not scared of a mine."

"It's a cave," says Clay. "Mines are man-made."

"I wish I was as smart as you," says Bobby. He gets a flashlight and tests it. He moves toward the opening, breathing through his mouth repeatedly, as if to inhale courage with the damp air. "You can sit here and die, or go with me. I'm getting the money and getting out of here."

"What about the girls?" asks Clay.

"If I find 'em, I'm not asking questions," says Bobby. "It's time they met Jesus."

"No such thing as Jesus," says Clay. "There's only what happens here and now."

"Jesus is what people like me never see, like a pile of money," says Bobby. "I'm gone."

He turns and heads down the passageway. Clay waits ten seconds and then gets a flashlight and heads out after Bobby Drake.


Lake Preston suddenly fills the entire chamber, and the battery lights are blinking. Sam lets Mary Beth go and strides toward a small ledge and reaches behind it. He takes out a Coleman flashlight.

"Better prepared than a Boy Scout," says Sam, and he clicks it on just as the water sparks a short in the light batteries. Mary Beth sloshes toward him. Water seems to be humming everywhere around them, draining, gurgling, rushing from the surface toward the center of the earth. "Come on."

She grasps his hand, and they go back out of the lake room down the passageway toward the sinkhole, but two hundred yards down it, long before the crossover trail, Sam stops and looks around. He flashes the light toward the fissured ceiling.

"What are you looking for?" asks Mary Beth.

"There's a crawlway up there," he says. "It's a belly crawl, but it goes a long way. I did it a while back and never went up again because it's blocked about half a mile in. It runs along the main cave and then parallel and just above the crossover cave. It cuts across from here. Hold the light."

He hands her the flashlight, and he reaches for knobs of speleothem, a slick curtain and a foothold. He climbs up the cave wall, and suddenly he seems almost lifted up and gone. Mary Beth strains to keep the light. He's gone inside the ceiling.

"Is that safe?" she asks. She shines the light briefly away from him down the passageway. "I think I hear something."

"What?"

"It almost sounded like singing," she says.

"Come on up," says Sam. "It's safer and drier than down there. We could hang around up here until they leave. Maybe we can tell ghost stories or something."

"Oh, great," says Mary Beth. He leans down and takes the flashlight from her, takes her hand, and pulls her up. The passageway is no more than three feet high here and seems to get smaller. Mary Beth is crowded up close to Sam, and she feels the immensity of the earth above them, the choking arch of this new crawlway.

Water splashes into the passageway below them.

---

Christiann hears Misty's receding song, realizes now that she cannot stay in this grotto alone. She's been crying in the solemn darkness since Misty left, feeling death very near. She can see her daddy in the yard being told they've found her body. Poor old Daddy. Her mother will have to lie in the back room, even though she and Christiann never got along. Her father got along with everyone because he asked nothing of them. He asked nothing of Christiann. He didn't care when she made F's on her report card.

"Momma," says Christiann, and she gets up to follow Misty, but she loses her sense of direction. The lack of light is nearly fluid, as if she could swim toward the surface like in a pool. She walks from the grotto into the breakdown passageway, scrambles up over the fallen rocks, and goes the wrong way.

The cave breathes and whispers names. Christiann emits a low, continuous groan and the name of Jesus over and over. She wonders if the streets of heaven are paved with gold. She could see herself as an angel, a plump bird with white wings and a halo, meeting her granny up there. Or her friend May, who died after an appendectomy when she was nine. They'd come to school Monday, and all they said was they couldn't stop the bleeding and May was dead. Death made no sense to any of them. They huddled in small reassuring clots on the playground and spoke of May in hushed tones. Already she was part of legend in that poor North Carolina town, that little Gregory girl who died. Because they were poor, the stone was a single chunk of granite with her name and dates and the word *Angel* beneath them. Her mother had always called her Angel, though no one else did. Christiann had never liked her, but after she died they all loved and pitied her, remembered her immortal soul in their prayers as the first of them to rise with God into his kingdom, a place they all feared and did not want to go.

Now, Christiann thinks she will soon see God, but she can't stop crawling and walking over the rubble, farther and farther into Blue Crystal Cave. She's crawling when she feels something cold and wet flow over her fingers, and she screams, a stinging shriek that echoes, comes back. Christiann moves to the high part of the breakdown and hears water running into the cave.

She starts singing "Amazing Grace" but can't remember anything beyond "how sweet the sound."


Misty has never quite felt so wonderful. She can't believe she lost faith in those boys! That Bobby was just kidding with her! She's known since she was thirteen that the boys loved her, that she could get things her way with a twisty smile, a flip of her hair. She never should have married so young! It just kind of happened. They all expected her to get married, so she did, but she was stupid to do it!

"Now I'm heading for Chicago!" she says. Her voice cheers her. She feels as if she's floating over the stones. Even in this night there's nothing to it.

Misty can't stop thinking of how it felt on the sofa with Bobby. She knew she could have him. He'd been watching her and thinking about her for the longest time, and all she had to do was smile at him and he'd follow her to hell. And they said being a woman was hard! *You could have the world eatin' out of your hand, idn't that what I told Christiann?*

Now, Misty hears the water, and it's beautiful! It's a twinkling sound full of diamonds and emeralds, maybe like Ruby Falls or something. Bobby and Clay will have the money by now and be up there waiting on her. Poo on Christiann. She'll wander out of here later today, and we'll be halfway to Missouri or Indiana or something.

Misty stops. She's astonished by a sight not far ahead: light. She sits on the rock and looks up there, but it's light, no question about that, and her eyes start to find it, follow it like a dog. She can see. She can see the stones around her and the water bubbling between them.

"Bobby!" she screams. "Wait, hon! Just hold on!"

Above them, in the ceiling chamber, Sam and Mary Beth hear human sounds and stop.

Bobby turns toward the sound. He and Clay have reached the crossover trail easily, and Bobby feels a churning terror. He's shaking all over.

"I hear her," hisses Bobby.

"Ice," whispers Clay. His shoulder is bleeding again, and the warm, sticky fluid runs down his chest, into his pants, and down his leg. "Ice, bro."

"Blade," says Bobby.

Misty waves at them and comes scrambling over the rocks, calling their names, babbling about money and Christiann. Bobby and Clay stand on the smooth floor of the original tunnel and shine the light on her, waiting for her to get there. Water is gurgling down the cave now, but it's not over Bobby's boots. It's leaking into Clay's shoes, and he's never felt such cold. Misty catches up with them in less than thirty seconds.

"We was lost in that cave without a light!" she squeals. "Poo on you for chasing us off!" She smiles and touches each of them on the arm. Clay thinks to warn her away, but he's feeling dizzy now, and he backs into the cave wall and leans there. "Did you get that old Nobody's money yet, hon?" She's looking at Bobby, up close to him.

Then something happens. It's his eyes. He's mad. An animal electricity spills from them, an incendiary rage that frightens her. She can't ever get things right. She never has understood how men think.

"Misty, it's cold in here," says Bobby. He's whispering. "I never been so cold in my life."

She thinks to hug him and looks at Clay, doesn't see the gun coming up at all. The twin gunshots slam into her rapidly. She staggers backward and can't take her eyes off Bobby. He's hit her in the stomach. It's taken her breath away. She glances down and sees the blood pouring out and then smells gunpowder. She wants to ask Bobby if that was his gun, if he shot something. For two seconds she knows, then falls over heavily into the passageway. Bobby's flashlight beam follows her down. She lands face first in the fetid flowing water, shakes violently once, then is still.

Sam holds Mary Beth as they lie in the ceiling crawlway. They cannot tell quite what has happened, but the gunshots are clear. Sam strokes her hair.

Bobby tries to feel something as he looks at Misty's body, to prick some fearful flow of guilt, but nothing happens. He doesn't care when Clay leans down to Misty, turns her over, and sees her open and sightless eyes. Her pupils are dilating, fixed. The wounds are terrible. He gently lays her back in the water.

"You son of a bitch," says Clay as he stands. Bobby points the gun at him. "How could you just kill her like that? What's the matter with you?"

"Something was always the matter with me," says Bobby. His gaze is level, his voice chilling. "Clay."

There's a sudden rush of water. It's up to their ankles and then to midcalf, and Bobby jumps and looks around with the light. Clay's still holding his own flashlight, and he touches the walls, believes it's nearly time for him to die.

Instead of trying to run out of the cave, Bobby moves through the water deeper into it, and Clay knows he must follow him. Soon, he or Bobby will kill each other. Clay stops for a moment and turns in time to see the water lift Misty's body and float it off down the passageway as if she were at a water park. Her hair waves in the water as she disappears from the light. Clay doesn't see it when her body reaches the place where the caves cross, flows left, falls into the pit. The water in it is ten feet deep now, and she lands not far from Hermie, and their motion around each other could almost pass for ballet.

213

Christiann hears the shots, like sharp raps on a door, and she crawls, crying, over the breakdown of the crossover trail. She knows Misty is dead. She was always running headlong into some tragedy. Once, they'd guessed about their own deaths, and Misty just knew she was going to die in a fast car with a bad boy.

"How about you, hon?" she had asked Christiann.

"Probably of VD," said Christiann, and Misty had laughed and laughed, hugged her close. Now, Christiann keeps blinking, trying to break through the walls of darkness, but it's no good. She tries to remember things she loved to see: the peach-colored smudge of sunset from her back porch; the familiar comfort of her room; bubbles on the surface of the bath between her legs.

The water spills on her ankles. The breakdown rubble seems to rise in levels like a cake, and Christiann steps lightly up it, hands out front, feeling with her hands. She hits her head on a stalagmite and squats and weeps. She's trembling. She can't say how she knows, but Misty's dead now. She might as well have jumped in front of a transfer truck. Something about that girl was headlong gone before she was ever born. You see people like her, thinks Christiann, and it's scary. They have signs around them like electricity that they can't last. Bobby had the most she'd ever seen. Those two couldn't live together very long.

Christiann folds her hands under her chin.

"Dearest Jesus, keep me safe," she chants, "and hear my prayer and cleanse my heart." She wants to cross herself but doesn't know how. She's seen that on TV, how Catholics make that cross on their chests, and she's always liked that but doesn't understand it.

She feels for the wall and realizes she can climb up the stones, higher here, and she does, until she's found a kind of

niche that she wedges herself in. She feels air coming from
above her. She reaches up and finds a fissure four inches wide
through which air moves downward. She's never been this cold
in her life. The niche has a smooth floor.

"I'm gone drown," she says. She doesn't want to drown. In
the ninth grade her friend Grady White had drowned in a farm
pond. It took them two days to find his body, and it was swollen
monstrously and black. The open coffin terrified them. It didn't
look like Grady, but they said it was. She lies down flat on her
back and listens to the water and wonders if she and Misty will
see each other in heaven, or if they will burn forever in the
flames of hell.

Sam and Mary Beth crawl quickly down the ceiling tube toward
the light of Sam's flashlight. His vision fades, then comes back;
now he can see reasonably well with his single good eye. The
gunshots have made his strong anger flare, and he feels his
shoulder muscles hunched with rage against them. He knows if
he has the chance he'll kill both the men with his hands.

"Stop," says Mary Beth. "Sam, stop."

He stops and looks back at her. There's not enough room
even to turn around, so he slides backward a little, and she
wiggles forward next to him until they're in each other's arms,
face to face. He's set the flashlight just ahead of them, pointing
down the tube.

"It's okay," he says. "We're okay."

"I'm scared," she whispers, and then she starts to cry. Sam
presses her face to his shoulder and holds her.

"Yeah, I bet you were scared on the Ferris wheel, too," he
says. "You got to get over worrying about these minor inconve-
niences."

"I'm serious," she whispers. "We're going to die. I can't
stand the thought. I love you so much."

Their faces move back, and then her lips are on his, a kiss

_215_

that lets them forget whose mouth is whose. Then her face is on his shoulder again.

"We are not going to die," says Sam. "We're going to live to be old." He suddenly thinks of those old headlines, of the children huddled against the collapsed cave, and he can't imagine what he's doing up here. He's running away. He shudders.

"You okay?" she asks. The alarm makes her voice shake.

"Come on," he says. "We got to move up in the tube a little bit more. Watch out. The floor splits up here, and you'll think you're falling, but it's never more than a few inches wide. Maybe we'll take a nap or something. This rain can't last forever. Then we'll get out of here. Probably a bright sunny day out there."

Mary Beth thinks of a bright sunny day, of her flowers bobbing and waving in the sun, of the coming of autumn when the trees turn to plum and gold. She thinks beyond all this to a wedding, with a chain of daisies in her hair and the soft light of spring on Sam Preston's gentle, broken face.


They've passed the crossover trail and the pit and are heading toward Lake Preston, but the water is now knee-deep and moving with brutal coldness around their legs. Bobby presses on and on, his pistol in one hand, flashlight in the other. He curses beneath his breath, laughs. His eyes are pale agates; he glances back at Clay. Clay thinks he looks blind, like the old man who shuffled around the town square back home. There's a slack-jawed and isolated madness about Bobby now.

The water rises. Bobby stops and tells Clay to shut up.

"We're gonna die here," says Clay softly. His blood is leaking out too much to live now, and he knows it. That's not pain beneath his shoulder; it's death gnawing away at him. Soon it will reach his heart.

"Shut up!" cries Bobby. "You hear that?" He turns around and around, sloshing in the water. Clay takes a step back and pulls his gun from the waistband with his left hand. He's thought about it long enough; he must kill Bobby now, but he'll make it as surgical as possible in honor of the old days. Between the eyes is best. The old cons in Reidsville called that a blanker shot: one instant you're alive, then it's a flat blank, a clean slate. No pain, they said. Clay will give Bobby a blanker.

"Hear what?" asks Clay. Bobby whirls violently, around and around.

"He's calling my name," says Bobby. "He's calling my name! He's still in here!"

"Who?"

"It's my father or it's Nobody."

"I thought your father was dead."

"Then it's Nobody."

"You're not making no sense, Bobby," Clay says. "If it's nobody, how can he talk?" Bobby takes a couple of steps down the cave, and Clay raises his pistol. He can't do a blanker; he can't watch Bobby's death swell over him down here, in his eyes. Bobby turns and sees Clay's gun up, his eyes filled with pity, something almost like grief.

The hissing sound turns to a muffled scream, and water blows a stone from the cave wall. The stone hits Clay's shoulder and then his head, knocks him flat down in the water, face-down into the icy flow. Bobby sees the cave start to fill.

"No you don't!" he screams. He pushes past Clay and heads back down the cave until he passes the pit and gets to the crossover tunnel and goes up it where the water is not so deep. He climbs over boulders and cracked stones, gets to the grotto, and stops. The water here is still only ankle-deep. "Daddy?"

Bobby puts the pistol to his head and whispers, *Daddy Daddy Daddy Daddy Daddy Daddy Daddy Daddy.*


The water sounds like a thousand lions. Christiann crosses her hands across her chest in the niche and thinks of God. The old

217

women all said that happiness was not for this earth, that we were born to suffer and that we would all be together in the sweet by and by. They lived on alone for so long, those women whose husbands died in their fifties. They might live another thirty years, remembering the swift passion of a hug in the kitchen, a picnic they took half a century before by some lake, long bulldozed for a subdivision. Christiann couldn't bear that. She couldn't bear to think of that long silent life. Now that she is going to die, she feels a kindness in her heart for the misery of this earth, for poor Misty, even for the unmarked graves of millions across the face of the earth.

Sam and Mary Beth reach a widened area in the ceiling crawl-way, and they straddle the fissure in the floor that goes below them into the crossover tunnel. Sam hasn't told Mary Beth the whole story, about how he came in here years before and got his foot caught in the fissure, how his carbide burned out and it took him nine agonized hours to free himself. Even now his breathing is hard and shallow, and he's afraid he might hyper-ventilate. He must get control of himself.

"Stop," says Sam. "Here's okay. Just roll back to the wall. The tunnel's a lot wider here. You feel the crack in the floor?"

"Yes," she says.

Below them, a few feet away, Christiann hears the voices of angels, and she smiles. They've come for her now. She lifts her arms up and whispers, *I'm ready,* but nothing happens for a long time. She opens her eyes and slides up in shock to a sitting position. It's light, up there above her in the ceiling. The glow is pale, like a robe on the streets of heaven. She hears voices now and knows who it is. She cannot orient herself, doesn't know if she's lying facedown or if Sam and Mary Beth are sideways in the wall or above her in the ceiling. She crawls to her knees and moves along the fissure until the light is bright and their voices are clear. She wants to hear them, ask

*218*

them something, but her instinct is for touch, for that human touch she never thought to have again. She reaches up through the fissure, gets to her knees and stretches completely up through it.

Mary Beth has her head on Sam's shoulder. His eyes are closed to rest, and she alone sees the terrible image before them. She sits up, gasps and grips Sam's arm, tries to scream, but only a high-pitched hiss escapes.

"What's wrong?" asks Sam. She groans and then opens her mouth and points at the hand, whose fingers are trying to touch the air. Sam backs up so hard into the wall that he cracks his head swiftly on the stone. For a moment they can't take in the sight. He shines the flashlight directly upon it.

"It's okay," Sam manages to say.

No angels, thinks Christiann. They are all women or talk with high, soft voices. This is a man.

"I'm Christiann Mizelle," she chokes. "I'm alone."

Mary Beth's tears fall over her cheeks, and she moves slowly toward the hand, reaches out for it, and then grasps it. The shock is electrical and full for both of them, a connection that dissolves fear but breaks down some defense. Christiann begins to weep. Sam comes to the edge of the fissure and shines the light down, careful not to point it near her eyes, and they see her, filthy, face bruised now, hair matted.

"I didn't never think I was gone see a human being again," says Christiann. She tries to muffle her sobs. She looks back behind her. "I think they killed Misty." She looks up. "How can I get up there with y'all?"

"You can't from there," says Sam. "Just sit tight. They can't stay in here forever. We just have to hold on until they leave. I'll get you out."

"The water's coming up," she says. "The water's coming up! Cain't you hear it? I'm gone drown down here."

Mary Beth looks at Sam as if to say, *Do something,* and Sam can scarcely bear it. When he caved alone, he only had to worry

*219*

about himself. Now two women's lives are in his hands, and he has only half an eye to help them.

"Sam?" says Mary Beth. He looks down through the fissure at the terrified woman. Churning groans fill the caves, as if the whole place were falling down.


Bobby decides not to kill himself yet, and he stands and howls and stamps his feet. The eyes are here in these walls by the billions, and they're laughing, *Oh my God in heaven, how they're laughing!* He walks out of the grotto and up the crossover trail. He goes twenty feet and stops at a cracking sound. Bobby whirls around, swinging the flashlight. Clay's there, gun up, face misshapen and monstrous from the rock's strike. His jaw is shattered and unhinged, and his tongue hangs out his mouth like a thick snake.

Because Bobby can't quite resolve the image, Clay shoots first and hits Bobby in the left collarbone. Bobby's eyes widen, his nostrils flare, and he fires a round that hits Clay just under the nose. The noise is deafening, echoing, roaring.

"Ice, bro!" screams Bobby.

Clay feels as if he's heading for a place far away, and he can almost see it. It's cold, and he's alone on this journey, and fires blaze, but he can't get near them. He looks back once and sees Bobby, small as a needle point, in pain. Clay feels no pain at all.

Bobby watches him hang for a moment and is going to shoot him again when Clay pitches heavily forward and lands with a splash in rocky water. He doesn't move.

The others hear the gunshots, and Christiann screams, then stifles it far down in her throat. She holds on to Mary Beth's hand more tightly, looks back down the cave. The shots seemed very close.

"They're coming to get me!" cries Christiann. "Sweet Jesus, don't let me die down here!"

"Sam?" says Mary Beth. Sam feels gooseflesh erupt along his legs and arms.

"I'm coming down," he says. "Just stay where you are. Mary Beth, keep the light."

"You can't do this without a flashlight!" she cries.

"Yeah, I can," says Sam, and he almost believes it. "For now, just turn it off and stay quiet. I'll do what I can."

"Kill them," says Christiann fiercely. "Please God kill those sonofabitches."

"I'll take care of you," he says. "We're gonna cut the light out now. You just sit back down."

"I'll be up here," says Mary Beth.

Sam hands the flashlight to Mary Beth, and she clicks it off.

"Is there anything you want me to do?" she asks.

"See if you can find that stupid blue crystal," says Sam. "I know it's around here somewhere."

She laughs but it feels wrong, like trying on a blouse that's the wrong size. Sam moves off in the darkness of the ceiling tunnel. Mary Beth lies down on the floor and lets her hand dangle through the fissure in the floor. She can feel her heart beating in the stone.

## 19

*Patricia's been home* for an hour, lying on the bed in her gown, when she hears the familiar sound of the back door opening. She gets up and comes to him. He's already in the den, sitting in his chair, when she gets there. He's unlacing his boots.

"I left," she said. "It had started to recede a little, and so I came on home. Are you all right? Is everything okay?"

A slow smile spreads across his face.

"It's down three feet already," he says. "Everybody's gone home but a few of them. The rain's stopped. Everything's going to be fine, Pattie."

She comes to him and touches his shoulder shyly, like a young girl. He leans back in the chair and then takes her hand. It's not quite five in the morning.

"Are you hungry?" she asks. "I could cook you some break-fast."

"I'm tired," he says. "Let's just sleep for a while, okay?"

"Okay," she says.

He's very slow undressing, as if everything hurts, but he won't complain. He lies on the bed in his shorts and white T-shirt, and she lies next to him and turns out the lamp on the headboard. The window is open, and they can hear the wind ruffling the higher limbs of the trees in their backyard. Tom wishes she would say something. He wants to do anything now, whisper her name.

"Why does the river go down so fast here?" she asks. He's surprised by the question and her voice; it should be drowsy, thick with sleep. Instead, it's bell-like, clear in the dark room.

"I don't know," he says thoughtfully. "I think somebody from the university said one time it all went into the caves, but I'm not sure."

"The water disappears down into the caves?" she says.

"I'm not sure," he says. "Something. Maybe that." He stretches and listens to the wind. "I went up the river and saw a cave I'd never seen. It went into the side of the bank, and it was full of beer cans and such. A kids' place. They'd found it. I've lived here my whole life and never heard of it. It reminded me of what Jesus's tomb must have looked like after the stone rolled away."

"You think there was a stone in front of it?" she whispers.

"No, it was more like a fissure," he says. "But you know how the caves are around here. Everything seems to lead some-where else. It's a restless thing down there. You think it's stopped, but then it never does. Sam won't quit because he thinks he's going to find his way out. Something."

He hasn't meant to hint at Blue Crystal Cave. He hasn't meant to speak Sam's name. He's missed Sam this long night, missed sharing with him the secrets of experience and age. Tom almost thinks that Sam could be sheriff someday. Tom tries not to see the picture of the children in his head, but he does

223

anyway. They are only sleeping now, not fearful or fleeing in this image. They are peaceful, at rest.

"I want to talk about him," she whispers.

"Sam?"

"Andy. Tom, it's so hard to stop hurting. It's like you become another person from the pain."

"I never got over it," he admits. "I kept telling myself that you were the one who couldn't deal with it, but it was me. It was like I was thinking he'd come back if I did enough good deeds for people. They all think I did it because I'm a nice guy."

"It was me, too," she says. She takes his hand. "I think I blamed you. It was how we were raised. All us girls thought the men could save things. I thought my daddy could stop anything bad from ever happening."

"Some things nobody can stop," says Tom. "You can't save everybody from harm or save the world, Pattie."

"Oh, I don't know," she says. She turns to him and lies very close now, her face on his shoulder. "You pretty well stopped that river tonight."

"I didn't do any of the work," he says.

"You were the lighthouse," she says. "That's what you've always been. You make people better than they think they are."

"Is that what I do?" he says with a small laugh. "God, I'm just trying to get by and live my life."

She kisses his cheek sweetly, and he turns to her and takes her in his weary arms. He wants to let go and cry like a child, but he won't. She buries her face in his chest.

"He went through me, Tommy," she says. She sobs and he strokes her hair. "He came there and went into my heart and then he left. Maybe it was from the lightning or something, but I won't ever believe that. I saw the stone, and I was not going to do anything, say anything. I wouldn't feel it. I was going to help and that was it. Then he came into me. I felt . . . It was like I was . . ."

"Shhhhhh," he says. He strokes her hair.

"It was like I was pregnant again, Tom," she says. She chokes and cries but pulls it under control. "It was that feeling of fullness and life and joy. Oh, Jesus, I wanted you to have grandchildren."

"We can talk this out," he says in her ear. "We have years to talk this out. We can start traveling. I'm going to let it go when my term is up."

"Are you sure?"

"Yes," he says. "You sleep now, dear. I got you now. It's going to be okay now."

"I know," she says. "I knew that the minute I saw you down at the cemetery. I'm so tired."

In less than two minutes she's asleep, breathing deeply in his arms as he strokes her hair.

Tom rolls slightly and looks through the parted curtains out the window. He can see the moon out there and stars. What was that children's rhyme about the cow and the moon? He remembers, *The little dog laughed to see such sport, and the dish ran away with the spoon.*

# 20

*Bobby swings* the flashlight from left to right, seeing the walls run with rainwater now, fantastic formations moving in colors of slate and blood. He stumbles along, forward, back, side to side like a drunken crab. He knows he must die now, but not until all life in the cave is dead before him. They will be laughing at him if he dies first. They'll find his body, stand over it and laugh and laugh. They said that about Jesus, that he died for Bobby, and it made him sick to think of it. He was nothing to die for, never had been. He was nothing to live for, either. Money was nothing to live for. There was no reason ever to have been born. That was the great lie: from birth you start inventing reasons that you were born, missions, righteous great things, but it was just like Clay said, marking time. Like scratching day-marks on a cell wall. You did that whether you were in prison or not, but most people didn't know it. Clay's gift was explaining that to Bobby, and now Bobby hates him, hates his life, hates his death, hates the pure misery of birth.

Nothing on this earth should be left alive. Bobby got all the books he could on nuclear war. He didn't understand the words, so he asked Clay, who explained that half the people on earth truly wanted it obliterated and that all this talk about peace and love was part of marking time. Bobby wanted it obliterated. He wanted to be laughing and sneering at the weaklings when the great arch of nuclear warheads swept across the sea. He could see mushrooms growing all over America, and he loved the sight. For a few minutes, when they knew it was coming, they'd feel as he did all his life. He'd talked about it all the time until he began to make drawings of mushrooms, and one day Clay had told him they grow mushrooms in caves and abandoned mines. Bobby had called him a liar, and they'd fought until Clay showed it to him in the prison library. Bobby's face had gone pale, nearly blue when he read it. Clay said there was no God, but he was wrong. God was up there all right, and he was a vindictive, monstrous alien who took precious delight in torturing everyone on this earth.

"Preston!" screams Bobby. He staggers around again.

He sounds very close, Christiann thinks, and she grips Mary Beth's hand and tries to stifle her sobs.

Bobby's mouth is terribly dry, and he can't get it wet. He wonders if anyone in the history of this world has ever been killed by a blind man. He's never heard of it. He wonders if mushrooms grow somewhere in Blue Crystal Cave.


"He's still a good ways off," whispers Mary Beth. "Just be still."

"Have you been in here a lot?" says Christiann. Her words are tiny, soft indentations in the silence.

---

227

"I'm going to turn off the flashlight now," says Mary Beth. She does, but the comfort of their hands cheers them both. The cave is cool, swirling with water, but their hands are hot and wet. "You okay?" The flashlight had only been on for a moment.

"Um-huh," says Christiann. "Have you been in here a lot?"

"Yes," lies Mary Beth. "I practically grew up in these caves."

"And you think we'll get out of here?"

"Yes."

"I don't know if I've got no tears left. I've never been so scared in my whole life. If God lets me out of here, I'm gone settle down and never run off with nobody again." She chokes off a cry. "Can he kill Bobby?"

"Yes."

"In the pitch black?"

"Yes."

For a time they are silent, holding hands, fingers fumbling one over the other, rubbing prints, touching palms. Mary Beth cannot believe how much a human touch helps her feel safe. She wishes she could hug Christiann.

"What's your name?"

"Mary Beth. What's yours?"

"Christiann." Suddenly they shake hands in greeting and both start to laugh a little. "I'm from Murphy, North Carolina. I don't want you thinking bad of me, because I don't know how come I went off with those boys except Misty asked me to and I did. I do a lot of things she asks me to."

"Are you close friends?"

"I think she's dead now," says Christiann. "Oh Lordy mercy, Mary Beth, I think she's dead. She couldn't stay away from things that was bad to her. If it was liable to hurt her, she ran after it like the ice cream man." Christiann sniffs. On her knees, Christiann can press Mary Beth's hand to her cheek, kiss it. She does. "I just come off with her, and she left a husband down there in Carolina."

"Why did she run off with them?"

———

228

"Bobby was working at the garage with her husband," says Christiann. "She and Bobby just had it in for one another the day he laid eyes on her. Anybody acted like they loved Misty, she'd follow them to the end of the earth. Plus J.D. was just so mean, and he hit her all the time. You never know about a man. You ain't married to that man?"

"No," whispers Mary Beth. "My husband died in an accident several years ago. Sam and I are just friends. Well, maybe more than that."

"That's his name, Sam?"

"Yes."

"You lucky you got a man, Mary Beth. When a woman finds a good man, she orta hold him and never let go. My granny told me that. I ain't never had a good man. I thought Clay was a good man, but there's something . . . missing with him. It's like you look into his eyes, and you can see right through his head and out the other side. He don't show you nothing about him. I guess he's dead, too. Bobby's crazy."

"Sshhhhhh," says Mary Beth. "He might be getting close. Just hold on to my hand now."

They're quiet for nearly a minute.

"Say a thing for me," whispers Christiann.

"What?"

"Say that you love me?"

"I love you, Christiann," says Mary Beth. Christiann's hand is shaking so badly that Mary Beth can barely hold it.

"Thank you," she says. "Here's love coming back to you, too."

The walls seem to be groaning, ready to give up the fight against gravity and the swollen rush of water from the angry storms.


Sam's elbowed back through the ceiling cave to where you can get out of it back near Lake Preston. He hears it. Spray pops and sizzles like bacon frying below him, and he wonders if he can even go down there without being swept away and drowning. Then he thinks of Christiann, and Bobby nearing her. Sam's rage sets his jaws. He slides down from the ceiling cave into the tunnel and finds the water is not quite waist-deep and that the current isn't very strong, instead moving majestically back toward the crossover tunnel.

It's hard to walk anyway, and his steps are heavy and slow, hands on the walls for balance. He didn't know such a flood ever came in here or had in decades. They are working on the roads near Bowling Green, grading and digging, and maybe that's where the flow comes from. Or maybe it is time for this cave to change. Maybe an underground river has diverted itself in the natural course of things and will soon and forever fill Blue Crystal Cave. The thought skims across Sam's mind, but he shakes it away, thinking instead about Bobby.

Sam isn't quite sure now if he can see at all. What if there is a sudden smear of light, then the laughter as he turns for its source, the stun of a bullet? What would happen then to Mary Beth and the other woman? Sam feels the walls, smooth outcroppings, messages from warm seas. He could be another skeleton deposited on the cave floor, turning to calcium.

Sam's surprised to pass the pit, which sounds full of water, and reach the crossover tunnel, knows he's here by the feel and sound. It's louder, and air is moving, a black wind. He moves to his right and immediately he feels the breakdown, comes up to ankle-deep water. He tries to walk without making a sound, and he's gone a hundred feet when something bumps his leg, a thick, dense, soft log, and he tentatively touches it, feels a face.

Sam's groaning shout slams up the trail, back down it, in the walls and the water.


He takes a step and falls into the jagged rocks, but the body seems to follow him, loose and flowing. Nothing more terrible has ever touched Sam in his life. He gets away from it, up the rocks to the cave wall, before he wonders which of them it might be. He puts his hand over his eyes. Every muscle trembles, and he feels death near him, inside his heart, dripping from all these walls.

"Help me," Sam chokes. He feels the trembling start to subside, like the dieseling of a car that finally shudders to a halt. He crawls down the rocks and feels for the body, and it's still there, and he finds it's heavy, thick, stiffening. He pulls it out of the swiftly shallow flow and up the stones. He wants to mumble a few words, but he's glad this body is lifeless, whoever it is. He wonders if it's the man he pushed into the pit. He can't quite believe he's killed a man. Maybe, geyserlike, the pit spit the man back up into the cave to confront his killer.

He gets the man as far as he can out of the water and then tries to feel his face; yes, it's the big one, the muscled man with the impassive glare. Sam feels his slick face, finds the gaping hole, sets the head gently on the rocks. He tries to find strength, moves away ten yards. This is hell. He's known it somehow all along, that this hole, this family pit, is hell itself, and the Prestons might run away from it, even move to Richmond, but it was always here, waiting for one of them to awaken into it and drown.

Sam shakes the touch of the dead man's face from his hands and moves slowly up the crossover tunnel. The oxygen might be dissolving with the rising water. He can't breathe. He can't remember how long it's been since he slept, but Sam suddenly isn't sure he's awake. He sits and blinks.

He's increasingly thick and immovable against the cave wall, not even yet to the grotto. His eyes are opened or closed; he realizes it does not much matter, and suddenly he's in Richmond, and Ginger is there; she's come back to say that leaving him was just a joke. She's back, but how does he tell her that he's now in love with Mary Beth? Does he love her? Yes, he sees lakes and autumns in her eyes. She has suffered too. Ginger looks at him kindly and says that it's okay he has found another love. Sam is numb with gratitude and hugs Ginger and tells her that in a way he'll always love her too. He's smiling at her. He softly calls her name.

Christiann's half asleep, and her voice is hypnotic to Mary Beth in the silence. Christiann can lie on her back and reach up and still hold Mary Beth's hand, but they've let go for a time.

"Misty was like a firecracker you lit, and it never did nothing but go poof," whispers Christiann. "She was always about to do something big, but it always went wrong. It was like her wedding. She told me just for days and days how wonderful that man was, how he loved her like nobody's business and that he was handsome and all. He was always away, and I'd only seen him once because I was taking a secretary course in Charlotte. He was from Raleigh, I think. A garage mechanic. Then, she brought him over a week before they's to get married, and he's this . . ." Christiann starts to giggle softly, has trouble stopping. "He's this little banty rooster with slicky-back hair and one thick shoe. He had a birth defect or something, and one leg was shorter than the othern, and he'd try to be nice to me. He'd say 'Miss Christiann this' and 'Miss Christiann that,' like he owned a plantation or something. It was weird. And when I looked at Misty, I knowed what it was. She just felt bad for him. Sometimes you look at somebody hard enough, you feel so bad for 'em you think it's love, but it ain't. And I was so jealous of him I wanted to kill him. Me and Misty was best friends from the beginning of time, you might say. I wanted to tell her she could do better, but it was almost like she was setting herself up for it on purpose. She'd have to leave him one day, and when Bobby come along, she didn't even think about it twice when he wanted to take her to bed. Misty always was missing something that makes folks hold things back. If anybody halfway acted like they loved her, she'd just fall down and die."

Christiann puts her hand over her face and sobs.

"Hush up now," says Mary Beth. She squeezes her hand, shakes it gently for emphasis. "You need to keep quiet."

"I'm gone die," says Christiann.

There's a sound to her right, like rocks bumping each other. Christiann turns sharply, and the light hits her in the eyes. She moves against the cave wall, nearly blinded. She makes groaning sounds, unable to comprehend what's beyond that light.

"Looky here," says Bobby. He's heard her voice and crawled up the breakdown. Now he's so close she can smell him. She feels nauseous, gets up and tries to stick her head through the crack and climb up to Mary Beth, but it's not even close. "What the hell." He scrambles over Christiann and looks upward to the hand that's just gone there like a toad retreating to its hole. "Who the hell is that?"

Mary Beth gets on her hands and knees and crawls back down the tunnel until she knows he cannot hurt her. She shakes, feels too weak and sick to breathe.

"Don't hurt me, Bobby," says Christiann. She tries to smile. Bobby moves long the floor fissure, looking wildly for a way up there.

"Come down here, dammit!" he screams. He waits, hears nothing, and his rage makes his head feel warped. He can't find a way up there, and he slaps his face over and over. Christiann has huddled, sitting up, as far back as she can go. Bobby's chest is covered with blood from his wound, and it's coming out all the time.

"Don't hurt me, Bobby," she says.

"They're up there," he says. His words drip spit. He shakes his head and foam flies. "They're making fun of me."

"Where's Misty?" asks Christiann. She knows it now. She can't stop shaking, and Bobby can't stop looking up at the fissure, fury in his heart. Eyes are up there. That hand might have been his father's. You can never quite be sure.

"Is this the northwest vein?" asks Bobby. He's serious, sits and puts the light in Christiann's face. She can't see him now or the blood.

"I don't know where we are," she cries. "The water's getting deeper. Bobby, don't hurt me. Please don't hurt me."

"It's the northwest vein," he shouts. "Daddy? Has he been in here?"

"Who?"

"My daddy!" he roars. "He smokes Camels, and he's tall." Bobby gulps. "How can you stand the eyes? My daddy brought me in here before. You just stay in here and dig until you die."

"Where's Misty?" She's not exactly asking Bobby now, just mouthing words that occur to her because it doesn't matter. Mary Beth's gone, and that one-eyed man can't save her now.

"Misty needed to die," says Bobby. He smiles now, turns the light off Christiann's face, swings it along the breakdown to the floor of the crossover trail, where the water is still no more than ankle-deep. "It was her time."

"Oh God, I knew it," says Christiann.

"Afraid I had to . . ." Bobby starts, but he's wracked by a stunning pain in his shot shoulder, and he grabs it and cries out. He looks back up and wonders where the bed is. Where is that boy? He should be telling him a few things now. He sees Christiann and clears up a little. "I had to shoot her. Don't worry." He starts to laugh and laugh and laugh. Christiann has never heard anything worse. "Don't worry, she's learning to swim."

Mary Beth can't bear it above them. Why has Sam not arrived there yet? What if Bobby kills him? She feels frozen to the floor now, unable to think of a direction to move.

"Oh my God," says Christiann. "Sweet Jesus. Oh, Misty, I'm sorry."

"Do you know how to swim?" he asks, but she can't understand the words, he's laughing so hard. The gun waves toward her, and she closes her eyes and thinks of Jesus. His stained-glass eyes are so calm and sweet at the church. He holds a lamb, and it has the same eyes, exactly the same eyes. Misty was the one who found that out. They made the same eye four times to save money.

"I can't understand you," she says. He looks at her, almost surprised to see her there. His eyes grow suddenly cold, his gaze level and flat.

"Come on, Christiann," he says. "We're going for a walk now."

"Where's Clay?"

Bobby starts laughing again, mouth open, and he helps her down into the calf-deep water of the crossover tunnel. He's almost like a gentleman.

"He's the one teachin' Misty to swim," chokes Bobby, and it's so funny he can't believe he said it; *he could be one of them stand-off comedians in Las Vegas or something*. He grabs Christiann from behind in a choke hold and puts the gun to her right ear. The air is cold and terrifying. He can't figure out how to shine the flashlight because it's in the hand of his choke arm, so he loosens the grip and tells her to take it and shine it down the path. She does, but she's shaking so badly that she can't point it straight. "Keep it on the path!"

"I'm doing the best I can," says Christiann, and Bobby hits her in the side of the head with the pistol butt. She staggers, but he holds her up. She starts to sing "Amazing Grace" again, but even to Christiann it's out of tune, terrible. Bobby hits her in the head again, enough to hurt but not so much as to knock her down. She tries to cry, but nothing comes. If she could just talk to Misty she'd be all right. When either of them was depressed, she'd call the other and talk it out. In high school, they'd talk for hours and hours on the phone.

The cave before them is full of boulders, broken from the ceiling thousands of centuries before, and climbing over them is slow, painful. Bobby's rage expands beyond its discovered territory.

"Preston!" he screams.

"What's that?" asks Christiann weakly. They're in a low

spot now, and the water is nearly to their knees, but it's not water she hears.

"Shut up," says Bobby. They turn in a small circle and hear it now: a guttural clicking and churning against the counterpoint of a skin-crawling screech. "What the . . ." Bobby wants to fire his gun, but he only has two rounds in the cylinder, two in his pants pocket. He takes the flashlight roughly from Christiann and shines it down the cave. The sound grows rapidly until it's nearly deafening. It's water, Bobby knows, the flood after all.

After his father died, Bobby's mother would sit in her starched black dress and read the Bible out loud. When Bobby got home from school she'd make him listen for an hour. One week she read the story of Noah for five straight days, over and over.

"It's the rain," whispers Christiann. Bobby's lips barely move.

"And the waters prevailed exceedingly upon the earth," he says, "and all the high hills, that were under the whole heaven, were covered . . . And all flesh died that moved upon the earth, both of fowl and of cattle, and of beast, and of every creeping thing that creepeth upon the earth, and every man. . . ."

He's in a trance, can't believe he's spoken words he has not read or heard in years. The sound grows. Christiann puts her hands over her ears. It's deafening.

Christiann raises her arms up. She's thinking that's how God comes and gets his children, but she's not sure. Maybe that was a movie, or a joke Misty played on her when they were in junior high school.


Sam sits up at the sound, realizes he's in the dark, perhaps has been asleep. He curses softly, stands, then falls because he can't feel what's vertical to the floor. He gets to his hands and knees, then to his feet. The water is knee-deep and rising. A dreamy wail echoes through the passageway.

"Damn," he says, too loud, and then he moves as quickly as he can up the cave, stepping firmly on each chunk of breakdown. "What is that?"

He knows that the woman must not be too far ahead, but he can't be sure how far it is. He tries to moves silently. The cave suddenly emits a shrieking, fluttering groan. Then he feels a familiar rising of the path and knows the ceiling tube is above him somewhere.

He can't call out and is thinking of getting a large rock to throw, when he sees a faint wash of light twenty yards ahead that blinks once and then goes off. He moves carefully against the noise and the water. He's gone fifty feet when the light swells up once more and then fades. He knows now that it's above him and must be Mary Beth.

"I'm here," he says. He moves up the breakdown toward the ledge where Christiann had been lying. "It's okay, lady, I'm here."

The light comes on again in the ceiling, then goes off. Sam thinks of Tinkerbell. He turns his head back and forth to the fluttering, listens beyond it to hear breathing, footsteps, any human sound. The wail is terrifying, but he can't decide what it is. Perhaps it's the final explosion of water, the breaking of an underground dam that has held a river away from Blue Crystal Cave all these centuries.

"Lady, I'm here," says Sam firmly. He moves to one side to dodge a gunshot in the dark, but it doesn't come. The flashlight above comes on.

"Sam?" Mary Beth says. "Sam, is it you?"

"Mary Beth?"

He moves toward the light up the breakdown but doesn't see the other woman. In ten seconds he's up to the fissure, looking around. He suddenly feels so tired he can barely move.

"Sam? Sam?"

He gets to his knees, stretches up and thrusts his arm up through the fissure. Mary Beth takes his hand, holds it and cries.

"He got her," says Mary Beth. "Sam, he got her. I think he's going to kill her."

"Hush up now," says Sam. "I've got to think. It's okay, honey, I'm here."

"What's that sound, Sam?"

"I don't know," he says. "I've never heard a thing like it before."

"I can't stand it," she says. "I don't think I can stand that sound much more. Is it the water?"

"I don't know," he says. He sighs, kisses her hand, tries to get past his indecision. "Look, I've got to go after him. He's already killed the other guy. I don't think that woman's friend is alive, either, the other woman."

"Sam, he's crazy," she says. "He's completely crazy. Just get me and take me out of here. There's nothing we can do for that woman. Just come on back now and get me out of here."

Sam holds her hand and thinks. They could be deep into the crossover tunnel now, finding that it finally dwindles to a series of small passageways, none of which goes anywhere. The sound could be water. They could already be drowned. Then he thinks of children huddled in this night against the fallen cave ceiling, waiting for help that would never come. He closes his eyes and sees, smiling and reaching out for him, the hands of Little Jackie Moss, trusting and precious, knowing that Sam would never leave him down here to die, that someone he loved or trusted would come anytime.

"I've got to get her," he says. "Anyway, I have to try."

Mary Beth's face is streaked with tears, but she understands and feels selfish, and calmer now that Sam is here. She just wishes he would hold her hand until they die. She could move across that gulf with him. She can't bear losing that late love in her life.

"Okay," she says. "I know. Come back and get me as soon as you can."

"I love you," says Sam. Mary Beth's tears fall through the fissure.

*  *  *

The roar deafens Christiann and Bobby. He takes the flashlight
from her and clamps his forearms over his ears. The beam hits
a row of stalactites that look like dragon's teeth, ready to bite.

"It's coming," she cries. "It's closer."

"It's the mark of the beast," says Bobby softly. His mother
had read him Revelation over and over, on cool winter eve-
nings, summer nights, Sunday mornings, before dinner, white
horses and seven seals, the mark of the beast. Trumpets shall
sound. Who knew what Satan's trumpets sounded like? "It's
the end of the world."

"You're scaring me," says Christiann. He swings the light
around.

"Preston!" he shouts. "It's the mark of the beast. It's the end
of the world."

But it's not the end of time. Christiann screams just as
Bobby feels gnats, flies, birds, thousands, millions of them in his
face and hair. The sound is deafening, a screeching roar that
seems yet far down in the cave. Bobby hears the groaning and
thinks of his father leaning over the bedside, sick in the night
before he died.

"It's bats!" screams Christiann. "It's bats!"

The air suddenly fills with them, millions of them. Bobby
and Christiann breathe wings, smell the stench of a million
wings. Bobby swings at them with the flashlight, cries in terror
and anguish. They are demons, monsters from below.

This is the night he always knew awaited him. He must die
now, and in that death leave no witnesses to his cowardice. He
thumbs the hammer back on the revolver.

# 21

*The early morning* filters into Tom's bedroom, where he still holds his wife in sleep. He awakens slowly. He hasn't slept enough, just three hours, but he feels a deep calmness now, and he smiles and strokes Patricia's hair. She groans in her sleep and rolls away from him and sighs heavily. Let her rest. He remembers how she looked in the light at the cemetery. He gets up easily and does not awaken her.

The shower feels wonderful, a warm, reassuring rain on his strong shoulders. He shaves the white stubble from his cheeks and skin and splashes on a little Old Spice to take the sting away. He dresses, takes a polished red apple from the bowl on the dining room table, and heads out the door.

The world trembles in jewels of sunny raindrops in the tree

limbs. A wind stirs the grass. For a summer morning, it's cool, fresh. Tom thinks of something that does not come clear at first, but then it does: Easter Sunday morning when Andy was a boy, getting ready for church, the reassurance against all logic that life was worth living, hopeful. He and Patricia had slowly quit going to church after the accident. A benevolent God could not have insisted on such a horror. It was pure meaninglessness. Such deaths were a part of no pattern: they were simple evil that no doctrine could dispel.

Now, though, he stretches and feels the air moving around the surface of the earth, and he knows that he can survive it. He gets in his car and drives, but it seems to make a softer sound. The edges are off everything here. He drives through Sheppard, and they're out already, sweeping the streets and putting up flags and bunting. Tom sees Douglas Dickens on the sidewalk, beaming. Douglas waves to Tom as if nothing ever happened. Tom smiles and waves back. Maybe the scene in the floodlights never did happen, or, if it did, can be forgiven. The town looks as if it had been rebuilt in the night, all new and shining.

Tom thinks to stop at the courthouse, then decides to drive down lower Main. All the people had started coming back well before dawn. The sandbags are still in place. Tom parks beneath a willow tree and walks to the breastworks and up the hill until he can see over them. The Coollawassee has shrunk back nearly to its banks already. Few rivers in eastern America rise or fall with such drama. Not a drop has escaped into lower Main or the houses there. Old women are out in their gardens. Across what was a lake just ten hours before, Tom can see the cemetery rising to the marble shafts in the oldest part. Its windswept majesty makes him nearly breathless for a moment.

He turns away from it. He has thought of going there to take a look, but he won't. He doesn't need to see it now. He's wondering about getting a sausage biscuit and taking it to the office, when he thinks of Sam Preston. He should have been at the sandbagging last night. It isn't like him. Even if his phone were out, he'd have driven down from the hills to see if there was a problem. He has a sense, a search for expiation perhaps, that drives him to help. Sometimes Sam and Tom are the only ones to volunteer for the Dunking Booth at the PTO fund-raisers, both childless. They make fun of each other, egg the crowd on until people can't wait for a chance. Sam's been at his side when they helped with brush fires. He should have come down.

Tom drives back through Sheppard and turns north. It's not yet nine A.M., but the sun is coming over the hills, beautiful and strong.


Tom pulls up in front of Sam's house and sees that he has company. Sam's truck is there, but so's a Cherokee and a Taurus with the doors open. He feels he's intruding, thinks of turning around, then stops. He can see rainwater on the seats of the Taurus. He turns off his car and walks around the cars. He recognizes the Cherokee, but he can't place the owner. The Taurus has no plates, and the inside is soaked. He walks up on the porch and finds the front door open.

"Sam?" he shouts. "It's Tom Meade. You in there?" No sound, not even a cricket. "Sam?"

He opens the screen door and walks into the hallway and calls Sam's name once more then listens. He goes left into the den and sees an ottoman turned over. The room seems wrong, as if rearranged by someone who doesn't live there. A saucer is full of cigarette butts. The room smells. Tom feels his senses rise, a pure fright that exceeds what his system may handle this morning. He goes back into the hall and down it to the library. There's some blood in there on the carpet. He follows the spatters into the kitchen. More blood.

"Sam?" he cries. He listens. The wind. This isn't true: He's still in bed asleep beside Patricia. He'll awaken and find her close to him, smiling in his arms. Yes. It's now, and something is terribly wrong. Tom goes swiftly down the hall and out to his car. He gets his gun from the trunk and straps it on. His heart is filling, rising beyond its fragile walls.

Tom walks around to the back of the house. The rain-dripping trees are dazzling in the sunlight, scattering jewels on the soft earth. He can see deep footprints in the mud, and he follows them up the hill, but they seem to go everywhere. He picks the deepest set to follow. That would be the heaviest man. He remembers his first days in the police academy and how much he liked them. He'd already been sheriff for twenty years before the first police academy opened in Kentucky. Careful not to step upon any of the prints, he goes on up the hill and finds himself near a large willow tree. A wind comes and shakes it. The dull thump of rainwater from it reminds him of something, maybe a hula dancer, but he's not sure.

The air up here seems charged. He feels something prod him forward.

"Sam?" he says too softly. Then louder, "Sam?" Nothing. He's been to Sam's house many times, and Sam's told him there's a sinkhole up here, but Tom's never seen it. He starts moving straight ahead, and now he begins to think of Blue Crystal Cave. He sees it soon. He walks to the edge of the sinkhole and sees a rope ladder descending into it. This country's full of sinkholes. Sometimes a cow will fall into one. Tom stands over it but can't see the bottom very well, so he squats and peers into it.

Water's down there. It looks like a swirling river. Bats suddenly erupt upward, hundreds of them, but he only half backs off because he thinks he's seen something floating down there. He waits until the wave of bats has subsided and looks again.

It's Misty. She's lying on her back, eyes open, floating, bobbing just beneath the surface and then coming back up. Her hair is matted with filth.

"Oh my God," Tom whispers. He sits up and backs off as more bats begin to emerge. "Mother of God." He looks back down, and Misty's staring at him. Then her body, moving with invisible currents, slides backward and disappears into the tunnel. Tom decides he can't wait. He feels a heaviness in his steps as he runs toward the house. He's seen flashlights there. Sam keeps a dozen of them at least. On the back porch he finds a large one, a Black & Decker, and he tries it, turns, and scrambles back up the hill. He can't believe how beautiful and light it is here.

The rope ladder goes down. He stands above it and looks. A few bats find their way out, then they're all gone. He feels a choking, can't breathe. He should call for help, call Leon or somebody. He could have a dozen men up here in twenty minutes. But that could be too late. A woman is dead down there. Sam could need help. Blood? What was the blood doing in Sam's house?

Tom turns around and starts to climb down the ladder. His hands tremble terribly, but he holds on. He can't believe this is happening. He can't bear the thought of going into this cave. At the bottom, waist-deep in water, he turns on the flashlight and shines it around the room. Fantastic shapes. The water is churning and roaring somewhere below him, back there in the walls. He shines it around looking for the dead woman, but he sees nothing. She has slipped beneath the water. He walks around the room following the flashlight beam. If he bumps into her body, he may not be able to stand it. He sees where the water goes; there is a passsageway at the rear of this room. Sam may be in there. He stands silently and thinks. Then he knows: *Sam is in there.*

The water is icy. It grips him as if to pull him down into the cave, down as far as anyone has ever been in the karstland of Kentucky. He can almost see it, his body disappearing forever and Patricia not quite knowing where he went, much less why. He heads for the passageway and can almost see it.

\* \* \*

Sam's ducking bats, thousands of them swirling down the passageway, wings flapping above the running water. The sound is terrible, a thick screech. He moves fast now in the complete darkness, hands beginning to know their way over the breakdown. Since the explosion, he's half known darkness and a deep fear that something might happen to his other eye. Now, eyes hardly matter.

"I'm here, you bastard!" Sam bellows. He doesn't quite know why he's done it.

A hundred yards ahead, gun still to Christiann's head, Bobby turns sharply, and a deeply creased grin breaks across his face.

"Preston," whispers Bobby, but the other noise is so loud that Christiann can't hear him. She's seen the gun come up in the flashlight's beam, felt the barrel on her temple, and she's still saying *Jesus Jesus Jesus* over and over. She can't believe she's not dead yet, or maybe she is. What does it feel like when you're dead, anyway? "Preston!" Bobby screams. This time, Christiann hears it. She opens her eyes just as Bobby roughly pushes her to the cave floor in the eddies of bitterly cold water.

Bobby looks back down the passageway and fires the gun. The report is thunderous, and Christiann shrieks terribly. Mary Beth trembles in the ceiling cave, puts her hands over her ears, then takes them off. Sam hears the shot ricochet past him in the cave. It seems to keep bouncing with dull pinging thuds down the boulders.

"You couldn't hit me!" cries Sam. He moves toward Bobby now, hanging close to the top of the breakdown. "You don't know anything about what's down here!" The bats have subsided, and even the noise from the water is easing. Sam's voice suddenly carries. Bobby believes he's very close now.

"You're the one don't know!" screams Bobby. Christiann gets up and moves off slowly on down the cave, lightly muttering to herself, saying *Jesus* and trying to sing "Amazing Grace." Bobby knows he must save his rounds, so he comes fitfully toward Sam in the water, holding his gun out like a probe into the darkness. "I known about this all my life!"

Sam doesn't stop. Bobby forgets completely that he was a snap away from killing Christiann, doesn't even think of her until he's gone twenty steps. He turns and shines the light for her, but she's dissolved in the passageway. To hell with her, he thinks.

Sam hears a scrambling not far ahead and tries to remember the man's face. He was thin and dark, had slightly crooked teeth and a violent, angry look. Sam is not afraid. The cave ceiling must be twenty feet high here, and breakdown rolls up to it in places. Sam crawls up as high as he can, finds a sharp hunk of rock, and holds it in silence. He will wait.


Mary Beth cannot wait. She comes forward once more to the split floor, turns and moves swiftly back down the ceiling tunnel following the flashlight beam. A few bats have come up through the fissure and brush by her as they head off down the passageway. Mary Beth begins to make noises, *unh, unh, unh,* as she walks on hands and knees back toward the tunnel's entrance near Lake Preston. She feels barely human and can't seem to get her breath. She doesn't stop until she's gone two or three hundred yards and only then because the flashlight slips from her hand and goes rolling down the gradual slope, stopping twenty feet away.

Her hands and knees may be anchored in some half-frozen liquid. She can't stop making noises, and the sound of them seems unholy, coming from somewhere else in the cave. She sees the flashlight, but she thinks she'll never get to it. When she touches it finally, her grip is wet, and it rolls gently away once more, as if repelled by some magnetic pole.

Mary Beth thinks she's halfway back to the main cave when

---

246

she's suddenly there, the ceiling passageway opening down into a grinding river littered with escaping bats that bounce down into darkness, and dead bats that float on the water like leaves after a storm. She sits up and shines the light down, then turns it off.

How could Sam save Christiann now? She wants to save herself, and she starts to think of her father, a stern man who spent most of his time in church. He always said that *No man can save himself,* by *man* meaning *Mary Beth,* and by *saving,* from the *corruption of original sin.* Mary Beth nearly dreams of her father, when she realizes her bottom is getting wet. She turns on the flashlight and shines it down between her legs at the crotch of her jeans. Water is running there, and she curses, gets to her hands and knees, and sees that it's trickling from behind her. She turns as well as she can in the small tunnel and sees that a rivulet shining like jewels runs from up where she was.

"Oh Jesus God in heaven," she whispers.

She sticks the flashlight into her waistband and lowers herself into the frigid waters of the main channel just as the trickle from above turns into a spray of foam that churns into the water at her waist.


Ten feet into the passageway, Tom leans against the wall, breathing heavily. He feels the water nearly to his waist, and it is very cold. He can see his breath. He wants to call Sam's name, but his throat is hard and dry. He peers down the passageway and sees nothing but boiling water.

He hears whisperings. Angels could be in there, groans in the flowing water, wind, wings beating, beating. He can't believe he is here or that the water is so cold. He thought he might never see this place again. There is darkness, and the earth, and the cave and water rising.

"Sam!" he cries, but his voice seems not to carry very far. "Sammy? You in there, Sammy?" There was blood in the house. Someone's been hurt. He should have called for help, called Leon, poor old Leon, but he had to come on down. He needs to move on into the cave. Just go back in there and keep calling. Sam could be hurt or trapped. He could be in there calling Tom's name.

Where is that woman who was floating down here? He walks back into the room at the foot of the ladder and feels around for her, but she's somewhere beneath the water now. She will not rise again. Her forehead will not break the surface of the water just ahead of her smile.

Tom walks back into the passageway. He tries to pray. He thinks of the small cave at the river's edge and Sam's name on the ceiling. Tom's never known such fear. It grips his heart. He listens to it speaking of faraway places, lives that were never properly lived, mysteries, terrible beauties. He feels something bump his leg, and he should reach down and see what it is, monster, animal, Sam's body, man, but it isn't there anymore. Log. It could be a log.

Tom hears something like a beast's panting last gasps. He realizes after a moment that he is the monster in the cave, and his power is anger and fear. It has always been there.


Christiann sits on the stones and rocks. She wants to grab Misty by the shoulders and shake her until some sense comes into that girl's head. Misty's always getting like this. She can do such stupid things, running off with boys, getting drunk, turning up in the wrong places. She got arrested once for vandalism, but her daddy got her off. Wait until he finds out what she's done now, leaving her husband and going off with a loser like Bobby Drake!

Except Misty's not coming back. Misty's dead. Christiann tries to think of Misty dead, but it just can't be. Nobody you love like that can die before you do. It's wrong in a way Christiann can't explain, in a way that can't be happening.

Christiann thinks maybe it's a dream, anyway.

All her life she's had fantastic dreams, flying chairs, curtains with voices like the church choir director's. She'll awaken to the night-light and believe it's the eye of a rabbit who lives in the frozen north and descends over America to kill. She'll dream of someone she knows, but with a slightly different face, as if to expose the hiding horror. Mr. Bilson, the math teacher, will flit through, except his eyes turn into pinwheels, and when he opens his mouth there's a vaguely familiar living room in there, sofas and chairs she once sat upon.

This feels as if it could be a dream, but no dream hurts so much. She has walked out of dreams before, into the kitchen for a bite, into the bathroom, where she'd awaken lying in the tub just before dawn. Now, she can walk out of this dream. She thinks of a man called Bobby Drake, and she almost giggles because he isn't real; he's part of this tortured, complex dream that's been spilling into her head all night. And that man with the eye patch like a pirate! Wait till she tells Misty about this one.

Misty seldom remembers her dreams.

Christiann climbs down from the boulders and finds that the water is still running on the cave floor, but perhaps not so swiftly, and she takes ten steps deeper into the cave, turns for no good reason, and starts walking out.

"It's not no dream," she says out loud. She's so sleepy, so deathly tired, so sunken in the noisy darkness, that nothing coheres. She tries to remember how she looks in the mirror but it's a blank to her. There's this pit up ahead somewhere, and there's death in it like a dragon, dreams she cannot bear. When the bad ones come, the invisible threats from which she runs all night, she awakens in deep breathing, bedsheets soaked with sweat. She will take the sheets straight to the laundry room, wash them in hot water with lots of Tide, but the stain and smell never quite come out. Christiann knows she smells like that now, a powerful wretched smell of sweat, urine, dirt. She'll have to wash the entire room when she's awake.

She feels the trail descending, and the water deepens slightly, the current running more strongly, but there may be a slackening now. She says, *Misty Misty Misty*, then she wonders about Clay, if he ever did really love her, and why she'd let Bobby make love to her.

She can't see Bobby, but their matched steps are only thirty yards apart now in the water, each slow slogging step lost in the underworld roar of water and the final filterings of bat wings. Bobby has his flashlight on, but the tunnel turns in subtle shifts, and the light never quite catches Christiann's eyes. She's looking down with her eyes closed anyway, moving easily through this dream. She thinks this is one of the bad ones, the kind that will have her stripping the sheets even before she showers.

Both of them pass Sam. He hears the sound, waits. With Mary Beth in the ceiling channel, he needs only to get behind Bobby. There could be two people, but sounds are strange down here. Sam's heard all manner of odd echoes, dull thuds far off into the earth.

Bobby gets to the crossover and swings his light left. He turns left, passes the gurgling pit, and goes toward Lake Preston, wondering if this is the northwest vein.

Christiann feels the change in the shape of air at the crossover. A slow-moving mass of wind spills over her left shoulder, seems to turn her right. She stops. A suction spills from footfalls somewhere, to her left, behind her, somewhere. Does it matter?

Her body moves right. *Hey, Puddintain*, calls Misty, *down here*, and Christiann starts to grin and knows it has to be Misty because that's her special name. Nobody's called her Puddintain all these years but Misty, and she calls Misty that, too. Christiann goes toward the opening of Blue Crystal Cave. When she awakens, she wants something to eat, sweet blackberry jelly, bacon, coffee that swirls steam out of a crockery mug.

* * *

Follow the light. Touch the walls. This water is a baptism. Tom
remembers baptisms at the church, how everyone expected to
come up different, shining, and then? Maybe a mild pleasure,
rarely a deep joy. No epiphanies but the ones we create. Follow
the light. It's all we are.

Tom's courage starts to come back. He moves farther and
farther into Blue Cyrstal Cave, but slowly. He moves against the
water like an old man. He shines the light back and forth. He
calls Sam's name very loud, but nothing comes back.

There's a knowledge now, though: Sam's inside this cave.
Tom knows it as surely as he breathes. He does not understand
the knowledge. His sidearm is getting wet, and he takes it out
in his right hand, shifting the powerful flashlight to his left.

He sees fantastic shapes. He does not think God lives in this
cave, perhaps not in the earth at all.


Mary Beth keeps turning as she walks slowly down the passageway, shining the light and whispering Sam's name over and
over. She thinks: what if he's already killed Sam? Her eyes fill
with tears, but she won't let them fall, instead tightening her
jaws until a grim glare steadies her gaze at the light's path. The
water's at crotch level, and rises an inch, falls three, comes back
up. She fears that the passageway will suddenly fill with water.

Before, in the days after Charles died, she had only feared
air, the absence of solid earth beneath her. She would awaken
soaked in sweat, seeing him drive off the cliff. There were no
skid marks. The sheriff suggested that he went to sleep. But if
he did, surely he must have awakened in time to know, to
understand what his carelessness had cost. He would have
steered the car in air as if that would change the course of his
death. Some nights, Mary Beth drives her Cherokee in the air.
She'll head off a steep mountain road and drive slowly above

*251*

the blue haze of valleys velvet with morning mist. She'll wonder why her late husband could not do what she clearly can, but then she knows that no one can live as she can, that she must be blessed or dead or both.

But lately she hasn't dreamed of her dead husband, and without the pictures his face has begun to seem vague, as indistinct as the hills when a storm descends. She will awaken having dreamed of Sam. And last night, they'd almost made love. Then this. Her mother's father, a dour old man named Isaac, had believed in the retribution of God and spoke of it so often that people called him Retribution Walters. He was merely eccentric until Mary Beth was nine, and then he'd suddenly slid completely into madness. He'd been at their house one Sunday afternoon when he'd come into the den and announced with calm determination that God had selected him to save the Japanese from themselves. He would pack and leave the next day. Nothing would dissuade him. By that night, he was raving about the dark night of ignorance. They hospitalized him. He spent four months in a rest home, and then one morning they found him frozen upright in bed holding a Bible open to Revelation, dead. They said it was a blessing, but Mary Beth could not forget his face as he lay in the coffin, or the fact that when they closed it, it would never be open again. When she remembered him, it was his dead face.

Now, Mary Beth feels barely sane. She's holding on to her fear, as if she'd rave and go mad if she opened her lips further.

She hears a sucking gurgle behind her and turns, shining the light and gasping, but there's nothing there but the cave and the water, which seems nearly to be lilting now, pulsing to an unheard melody. When she turns back around, Bobby Drake is two feet from her, pointing his light down and his gun at her chest.

Mary Beth turns and tries to run and falls into the water. When she stands again, Bobby's on her, pressing his gun into her stomach.

"Well, well," he says. "Look what I got."

"Sam!" she screams. Her voice comes out with such force that it frightens them both, deeper than it seems possible. "Sam! Sam!"

Bobby's anger erupts. He hits her in the face with the back of his gun hand, and her flashlight falls as she does. Bobby watches the light going under the water. She gains her feet and sees him. His eyes show no anger. They are merely predatory, ready. He almost seems to be shrinking down before her into taut ropes of muscles, coiling.

Sam hears Mary Beth's scream, but he cannot tell where she is. If he shouts, Bobby may be on him instantly, kill him. He heads down the crossover tunnel, but she doesn't scream again. He can't think in that darkness. He tries to place a calm anger in his heart, but it's a burning rage now. He could storm rocks, churn through here making his own cave, straight into the solid wall of stone.

Christiann sings softly, half hums as she moves toward the opening of the cave. She's in this dream. Wait till she tells Misty about this one! *Looky here, Puddintain, this one was the worst one I ever did have! I was in this awful, awful cave!*

She stops because something's changed. She peers ahead, and there's light up there. It's waving at her. She yawns and wonders if it's almost morning. She walks a few steps farther and waits until she realizes that she can see now in the dimmest of light. The ceiling hovers over her like the wings of a great bird. The water here seems to be moving faster.

Christiann stops and shakes her head as if to awaken, then she understands that she is not in a dream, and she remembers. She trembles violently. She wants to move ahead, but she's never before been so scared in her life. Her hands hang by her side, touch the surface of the water.

She can see better and better now. There were lights in here, but they must have shorted out. Misty's probably out there somewhere waiting. . . . She can't think of anything sequentially. She's about to call out someone's name when Hermie's body drifts up and bumps her leg.

She looks down and can see his face. His eyes are open. She screams and screams, and slogs through the water toward the light, shaking so badly her knees buckle at every step. She sees that someone is coming toward her.

She thinks of turning and going back into the cave. She's frozen to the spot, and that's when Misty's body surfaces, not two feet away. She wants to say something, but she feels sleep coming to her once more, the deepest sleep she's ever known.

She's just starting to fall down into the water when Tom Meade reaches her, lifts her from it, saves her.

## 22

*Bobby puts his arm* around Mary Beth's neck and holds her so tightly she can barely breathe. She struggles, but it's no use. He's much stronger, and her face aches where he hit her. No one has ever hit her face before, and the stun and humiliation disorient her. She still calls for Sam, but her voice is weak. They're moving toward Lake Preston now through the water. He's having trouble holding the flashlight and the gun, so he stops.

"Take the light," he says.

"What?" asks Mary Beth. Something about light?

"Here," he says. He loosens his grip and hands it to her; she instinctively shines it down the passageway. She can hear the water spilling behind them from the ceiling cave where she and

Sam had lain. It splashes into the stream, and the water level is rising.

"Why are you doing this?" Mary Beth asks. Bobby keeps peering ahead, looking behind himself, gun out for Sam.

"Blade," he whispers.

"Blade?" she says. She's trying to get her fingers beneath his arm so it won't hurt so much. He tightens the grip. Then he shakes her violently.

"Don't say that!" he screams. "You can't say that! That's for me and Clay! You can't say that!"

"Don't hurt me," she says. He realizes that he may be killing her and loosens his grip slightly. She won't be worth a thing if she is not breathing. They slog through the water until the passageway widens, and they're standing in the room where Lake Preston now fills every corner.

"Shine it around," says Bobby. She can't bear his closeness, but she shines it around anyway. The room is enclosed, no way to escape.

"There's nothing here," she says.

"Dammit," says Bobby. His voice is shaking. He lets Mary Beth go, then grasps the front of her shirt and holds her tightly. She shines the light in his face, but it doesn't seem to bother him. "Call him. You call him right now." He brings the gun up toward her stomach. "You tell him it's all right to come and get you."

"Please," she sobs.

"You call him right now, or I'll blow a hole in your stomach," he says softly.

She glances back and sees the ice in his eyes, solemn intensity like a lowered flame.

"Sam," she says. Then, louder, "Sam? I'm at the lake. Sam? I'm all right. I think he's gone."

The voice is not hers, a disembodied string of words that could not be spoken by anyone. She says it again, and she knows that the water level is rising beneath her. Soon, the earth will give way and she'll be flying out over the edge of some horror, and when she looks down, nothing will be there below her but her own death.


God pulls Christiann Mizelle up into heaven.

That's her first thought, anyway, when the white-haired man is lifting her up by the shoulders into the dim light. She coughs and chokes and spits water. Her arms wave, and she sees them but cannot connect the action to her own body. She's awakening slowly. She stops thrashing when she knows it's God and looks around for clouds and golden streets and white-robed angels with harps.

She smiles dreamily at Tom Meade.

"It's okay, lady," he says. "I got you now."

When he'd heard her, his blood seemed to flow out in one great heave from his heart and not return. Now, he cradles her. She looks at him and thinks of Misty and begins to struggle against him with what strength she has left.

"Leave me alone!" she cries. Her voice is husky, not very loud. She cannot break his hold.

"I'm the sheriff," he says. "Come on now. We're going to get you out."

He takes her down the passageway. She stumbles in the water, and he holds on to her. Christiann coughs water. They get to the entrance room, and Tom leads her to the rope ladder. She says she can't get up it, and he says she must.

"I don't have no strength left," she says.

"Can you hold around my neck?" he asks. He turns his back to her, and she reaches around him and holds his neck. She's shivering and soaked. Her hair is matted to her face.

Tom begins to climb up the rope ladder, but it strains terribly beneath their weight. He closes his eyes and ascends toward the light. She starts to slip.

"I can't hold it," she says.

———

"You hold on tighter!" he barks. She wraps her legs around his waist and squeezes his neck and cries. A few feet from the top, Tom thinks he's not going to make it. He clears his head and hunches his shoulders, and in thirty seconds he's helping Christiann out, onto the soaking, spongy ground.

"They're dead," whispers Christiann. She lies on her back. Tom leans down on hands and knees, wheezing.

"Who's dead?" he asks.

"They're dead," she says.

"Is Sam Preston in there?" he asks. Christiann turns and looks at him.

"Sam," she says. "Yes. And Mary Beth. She's my friend now. Mary Beth's in the roof."

"Are they alive?" he asks.

"I'm cold," she says. "I ain't never been this cold. Misty? Misty?"

She sits up and looks around wildly. Tom sees that she needs help, so he takes her back to Sam's house, puts her on the bed, and covers her with a blanket. He tries to call Leon, but the phone's still out. Something propels him out the door. He stumbles back up the hill and descends the rope ladder.

He thinks of the children.

Sam hears Mary Beth's voice, and she sounds calm, but something jagged is there, too, and he cannot understand why she's even come down from the ceiling cave. Sam's at the crossover spot now, where the two cave channels meet. He listens very carefully and knows she's calling from Lake Preston. He holds to the edges of the wall.

Only a few bats flit around, and a gurgling groan echoes throughout the cave. The water is rising but still pouring down to a lower level now, down where he's never been. You can go down six levels in Mammoth Cave, but Blue Crystal slopes and wanders on a single, endless level. After they'd opened it in the twenties they quit exploring it, and then the accident happened. Sam's the only one who's ever seen most of the formations.

For a moment he slips into a drift, a suspension of light and darkness that is silver and cold; awakening or dreaming spills into a single stream. He bites his lower lip with such force that pain angles through his cheek and down his neck. He hears Mary Beth calling again.

She says everything's okay, and so he knows that everything is wrong. At some instant he will collapse. Now, he tries to think of a way to save her.

Sam comes up the tunnel now, touching the low draperies and speleothems, wondering exactly where the gypsum needles are on the ceiling along here. What if the voice is the other woman's? No, already he knows Mary Beth's sounds like a fingerprint.

A light glows softly ahead. The smudge is sweet. He can nearly taste it. The cave walls are barely luminous, like an old watch dial, and he looks at them with his single eye as he walks, unaware that he's in the room with Lake Preston until he turns and sees them, Bobby with his hand around Mary Beth's neck, and she holding the flashlight down toward the unsettled water.

"Now," says Bobby. Mary Beth feels his breath on her neck. "It's time to end all this."


"Let her go," says Sam. He takes a few steps toward them, and Bobby tightens his grip on Mary Beth's neck. "Please don't hurt her. There's not any money. Dammit, there's not any money. There's not even a blue crystal. There never was."

"You're lying," says Bobby. "I'm going to kill her." His voice starts to wobble, almost fade. "I'm going to kill myself."

"Sam," says Mary Beth.

"Just let her go," says Sam. "Please don't hurt her."

---

"What's that?" asks Bobby. The cave fills with a frightening roar. Rocks tremble. "What the hell is that?"

Sam backs up and places his palms on the cold stone. It is vibrating continuously now, like nothing he has ever known. The cave feels as if it will dissolve now, collapse into itself from the flood.

"Sam," she says again.

"It's dying," he says. "The cave is falling apart."

"You're lying," Bobby whispers. But he knows that he has stumbled into the northwest vein. He believes it more than anything he's ever believed in his life.


Tom follows the flashlight beam. He is silent. Something beyond imagination is down here, powerful and violent. As he walks he hears the water rushing in the walls and below him. It's to his waist. He holds the flashlight in his left hand, the gun in his right.

He's thinking of Patricia, of sunlight on red, white, and blue bunting when Clay's body surfaces near him. The face is impossibly white, eyes open and staring.

"My God," says Tom, and he backs up to the wall to escape the body. His left hand hits the stone, and the light falls into the water. For a brief moment he sees Clay's face in the light underwater, stilled like a bee in amber. Tom falls to his knees and reaches into the swelling rush of water and grabs the light before it can be swept away. It still works. He looks both ways now, farther into the cave and out.

Tom knows. *He knows.*

He moves as quickly as he can toward the heart of Blue Crystal Cave, moving the light back and forth. He reaches the crossover tunnel, and he looks up it to his left and sees that it rises toward the farthest reach of his light. The water is not as deep. He cannot know which way to go, but he is borne along by an imperative, a certainty. The rising water sparkles in the flashlight beam. His legs are freezing.

He moves straight ahead, keeping in the main passageway. The cave groans and cries out now, names intermingled with whispers and shouts. The stone sings. Calcite wings fold down, draperies of angels. Tom hears angels.

The exhaustion that had sunk his shoulders a moment before seems to recede now. He feels as if he is growing taller, second by second, stronger. He realizes that he is not afraid.

He goes another hundred feet, thinking of angels' wings, spokes of light from the sun, dazzling dreams he's had of this for his entire life. The shouting comes back, two voices, both men's. Someone is alive down here.

Someone is left alive.

Sam doesn't know what to do. You can't attack a man who has a gun when you have only a rock. He drops it.

"Daddy?" cries Bobby. "Daddy?" He looks around the room. He mumbles about mines and dust and coughing and being docked a day's pay. He talks about Clay and Reidsville.

"Just let her go," says Sam.

"Sam," says Mary Beth in a hoarse whisper. She wonders if each word she says now will be her last. "Sam. Sam."

Bobby is looking wildly around the room when the flashlight beam hits his face. Mary Beth flinches in pain. Sam turns.

"Clay?" says Bobby. He starts to laugh. "Clay, is that you, bro?"

"Let her go," says Tom. He sees the man, sees Mary Beth. Sam is to his right. Bobby can't believe the sound of the voice. The cave shudders now. The water is trembling around them. "Sam, get out of the way."

Tom shines the light upon his own face. Sam knows at once. Bobby thinks his father has come for him. Gray hair, an older face. Bobby's gasp rises over the cave's groans. Tom turns the light back on Bobby's face. Mary Beth Price? Tom wonders what in God's name is happening here, but Sam is alive. Alive. Mary Beth is alive.

"Daddy," says Bobby. "Don't touch me."

"It's about to give way, Tom," says Sam. "We got to get out of here."

"Let her go now," says Tom evenly, not taking his eyes or the light off Bobby. Bobby's face twists into a fierce grin. He looks around and then starts to cry, and then he laughs. The gun is hard against Mary Beth's temple. She closes her eyes and prays to Jesus for strength. She does not pray for deliverance.

"I don't understand why this is happening to me," says Bobby. He seems almost sad. "It's going to be this way. I could always see that coming, Daddy. It was you. You were always coming for me." He loosens his grip on Mary Beth's neck. "It was going to be this way."

Mary Beth suddenly falls, letting her weight take her downward to darkness, toward the earth's hot core. Bobby grabs for her, misses, looks up, raises his gun and points it at the light in his eyes. Sam leans against the wall, trying to see where Mary Beth's gone. An orange-blue flame leaps from the end of Tom Meade's pistol. His light's still on Bobby, who has been hit in the throat. He falls to his knees. Sam turns his head wildly back and forth to take in the scene. Bobby's still there for a moment, head up. He could be smiling or crying. His left eye closes, and the right one rolls into his head. He slides soundlessly into the water.

Mary Beth tries to scream as she splashes forward, but the sound won't come out. Tom gathers her in his arms.

"It's okay now," he says. "Sam? You okay? Are there others?"

"No, no," he says. He gasps and stumbles toward them, takes Mary Beth from Tom and holds her. She's crying, clinging to him tightly. "They're all gone now."

Mary Beth coughs, looks around for Bobby, but his body does not resurface.

"Tom, we got to get out of here," says Sam.

The water is suddenly rising with a terrifying swiftness. It is waist high, and fifteen seconds later it's to their chests. A cracking roar deafens them.

They turn and move quickly down the cave. Water starts to escape from fissures in the walls and ceilings. They feel spray on their shoulders and faces. Sam stays close to Tom. Mary Beth struggles at his side.

They reach the crossover cave and go up it since the way back to the main entrance is disappearing under water. Just ahead, the rock is shaking. A creak. A subtle shifting and a groan.

They're back in waist-deep water when it breaks.

A blast of water, a moving wall of force, heads toward them, but Tom has time to back up to the wall and reach for Sam, who grabs Mary Beth and holds her tight with his right arm.

Water fills the crossover trail cave. They are completely underwater. They hold their breaths. Mary Beth manages to put her face against Sam's shoulder. Tom wedges his knee into a small crack in the wall and holds them all.

*Hold it, just hold it. Clear your head and try not to pass out. Don't swim off, don't let go. Hold it.*

The water recedes below their necks. They gasp for breath, choke and spit.

"It's not as deep up there," Sam says, nodding forward. "We should go on ahead this way."

The current seems to be eddying suddenly, not moving from one place to another. Moving up the crossover cave is not so hard. As they walk, the water level drops rapidly. They hear a tremendous rockfall behind them and turn in time to see the cave collapsing, tons of rock breaking down from the ceiling. They move faster, and the sound begins to subside. Water is past their waists, falling. A wave of rock dust envelopes them, then settles on the water. Tom still grimly holds the flashlight.

They walk without speaking. A hundred feet farther and the water has disappeared completely except for a trickle at their feet. The air is thin. Boulders surround them. Tom sits, breathing hard, wheezing. Sam and Mary Beth sit near him.

"You okay?" Sam asks her. She nods and coughs more.

"I thought we were dead back there," she says. "I never was that close to being dead."

"Tom, you all right?" Sam asks.

"I've had better days," he says, and Sam laughs. "What happened back there? Who are those people? What happened to your face? God, you must have taken a terrible beating."

Sam tells him as they listen to the cave's now-distant sounds. Tom says he helped a woman out of the sinkhole and took her back to the house. "That's Christiann," says Mary Beth. She notices for the first time that Sam's eye patch has washed away. Without it, with his sightless eye, he looks fragile. They talk about the cave, about floods.

"What's up ahead?" asks Tom. They've been sitting for a few minutes now. Sam doesn't want to say it.

"Why don't you turn off the light to save the batteries?" Sam says. "We're okay here now."

"Right," says Tom. "Y'all ready?" Ready, they say. Tom switches off the light, and a blackness that penetrates the bone sweeps around them. For a moment, no one makes even the briefest sound.

"Nothing's up ahead," says Sam. "It ends here. It just ends here's all."

"Well," says Tom. He thinks about it. He thinks of the color of sky, about the storms passing, of Patricia still restless in her dreams.


Five minutes pass without a word. Sam strokes Mary Beth's wet hair and kisses her. She's cold and shivers in his arms. Tom wants to find the proper words for farewell, but he can't bring himself to say them.

They all feel the moving air at the same time.

"Hey," cries Sam.

"Where's that coming from?" asks Tom. He turns the flashlight back on and shines it around them.

"I feel it," says Mary Beth.

"Go on ahead," says Sam. They get up and walk up the rock-littered trail, creeping over the stones. They get to the tunnel's end, and a crack has developed in the wall; fresh air whirls through it.

"Let me go through first," says Sam. Tom gives him the flashlight and puts his arm around Mary Beth. They watch as Sam disappears into the wall with the light.

It's only ten feet through, snug but wide enough. He comes out of the fissure into a room of stunning magnificence. A gentle slope leads downward; the ceiling is forty feet over Sam. The floor is dry. The flood has not come through here, even though the wall has cracked. Sam sees pillars and flowstone, calcite curtains, crystalline hackling in toothed rows along the ceiling far above. He knows instantly: this is virgin, the wilderness of John the Baptist.

"What do you see?" asks Tom from the other side.

"Wonderful things," says Sam. "Come on through." He turns and helps them into the room with its dusty silences. He shines the flashlight around them. Millions of years have passed since the cave formed, and yet no human has ever been here.

"My God," Tom says. "This makes Sweet Sally look like a sewer tunnel."

"It's easy," says Sam. "Stay right behind me. It's just a dusty floor. Let's see where this sucker goes."

They descend. Mary Beth feels a dazzled fearlessness, just behind Sam Preston. If it's part of Blue Crystal Cave, no one's ever been here or knows how it connects. They reach a low spot, and Sam tells them to stop. He shines the light up and around them, and the formations are breathtaking. Sam lets the light beam drop. He's giving a running commentary on geology, limestone caves, basalt, flow zones, and lava tubes when the light catches something odd.

"Go back," says Mary Beth. "What was that?"

Her voice reverberates in the room. Sam sweeps the light back, half expecting to see the blue crystal. Instead, the light comes to rest on a shoe.

It's a child's sneaker.

"Sweet Jesus," says Tom Meade. "Sam?" He doesn't know if he's asking Sam a question.

"Looks like a shoe," says Sam. He walks to it and kneels. Mary Beth and Tom are just behind him. He shines the light past it, but he sees no footprints. The dust on the floor is thick and even. There is one smudge nearby. The shoe rests on its sole. Sam picks it up and turns it over and over. It's nearly new.

"Lord," says Tom. "How in the world could that get in here, Sam?" Then, a moment later, "Sam?"

"I don't understand this," Sam says.

"There's got to be a way out," Mary Beth whispers.

"A way out," says Tom.

They stand and look around as Sam shines the flashlight. He starts to walk through a forest of ten-foot-high stalagmites. They walk slowly. Sam holds the sneaker in his left hand. They rise now, upward and around, higher with each step. They come to a sheer wall, solid before them.

"This won't work," says Sam.

They keep walking around the wall, find that the room has walkable limits. Sam stops and makes a mark on the wall with his pocketknife. They keep walking, then pass the crack by which they entered the room. They move slowly. Water drips. A few minutes later Sam stops and shines the light on his mark. Tom sighs.

"Hell," says Tom. "There's got to be a way in here."

"Then it's up there," Sam says. He steps farther into the room away from the wall and shines the light up into the ceiling, which is mottled with draperies and speleothems. "It's by God up there somewhere."

"Up where?" asks Mary Beth. "I don't understand."

"Somebody threw the shoe into the room from up there," Sam says. "It's the only way." Sam can almost read Tom's thoughts. "It could have been anybody."

"Now what?" asks Tom.

"I'm going up and see what I can do," says Sam. "Could you two stay here in the dark for a while?"

"You can't get up that wall," says Mary Beth. "I don't even see a ledge up there or anything."

"Well, I have to try," says Sam.

"I'll go," says Tom. "You stay here with Mary Beth."

"Don't be ridiculous," Sam says. "Even with one eye I'm a better climber than you are. It's the only thing that makes sense. We could yell until we turned blue. Nobody'd hear us."

"You're right," admits Tom.

"Sam, be careful," says Mary Beth. He hugs her.

"You worry too much," he says. He hands Tom the shoe. "That ain't my size." Tom tosses the shoe behind him. He can't stand how it feels in his hands, rubbery and cool.


Sam finds a place in the wall with a few cracks and crevices. He leaves the flashlight turned on but puts it in the front of his jeans so it will shine straight up. He goes up twelve feet and finds there are no more holds, so he slowly comes back down.

"I'll find it," he calls back to them. They're twenty feet from him, sitting in the dust, holding hands.

He moves along the wall and finds another likely spot and begins to ascend. His arms and legs are heavy beyond memory. Each toehold is small as he free-climbs up the wall. He goes up ten feet, fifteen, eighteen, twenty-two. The flashlight barely helps him see the next space for his fingers.

*I can't make it,* he thinks. *I'm going to fall.* He's at twenty-eight feet. *I knew this wasn't going to work, and I can't get back down without dropping. No. Be strong. Be strong.*

Sam feels as if he's going to sleep. He turns his head sharply to the right and bites his deltoid so hard he tastes his own blood in his mouth. The adrenaline hits him like a floodlight. He starts climbing without seeing the next handhold. He finds it anyway.

He's sitting on a ledge. He's reached a shelf. Blood runs down his arm and into his shirt. He backs up and up, six feet. He can't tell if it goes anywhere. He takes the flashlight from his pants and shines it around. The shelf isn't much larger than he is. The wall behind him is solid.

Air moves over his head. He can hear it, a bare whistling. He tries to stand, but his legs are too weak. He gets to his knees and then stands. He holds the light up. Just above him is a tube, more than large enough to climb into.

"I see a way out," he shouts.

Down below, Mary Beth starts to cry for joy, and Tom takes her in his arms.

"Okay, Sam," he shouts back. "We're fine here. You go on and see what you can do."

"Okay," he says. "I'll be back."

Sam throws the flashlight above and into the tube. He reaches and hauls himself up. The tube is about four feet high. The flashlight has rolled ten feet. He picks it up and shines the light on the floor and sees a perfect pair of footsteps coming up to the opening to the great room and then returning. One shoed foot and one bare foot point the way out.

The tube widens after twenty yards, becomes nearly six feet high. Then it narrows down to no more than thirty inches wide and four feet high. A few yards later it opens again.

"Hey," says Sam. He shines the light around. He's in a small room littered with beer cans, cigarette butts, and pieces of food. He walks past the room and continues down the tunnel. It has a sharp bend, and he's almost running around it when he comes to rockfall that has completely closed off the tube.

"No," says Sam weakly.

He falls to his seat and starts to hyperventilate. He cups his hand over his mouth and breathes into it, and the panic begins to subside.

Sam hears a squeak. He turns the light slightly. A mouse sits up on its haunches, then scampers off down the tube. Sam thinks to follow it for no good reason. He goes back into the small room with the beer cans and sees the mouse scamper to one side, run up a slope of dirt, then disappear. Sam sees that part of the ceiling has collapsed here. He moves up over the breakdown and finds a small shaft of faint light. He puts the light on the fallen stones and digs upward with both hands.

He breaks through into fresh air. He enlarges the hole enough to wedge through and finds himself in the bottom of a shallow sinkhole in a deep forest. He's maybe twelve feet deep. He climbs up and out easily.

He stands in the woods and feels the wind and sees the blue Kentucky sky above him.


Tom and Mary Beth sit, holding hands in the absolute darkness of the cavern.

He wants to speak to her, as she does to him, but the silence is their ally now.

She feels his strength, his undemanding love.


Sam can't quite believe it: he's only a quarter mile from his own sinkhole, up the hill on Ezra Thompson's property. He gets to his sinkhole and sees dust settling around it. He looks down: rockfall has choked the entrance. Sam cuts the rope ladder from its pitons and rolls it up. He's exhausted and his vision swings from crystal clear to hazy. He wants to hurry, but his bones move like an old man's, not responding to his mind's command.

He'll have to find another way to anchor the ladder to the rocks above the room where Tom and Mary Beth sit. He knows: Loose rocks litter that edge. Pull out these pitons and hammer them into the hard earth with those stones and bring Tom and Mary Beth up.

*269*

Sam carries the heavy rolled-up ladder on his back. He glances once down the hill toward his house. The wind seems to pulse around him, urging him to go higher. He feels this light in the center of his bones.

## 23

*M*ary *Beth awakens* to the warmth of sun-light on the bed. The window's open, and the rich aroma of honeysuckle fills the room. Her face, still on Sam's chest, rises and falls with his steady breathing. Birds sing quietly. She feels unwilling to move away from him even an inch. She smiles as his fingers begin to fumble through her hair, stroke it gently from the crown of her head and down over her ear, to her neck and back again.

"Morning," she says.

"Morning," he repeats, and she feels the shape of his words through his chest. "You hungry?"

"Ravenous," she says. "I wonder why."

"Probably a glandular condition or something," he says languidly, and Mary Beth laughs. He can't believe what a lovely sound it is.

She sits up cross-legged next to him and leans down and takes his face in her hands and kisses his lips gently. The swelling has gone down, and a small white bandage covers the burned spot. He's wearing the eye patch. She likes it. Her ankle is better and not broken after all. He puts his hands behind her head and kisses the soft spot in front of her left ear. She sits back and a cloudy look passes over her eyes.

"What?" he asks.

"I dreamed about it last night," she says. "It's been two weeks, and it was the first time I dreamed about it."

"I dream about it all the time," says Sam.

"It was about Christiann," says Mary Beth. She lies down and puts her face next to Sam's. A light breeze lifts the curtains, but they fall back and do not move again. "When we were up above her and couldn't get to her."

"That part," says Sam.

"The dream was just like it happened," she says. "I mean, nothing weird happened like it does in dreams. It was just about her lying there and crying and me holding her hand. I worry about what's going to happen to her."

"Nothing's going to happen to her," says Sam. "Since we aren't filing charges, it's just a matter of her learning to live all over again."

"I wish I hadn't gone to see her at the hospital," says Mary Beth. "She was so pitiful. She didn't even look human somehow. I don't think she's going to have much of a life."

"She probably never had much of a life," whispers Sam, stroking her hair again.

"Lot of that going around," says Mary Beth.

He rolls to her, and their bodies meet at full length, and when the breeze lifts the curtains again, she doesn't see them rise or fall.

Tom kneels at the foot of the grave and pulls a few dande-
lions. He lifts one to his lips and blows. The feathery tufts
drift on the sunny still air across the muddy field toward the
Coollawassee. The river winds placidly through its ancient
channel.

Patricia has finished planting zinnias near the headstone.
She stands, brushes the dirt from her jeans, and looks down at
them.

"I like zinnias," she says. "They look good until frost. Maybe
we can plant some perennials out here, too, Tom. I kind of like
the idea. Something coming back every year."

"Let's go get something to eat," he says. "I'm ready to leave
this place for a while. I don't think he's going to mind now." He
nods toward the headstone as if it were a living thing. Patricia
laughs lightly.

"He probably never did," she says. "We learn our lessons
awful slow."

"But we learn our lessons anyway," says Tom. "I tell you
what I learned." She comes to her husband and stays very
close. "I learned that we have reservations for the next ten days
on Amelia Island."

"You didn't," she says with delight.

"I did," he says. "By God, I did."

"Don't you think Sheppard County's going to fall to pieces
without you here to take care of it?" she asks.

"Sure," he says. "But nobody would notice. Douglas Dickens is so happy that Sheppard Dollar Days went well he'll
probably do all my work, too. Now, let's go eat. I'm going up to
see Sam. We're leaving on Friday, lady, and you got packing
to do."

She gets her small spade and the box of fertilizer. As they
pass from the plot, her hand trails lightly along the stone, just
touching it, as if caressing a child's head.

* * *

It's Friday, and Sam Preston no longer has a cave to explore. Still, he's left the hardware store to Jimmy Jones while he cleans his house. Mary Beth's in town at Mountain Pages. She's tired of answering questions about the ordeal, but she does it anyway with as much patience as she possesses.

The media had been in Sheppard for ten days, even the *New York Times* and *Newsweek*. The *CBS Evening News* called it a tragedy and spent two minutes of a three-minute piece on the life of Bobby Drake. Everyone in Sheppard was disgusted. Ezra Thompson wouldn't let anyone on his property to see where Sam, Tom, and Mary Beth got out. He hates caves, didn't even want to see the sinkhole.

Tom and Sam sit on the front porch of Sam's house and look south down the slope toward town. Sunlight sweeps the countryside with a sweet insistence.

"It's not caves," Sam says finally. "It's not the children, Tom. I always thought it was the children. Little Jackie Moss. Your Andrew. When I really understood what had happened, when I was back there in Richmond, I fell to pieces. Family blood guilt or something."

"We just do the same things over and over," says Tom. "It's the way of the world, I guess."

"I'm glad they decided not to exhume those bodies," says Sam. "Let them be. Just let them stay there. It's as good a place as any."

"Yeah," says Tom.

A hawk's shrill cry echoes high above them. Sam stretches and touches the side of his face. It doesn't hurt much anymore.

"Like to be able to fly," says Sam. Tom seems to be thinking.

"I'm not going to run for reelection," Tom says.

"I heard," says Sam. "I think you're smart."

"Next spring, I was thinking of taking Patricia on a tour of Civil War battlefields," says Tom. "You know, Shiloh, Chancellorsville, Bull Run, like that. You think you might, you know, be able to get away and go with us? We'd love the company."

Tom and Sam don't look at each other. They stare at the countryside, the green and gold of summer.

"Tell me when, and I'll start packing," says Sam.

Tom says, "Sounds good," and he walks back to the car. He opens the door. "You take care of yourself, Sam."

"You too, Tom," says Sam. They shake hands and look at each other. Tom gets in the car and then starts to laugh.

"I was just thinking," says Tom. He leans slightly out the window and looks down at the earth and then up at Sam. "You know, about down there. It's never what it seems like, is it?"

"No," says Sam. "Never is."

Sam watches the car until it disappears down the hills toward town.

# About the Author

Philip Lee Williams is the author of six previous novels. He lives with his wife, Linda, son, Brandon, and daughter, Megan, near Athens, Georgia.